THE VISCOUNT'S PLEASURE HOUSE

IRRESISTIBLE ARISTOCRATS
BOOK 1

SUZI LOVE

THE VISCOUNT'S PLEASURE HOUSE

An erotic story set in England in the risqué early Victorian era.

In exchange for information about his mother and sisters, London's most notorious Viscount is coerced into allowing three respectable women to visit his Pleasure Houses.

The goal of the ladies is to learn how to hold men's attention by giving them exquisite pleasure. Each lady comes to the pleasure gardens a little naïve, but leaves as knowledgeable as a well schooled courtesan.

Though the world-weary viscount falls in head over heels in love with one of the ladies, he struggles to find reasons to convince her to trust him, and to marry him, after their visit to his country Pleasure House is over.

The Viscount's Pleasure House

Copyright @2013 Suzi Love
Cover by Anna Scheuringer

eBook: 9780992345600

Paperback: 9780992345617

❀ Formatted with Vellum

1

E arly in the reign of Queen Victoria
Hawkesbury House in Belgravia, London

"REMOVE THAT HIDEOUS GOWN!" Justin Tremayne, known in amusement- seeking society as Handsome Hawkesbury or the Virile Viscount, struggled to hide his rising frustration. "I need to examine your body. All of it."

The woman, clad in unrelenting black and looking more like a newly grieving widow than an enchanting bird of paradise, had pushed past his butler and stormed into his library as though claiming her right to be seen and heard. As if she feared her late arrival might have cost her the chance to strut around the room with the other peacocks and show her wares. And as if her life depended on him offering her employment.

He, of all people, knew how fear of failing drove a person to take rash chances and how desperation to achieve something could drive a man, or woman, to extreme lengths. But to his surprise, the strange woman had come to a dead stop a few feet inside the room, dug her feet into the carpet as solidly as a scarecrow staked into soil, and turned her head, ever so slowly, to stare at the girls posing around the periphery of his library.

Below the chin length veils, Justin could see her long, thin neck rise and fall in pronounced swallows. He watched, amazed, as she clenched and released her fists. After her headlong rush into their presence, she now appeared to be waging some sort of inner battle, most likely torn between picking up those ghastly skirts and leaving or tossing off that ugly outfit, and her inhibitions, and joining the other girls.

Justin stood before the woman in his rumpled disarray—evening coat discarded, shirt tails hanging, booted legs spread—and threw his arms wide. Looking up, he appealed to the smiling gold cupids frolicking in naked abandon across his plastered ceiling. "Why me? Do I not have enough problems in my life?"

The gala at his club opened in three weeks—his grand finale—and the smallest disruption to his schedule could mean everything he'd worked so hard for could slip through his fingers. During week-long performances at the Pleasure House, every fat-pursed gentleman in the city would visit, drawn by promises of spectacles more ribald than any of their fantasies. His potential buyers would be so impressed with the club's earnings that they'd throw their money at him and fall to their knees and beg him to sell the club to them.

After four hide-thickening years, Justin could retire from the loathsome industry of flesh- peddling and be free to concentrate all his energies on locating his lost family. But he'd expected to be hiring his thirty extra girls tonight and setting them to work practicing their parts in the exotic fantasies he had planned. His annoyance rose once more and he felt ready to erupt, much like the storm threatening to explode in the square outside.

At least six of the twenty girls parading around his library pretended to earn their daily bread and butter by hawking oranges to theatre patrons around Covent Garden. In truth, their money was earned by enticing well-heeled gents away from their friends and giving them some extra entertainment in the surrounding alleys. It worried him that performing as a group wasn't their usual field of expertise but with time running out, he'd decided if he couldn't provide top quality ladybirds for his customers, he'd have the men's eyes popping out of their heads and their senses overwhelmed with a large quantity of performers.

Dammit. That meant he couldn't afford to kick anyone out of his house and back to the street. Perhaps the woman in black truly was a widow. City streets teemed with women left in dire financial straits by men who gambled or drank too much and forced the women to take up streetwalking to feed their family. The cumbersome layers of neck to ankle clothing proved she wasn't comfortable with flaunting her body like the more seasoned girls were doing.

He tried for a more encouraging tone this time. "I'm rather short of time, my love, but I need workers, and you need work. Now, let's remove that repulsive costume so we can see what you've been hiding."

The woman straightened her shoulders and appeared ready to speak, but instead of words coming out her lace veil sucked into her mouth and she choked and coughed. Justin moved to help but the woman frantically waved her hand to keep him away.

He turned away to allow her time to recover her breath and spoke to Bart and Thomas, his best friends since their days at Eton when they'd banded together to fight off bullies. Lord Bartholomew Branxton, now the tenth Earl of Brimley and as comfortable in low-class brothels as high-class ballrooms, lay sprawled across an elegant French settee with one long leg dangling over a spindly arm. Thomas, outranking them both since becoming the Duke of Rowbrough after the recent death of his father, balanced his considerable girth in an armchair that was equally unsuited to hold anyone but a petite lady.

"What the hell am I going to do? Billy used all my spare money to grease the palms of those madams. And all he managed to find me is twenty performers."

"Brothel keepers can never be trusted," Bart said with a grin.

"Giving money to your competitors was bound to come back and bite you in the bum."

"The alternative was standing on street corners and doing my own procuring."

"That would have only earned you a knife in the ribs, not any hirelings."

"And," Thomas said, "it's far too dangerous for a gentleman to loiter on any street in those seedier districts. Sort of thing only thieves and brothel keepers do."

Justin looked at Bart and rolled his eyes. No point reminding Thomas that Justin had owned his own bawdy house for the past four years, because Thomas preferred to cover his ears rather than discuss the seedy ways a viscount had been forced to earn his money. To some extent, Justin agreed with his friend. Owning a Pleasure House, the haunt of the richest of the upper ten thousand, and catering to a vastly different clientele than a common whorehouse, didn't make him a brothel keeper ... though he'd collected his first real money on his back and servicing the rich and lustful, just as his girls did now.

Ignoring Thomas's well-meant but always uncomprehending comments, Justin spoke to Bart. "The three rooms for the Sultan's Harem require a minimum of twenty slave girls. And the fetish rooms will be open all week."

He watched the girls strut around the room's perimeter, bodices removed or pulled wide to display their bountiful assets, thoroughly enjoying themselves. They played to their audience, only three men this evening, but they flaunted and posed as if the room were filled with eager patrons. Billy had followed his orders to some extent because they all had vibrant coloring and, as prostitutes rarely wore undergarments, each time one bent, lifted, arched, or pointed a leg, they revealed swatches of hair, often dyed in vibrant colors to match their head. But for Justin, pussies—painted, plaited, bald, or plain— had become commonplace.

"Lovely girls," Justin said, summoning his most winning smile. "You are all exquisite. Gentlemen attending my gala will be charmed by your beauty." Their squeals of delight made him laugh. "So yes, you're all hired. You'll be given lessons on how to act like harem slaves and taught to dance with veils." More tittering from the girls. He glanced back at the ghoulishly dressed woman and shuddered. "Unfortunately, we don't have enough performers yet. And it appears my man found the only working girl in London who is too shy to disrobe before a crowd."

"My lord! You misunderstand!"

Her words surprised him. "Ah! Finally. She speaks." The woman sounded confused and upset, yet she spoke with a cultured voice.

She hurried forward a few steps to the center of the room. "I'm not one of them." She waved a hand toward the other girls. "I'm not a pr... pros ... "

She broke off and looked around the line of girls who stared back at her. Their faces showed a mix of defiance, anger, or amusement but hers showed terror. Her gaze fixed on the wall above the girl's heads, as if she'd swoon if she focused on their bared chests.

Sucking in deep breaths, Justin prayed for patience. "Everyone here tonight is auditioning for a role in my theatrical. Slaves for the Sultan's Palace." Her eyes went wide and she gasped. For the first time he considered the possibility that she may not be a working girl of any description, experienced or newcomer, and that she may not be one of the endless parade of rich women who tried to sneak into his bed. "Why have you come, if not for that?"

She appeared to be again searching for words. Uneducated, or merely shy? He circled around her and inspected her figure and face. Whoever she may be, her above average height and long straight neck would make the perfect employee for the discipline room. It never ceased to amaze him how gentlemen who suffered daily haranguing from their wives at home appeared on his doorstep the moment they heard a more ferocious whip-wielding female had been hired. Majestic women he could appreciate. Stern or brutal ones, never.

Justin's favorites were like those now being appreciated by his two friends. Or at least, his tastes had run toward large breasted and loud-laughing women in the past. His two friends presently wore identical grins of blissful contentment as their laps overflowed with the ample rear ends and bouncing breasts belonging to four Covent Garden actresses. Though Bart and Thomas were as different as the devil and an angel, both loved having this unique chance of helping Justin cast ladybirds to act in his exotically named Sultan's Harem.

Justin studied the woman again, uncaring that his scrutiny seemed to make her uncomfortable. Any female who brazenly pushed her way into a viscount's residence deserved to suffer the consequences. He'd been forced to reveal his address to several people tonight, knowing his stern and forceful butler usually delighted in evicting any unwanted intruders, but he already regretted breaking his own rule.

"What do you think?" Justin decided that if the woman weren't going to reveal her true identity, he'd continue treating her as a prostitute. "She'd make a fine whip- cracker."

"Hard to tell," Bart said. He and Thomas gave the woman an even closer scrutiny. "Not without showing us what sort of body is under that mountain of fabric."

With a wave of his hand, Justin said, "If you're new to the profession, love, there's no need for modesty. We've seen it all before." He indicated the high flyers that filled his room with cheap perfume, cheap clothing, and hopeful looks. "As these girls know, you'll earn better coin performing for me for a short time than a year's worth of peddling yourself on the streets." He flicked a glance at the ornate clock, another thing he'd inherited that he didn't particularly like but that he had, either from apathy or defiance, left in that same position since his mother had been banished by his father years ago. "But please, if you're staying, get rid of your clothing. If you're going, leave now."

A buxom redhead sat, straddling the arm of his wing chair, and waited for Justin's return. Naked to the waist, she'd spread her legs wide in a blatant bribe to hire her as one of his dancers. Justin grinned at her, though he spoke to the black-clad woman. "I've several pressing matters to attend to."

"Pressing matters, indeed," she said, rolling her eyes and not trying to hide her scorn. "I promise to not take up more than ten minutes of your ... valuable time."

He gave a small snort of laughter. In response, the strumpet in his chair giggled, an out-of-place girlish sound, cupped both her large breasts, and lifted them higher, to better display her claret nipples. Like lush cherries, they were waiting for a man to open his mouth around them and suck.

"Justin, old boy," Bart said, his face split with a grin. "You'd better hustle. Those titties are so ripe they're about to drop off their stalks. If you don't come, it'll be my tongue under there and catching them as they fall."

Justin chuckled. The three men trusted each other implicitly, whether it was with their fortunes or their women. They'd combined their talents, their earnings, and had taken enormous risks in the money market until now—though they didn't advertise this fact, they owned sizable slices of London property and English factories. Without his friends' unflagging support over the past three years, Justin would never have had enough coin to employ dozens of investigators to search across England and Scotland for his mother and sisters.

The woman cleared her throat, loudly, clearly determined to pull Justin's attention back to her. "My lord, please listen to me. I have a proposal to discuss with you."

"Look around, pet." He waved at the posturing demireps. "Every girl here is offering me something tonight."

Desperate for well-paid employment, the girls took their cue and swarmed around Justin, draping themselves suggestively all over him. There was a chorus of cries and entreaties. "Oooh, yes, yes, my lord" or "Pick me, my lord." Added to these were many highly exaggerated tributes to his manly physique and his awe-inspiring sexual prowess.

Hearing the outrageous compliments the girls were flinging at him, Bart and Thomas roared with laughter. Above the women's loud and flattering cries, Justin heard several loud sniggers. Ah ha! His mysterious lady paid attention, even if she declined to reveal herself, or her intentions, quite yet. He smiled inwardly and, as her height was only a couple of inches less than his, looked at her over the tops of several bent female heads. The girls were occupying themselves by licking or kissing every inch of his bare skin they could find. He squirmed, but more from being tickled than from arousal.

"What makes your offer any different?"

"In contrast to these ... eh ...women," she said, her eyebrows rising to show what she thought of their antics. "My proposal doesn't involve anyone undressing. Or at least, not tonight. Perhaps later, though I'm not certain about the specifics."

It was damned hard to concentrate on the woman's stumbling explanation, but her insecurities intrigued him. Such a refreshing change from the brazen claims made by many of the titled bitches he'd been forced to deal with. He clasped the hands of the girl intent on unbuttoning the flap of his trousers so he could listen. "I'm offering you an exchange of information and services. One of benefit to us both."

He was distracted again by a saucy raven-haired temptress creating a ruckus in the middle of the room, a determined effort to claim his attention. She dragged back a large corner of Persian carpet and stood posed, center stage, until she could catch his gaze with her mesmerizing eyes, the obsidian color found in nomadic gypsy tribes. After raising her bare arms, she began to clap and dance and sing in the wild and passionate rhythm of the Rom, the one the gypsies used for arousal. He shrugged an indifferent shoulder and was amused when the fiery gypsy hissed at him.

The teasing vixen reached down to drag her gaily ribboned skirts to her waist, lifted her leg, and proffered her toes for him to suck. She struck an eloquent pose and waited for him to acknowledge the sensual heat of her performance, her compelling eyes issuing a blatant invitation to him for her to join him for more intimate acts later. Justin happily obliged her first demand by drawing her toes, one by one, into his mouth and making loud sucking sounds. Her other, unspoken, demand he ignored.

Muttered but angry-sounding words beside him reminded him it was past time to deal with the black widow, and his throbbing head told him to ignore her proposal, whatever it was, and call a finish to the evening. By now, he should have chosen his line-up of Cyprians and sent them away so he could crawl into bed—alone.

He addressed his assembly. "I apologize for being out of sorts tonight, but this shall be my pièce de résistance. You'll form the most exotic group of harem slaves ever seen in England, created to entertain the crème de la crème of our society. I shall then be retiring from the Pleasure House."

"Dammit, Justin, I wish you would reconsider selling the club." Bart lifted his blond head and fixed him with piercing blue eyes. "I do so enjoy our evenings at the house." Justin turned to the woman and gave a half-bow. "So you see, madam, I really don't care who you are, or what you have to offer. My time in this noble profession is about to come to an end. It appears that you like to watch, though. Stay until we are finished, if it entertains you. Otherwise, my butler will show you out."

At that moment, Justin pitied his intruder. There was something in her eyes, a weariness that matched his own, and for a split second she'd looked as weighed down with worry as he felt. As if, despite her head making a decision to leave, her body hadn't agreed and kept her feet nailed to his floor. A lion cub hovering near the shelter of its den while it summoned up the courage to venture into the unknown. Nevertheless, her standoffish attitude had far out- lasted his small store of patience.

He stepped closer and in reaction she moved back. As if remembering her reasons for coming, she shook her head and moved that same pace forward. Not as close as before, yet near enough to appear fearless. He sighed, and rubbed a fist across his aching eyes. "I'm fatigued, out of sorts, and my friends and I have business to conduct. Either join in, or leave."

He waved toward the door, hoping she'd walk out and leave him in peace, but also hoping, ridiculously, that she'd unveil, undress, and stay. Because something about this particular woman was different.

Something about her stirred his first true sexual interest in many months.

He smiled a little. "I'd still like to see a little more of you. I can't even see the color of your hair." He pointed toward her groin. "Top or bottom. Here, let me unbutton you," he said, his fingers set to work on her top button, brushing the soft skin of her nape as he did so.

She flinched and held tight to the gaping neck of her dress with clenched fists. "Please. Listen to me. I'm not seeking employment."

"Ah, then you're simply a bitch in heat like all the others. Wanting a lusty tale to recount to your upper- class friends over tea and cake. Perhaps compare notes on Viscount Hawkesbury's infamous prowess."

Her quick series of breaths hissed and sizzled like water spitting on hot coals. He heard the girls tut-tutting nearby, but taunting, teasing, and arousing the lioness who'd dared brave his den so late at night had proved too delicious a temptation to resist. Only one more jest at her expense and then he'd summon the butler and a couple of strong footmen, and bid her farewell.

He turned, slowly and deliberately, and spoke to his two friends. "Gentlemen, which of you is capable of keeping your prick upright long enough to provide such a lusty lady with the thrill she so clearly came to my house seeking?"

Justin knew that in their heightened state of inebriation, neither Bart nor Thomas would be capable of servicing any girl tonight. And the Virile Viscount had given up such jaunts. The only business he involved himself in now was the palace and even then he kept a very low profile. By next month, he'd no longer own that either. His pleasuring days were finished. Investing in the rapidly expanding railway tracks and steam engines was far more profitable, and respectable, for a man who hoped to bring his mother and sisters home to live with him.

Thomas, red-faced, lurched to his feet. "I say, Justin, she seems like a lady."

"Thomas, you should know by now, on the outside they're all ladies. However, underneath they all seek the same thing."

The woman flinched. Justin yawned, not bothering to cover his mouth, and then collapsed back into his armchair. Leaning his head back on the headrest, he laughed. "My love, if you've better to show me than them, do as I've asked. Undress!"

She muttered something that sounded like, "Rude swine."

He laughed and indicated the empty space on the chaise longue beside Bart. "If you're suffering personal timidity, at least take a seat and watch. Give the girls your opinion on what tricks attract gentlemen the fastest. What do you do to entice a man?"

Her hands fisted at her sides but she stood her ground. "I realize you're amusing yourself at my expense, but I give you fair warning, my lord. If you continue with these childish taunts and force me to leave without letting me speak to you, in private, you'll regret it later."

He pointed to the door. "And I'm also issuing a warning. Join in or leave. Perkins will show you out. I've run out of patience with the so-called weaker sex and the schemes and lies that women seem to delight in bringing to my door."

Bart spat out an uncouth curse while Thomas muttered under his breath, both scolding him for his rudeness. Disgust suddenly flooded Justin's body and the heart he'd assumed was frozen in his chest clenched, hard. Despite being forced into unseemly money-making ventures, the three of them had vowed to remain, at heart at least, gentlemen. They all needed to take their places in society, which was why Justin never usually entertained this sort of female at his house. Too many watching neighbors and too many wagging tongues in this respectable neighborhood.

Had he now passed the point of no return? Had the indecent acts he'd committed, all to either survive or earn his some of the ready, tainted his thinking to this extent? It terrified him that his morals were as lost as those idiots who assumed a title and riches gave a man leeway to be rude, arrogant, and even to inflict pain on those they considered inferior.

He'd picked out this woman and had intended on using her as an example, encouraging her to pass along his message to the long line of societal whores who would continue to plague him. He wanted to stand in the street and scream and yell, "The Virile Viscount is finished!"

Behavior such as his here showed the arrogance he'd always deplored. Rude attacks on a woman were despicable, and it was especially ill-bred of him to tease and taunt what he now suspected was a well-bred lady. But he'd underestimated the woman's pluck, or perhaps her determination to make herself heard.

"Be warned, my lord, I shall return. Tomorrow. Early. Very early. And if you refuse to speak with me, I'll haunt your house until you are prepared to listen to me."

Her ferocious expression made him burst out laughing again. Bart wiggled his eyebrows in a suggestive manner and held out his hand to encourage the woman to take a seat on the thigh of the woman he still held.

"I like her, Justin. Can I have her?"

"Feel free, Bart. If you dare! Though I suspect Thomas is correct. I've come to the unwilling, and unfortunate, conclusion that she's not here to audition for the Harem."

"Certainly not." Her tone was icy. "I'm offering you an exchange. Your skill in tutoring my friends in return for information."

"Regrettably, my services are no longer for hire."

She inhaled so sharply he swore her ribs vibrated. Then she made her announcement. "If I leave this room, I'll take with me what may be your last chance to see your mother. Alive, at any rate."

Justin felt the air suck out of the room. Movements ceased, breaths held, no one spoke. Every person in the room, including the courtesans, was aware of the reason he'd spent four years debasing himself before the wealthiest members of the ton. The reason he forced himself to get out of bed each day, to place one foot in front of the other and go through the rituals, the pretense of living a normal life. Why he arranged wild bedroom antics for women and men that he barely knew and certainly didn't like or respect. His guilt festered like an open wound and the pain never lessened. His obsession was to locate his mother and two sisters, to bring them home, and try to make amends for his absence at the time his deranged father had evicted them.

Unable to reply, he shook his head, robbed of coherent thought, unable to believe her declaration. Unable to convince himself it wasn't another misery-causing lie. Unable to gather the energy to conclude his night's business. Nothing mattered above the bait she dangled before his nose, the thing he yearned for more than any other—to bring his family back to him. This tiny despot had forced him into negotiating with her.

"Bart, Thomas. I ask you to leave me to my visitor. Then I'm off to find my bed."

The busty redhead jumped to her feet, leaned her lush body down his side, and rubbed the enormous mounds of her breasts against his shirt. "Oh no, my handsome one. I made you a promise." She grinned, exposing wide gaps in her teeth. "To please you all night, remember?"

He pulled some coins from his pocket and pressed them into her hand, calling Perkins as he did so. With a wet kiss to her pouty lips, he tugged together her gaping bodice. "Perkins, please see my guests out. Also, call the carriages to drive the girls to their lodgings. We'll conclude our transactions tomorrow, when I'm more awake."

Amid good-natured ribbing and backslapping, his friends departed. The girls complained, disappointed not to have confirmation of their positions in his harem. Several made brazen offers, with lurid descriptions of their favored activities, if allowed to spend the night.

With a husky laugh, a pat on a bottom, or a caress of a breast, he dispatched them, one by one.

2

J ustin leaned against his mantelpiece, stared down at the diminishing fire, and took stock. Ironic that when he reached out to touch his craved return to normal life, almost held it in his hands, something—or, rather, someone—arrived to shatter the fragile harmony. Women had tried to feed him the same falsehoods she offered too many times before, and always for the same reason. His gullibility astounded him, each and every time, but desperation invariably blanked out reason.

"Why don't you be a good girl and go? Just go!" he called over his shoulder. "And please, I beg you, tell your friends the Virile Viscount no longer exists." When she didn't move, he peered over his shoulder and saw her puzzled frown. "You, my dear, have obviously been in the country."

"How ... how did you know that?"

He laughed, a dry hollow sound. "If you'd visited any tonnish house in London during the past week, you'd have heard my comic situation discussed and know that some of my previous customers are incensed that I've announced my retirement."

When she gave him another uncomprehending look, he shook his head and sighed. "My overused sexual appendage hangs in my breeches as limply as a wrung out dishcloth and yet they expect me to continue in the time-honored profession of servicing the rich and perverted. You're not the first to use devious means this week to gain entrance to my house. I've been inundated with women convinced their unique sexual talents will rouse the sleeping beast in my breeches. They want me to be the whore who panders to their perversions and satisfies their perverted appetites."

He glanced to the door where Perkins hovered, with Johnson visible outside, both ready to escort the woman to the street as soon as he lifted a finger. "Perkins, inform the lady of how many women —" He gave a harsh laugh. "And men— " She exclaimed, sharp and loud, so she understood his reference. "— have thought to slip past you." Perkins stepped from his darkened post into the light of the room and dipped his head. "Four and twenty, my lady."

"And how many of those intrepid souls gained admittance?" "None, my lord. None at all until now." Perkins glanced at the lady with a look that appeared half- sneer and half-admiration.

"Let this be a lesson to us, Perkins. We let down our guard." He presented her with a low bow, an ironic gesture. "You caught us all off-footed. You alone breached our fortress. If I wore a hat, I'd tip it in salute to your fortitude. But now, I'm afraid I must ask my servants to remove you because the Virile Viscount has retired. And will remain so no matter what fairy tale about my mother you'd intended telling me. I've heard them all. I believe few."

Perkins walked to the sideboard to pour him another brandy, though one more glass wouldn't dull the spark of interest he'd felt at her subtle scent ... and at the throaty timbre of her voice. It'd been a long time since he'd felt the tiniest flicker of interest in resuming his sex life. When a hand touched the small of his back, he jumped. A light touch, yet even through his velvet evening coat, it jolted. He stiffened, but didn't turn.

"Perkins, please escort the lady to her carriage."

"I'm not leaving. Not until you agree to my proposal."

Her demeanor was determined and, dare he think it, passionate, but he wasn't going down that path. Not again. No, no, no. Never again. Before he could disagree, she slipped around him and stood under his chin. Her billowing clothing pressed so close that he smelled the same violet scent on her person as had clung to his mother's gowns. He closed his eyes, willing her to be gone when he reopened them. From under his nose, he heard her chuckle.

"I'll still be standing here when you open them."

He lifted his eyelids slowly, resigned to removing the pesky woman by force. Perkins hovered at his elbow, flustered, out of his depth. Not his normal display of proficiency. The lady placed her small gloved hand on his sleeve and looked up, although he could still discern nothing of her face through the lace.

"Please, I only need five minutes."

Justin raised his eyebrows to show sardonic amusement. "Madam, you certainly must be from the country to assume that five minutes with the Virile Viscount would be enough to satisfy you. I'm good. I'm very good. But I refuse to be that rushed."

Her hand dropped as if burned. "This isn't a jest, my lord. I have a serious proposition to discuss with you."

He paused, intrigued despite himself. His world-weariness had dipped to new lows if a five-minute discussion with a woman of nondescript appearance sounded an enticing prospect.

"Very well. You've five minutes in which to entertain me."

Crossing back to his favorite armchair before the fire and disregarding manners, he sat. He waved a lazy hand toward the matching chair, then leaned back. Good manners dictated a gentleman never seated himself before a lady. It also dictated that a bachelor 's library shouldn't be invaded after midnight by unknown women.

From under half-closed lids, he observed her jerky body movements and considered her long moments of vacillation. Decision made, his unwanted visitor perched on the chair 's edge and spread her skirts. The unconscious gesture reinforced his impression that she mixed in the highest echelons of society.

"You may wait at the door, Perkins. The lady shall leave in five minutes."

Glancing at her again, he noted the precise way she sat, feet placed together and spine as rigid as his brass fire poker. Her whole appearance was far too upright—almost uptight—to be one of the indolent and immoral women of higher society that he despised in secret.

He fixed her with his fiercest lordly gaze, designed to make her squirm in her seat. The irritating woman neither moved a muscle nor rushed to fill the silence, as many women felt the need to do. His fingers clenched hard around his glass until he feared it would break while he tried to outwait her. Impossible woman. He broke the silence himself.

"Please, go ahead. You've only four minutes remaining. No, no, stop!" He held up a hand to her. "I refuse to discuss any sort of proposition without knowing who you are."

"That is not necessary."

He smiled a predatory grin. "Oh, but it is. My reputation may have mislead you to think that I'm indiscriminate in the women I befriend—"

"Nor, my lord, do we need to become friends to meet the terms of my proposal."

"Nevertheless, you'll remove your veils before we go any further."

"No. I told you it's not necess— "

"Very well." He pushed to his feet. "Perkins, we're finished here." She muttered something under her breath that wasn't at all ladylike. "P-pardon me?" He didn't bother to hide his amusement. "Did I hear you repeat a favorite seamen's curse? Tut, tut, my dear. Shame on you."

Her breath blew out in a loud rush. She hesitated, then reached up to the ends of her veil. With the slow precision of an experienced whore exposing herself in an East End brothel, she peeled back the remaining layer of black lace and chiffon to reveal her face.

Damnation! What had he done? His breath caught as a rush of lust and longing swamped him, one he'd not experienced in a very long time. He absently rubbed at the ache in the middle of his chest. No, she didn't have the cherubic prettiness of a seventeen-year-old blond and blue-eyed chit just blossoming into womanhood. Nor was his widow what fashion dictated as of the first stare because, at present, that leaned to women with hourglass figures. Women petite enough to make a man feel like a true male, a protector.

Instead, when she'd looked up at him, she'd tilted her head scant inches to meet his eyes. No fragile fairy, then. Plenty of women seemed either threatened by his above- average size, or alternatively titillated by the thought. Belief in the old adage of large feet and large hands leading to large other parts encouraged many women to make advances to test the theory. He guessed her age to be around his own, a tad over thirty years, give or take a year or two, but her clothing made it hard to decipher. She could be older than him by a few years, which would mean edging toward forty years and what the older generation called the mature years.

Yet, something about this woman snared his attention with an intensity that shocked him. If being unkind, her hair would be described as plain brown. But, strangely, he considered it anything but ordinary, with streaks of auburn throwing up gleaming red glints in the firelight.

His own dark eyes matched his near black hair and while hers were also dark, they were different, so very different to his. Where his inclined to the blackest of nights, hers glowed brown like sunsets, with luminescent rings of green and gold that matched the glinting sparks from her hair. The combination robbed him of breath.

No, no, no! He shook his head. He only noticed because of late he'd stopped looking at the array of morsels dangled before him. Redheads with green eyes, dark- haired gypsies, and other exotic combinations of coloring he used to enjoy. Swallowing hard, twice, he tried to recover his voice.

"I'm afraid you have me at the disadvantage. I cannot remember if, or where, we might have met."

She looked away and then back at him. "You were correct. I'm only recently arrived from the country."

"Which part of the country would that be exactly?"

Her brown brows nearly met in the middle of her forehead when she frowned so deeply, her irritation evident. Rousing this woman was a delight.

"Where I'm from is of no consequence. I wish to discuss something of importance with you, and I've little time."

He glanced at the clock. "Actually, your time is up."

"Oooh!" Her fists clenched at her sides. "Do you delight in always being difficult?"

He grinned, entertained. "Yes. Always."

She narrowed her gaze and sucked in a breath. Once more his own breath caught in his chest as he watched her breasts rise, then fall. Full and heavy. Even the misshapen black dress couldn't conceal their shape from his practiced gaze.

Noticing where his eyes focused, she glanced down. "Damn you, this is more difficult than I believed. My informant said you were open to business arrangements. That you didn't create unnecessary difficulties."

"Not any longer."

"Excuse me?" She frowned again and once more, he enjoyed it. "Not any longer for what?"

Leaning forward in his chair, he pressed his face closer to hers. "I now delight in creating difficulties." He smirked. "Take. Off. Your. Gown."

She jumped to her feet. "What did you say?"

"You heard me. I said, undress. If you expect me to make some sort of bargain, I need to inspect what you're offering."

"My lord, you're talking at cross purposes. Again. To deliberately disconcert me. I'm not offering my—" Fists clenched into the folds of her skirt. "I'm not offering that sort of bargain. My friends and I need your help. Your ... expertise."

"Ah. You want me to entertain a group of you."

"No! I don't want that at all." One booted foot stomped on the carpeted floor. "Oooh! Stop putting words into my mouth."

"Mmm. Nasty temper. See, I learn a little more about you each minute we're together."

"In everything I was told, nobody explained you were so exasperating. A gentleman who delights in tying my mind in knots."

"Who's been telling tales about me? And what did they say to entice a country mouse to leave her haystack and scurry to my fireside in the dead of night?"

With a whoosh, she sank back down into the chair across from him, frustration and need warring on her face. "My two friends are having difficulties. With your wide experience, we feel you're the ideal person to assist us. To broaden our education. In exchange for your help, I shall provide you with information regarding your mother and two sisters. Proof they are living in a region of England that your investigators previously searched but didn't locate them."

He rose to his feet. "The last person offering that sort of information was telling lies. All that so-called lady offered was her body and frankly, a romp in bed with another deceitful aristocrat didn't interest me. Although, she did promise five of her very best friends would join us for the week." Her eyes opened wide, very wide, and her question was an astonished squeak. "Five?"

"Yes, sadly, some higher class of ladies want to invite all their friends to test my stamina. There's a reason they called me the Virile Viscount."

"You mean ... You ... " She fluttered fingers at his groin area. "You and six ladies?"

"Yes, on one memorable occasion. But only because I needed money to buy extra shares in a new railway venture. I did enlist assistance. From friends, from staff."

She audibly gulped. "Staff?" Another adorable little squeak.

Sweet, refreshing. His country mouse brazenly invaded his house and pretended sophistication, yet failed to comprehend real levels of depravity.

"Oh yes, my lady, I employ several large, and well-endowed, footmen at my estate."

She nodded with such enthusiasm that her odious hat bobbed. "That's why we must attend one of the parties at your house. I've heard it called your Pleasure House."

"Naïve little lady, have you any inkling of the events taking place at those weekends?"

"Of course." Her proud little nose tilted higher. "You hold orgies."

"Held! I'm finished with having visitors to the Pleasure House." He laughed without mirth. "In the past, bored gentry paid me well for their dreams." He ticked off the numbers on his fingers. "Husbands escaping eagle-eyed wives. Rakes who've sampled every whorehouse in town. Green lads with money in their pockets and randy cocks in their pants. And then, of course, we've the women."

The red in her cheeks heightened. "What do the women want?"

"Are you sure you want to hear this?"

She looked him in the eye and nodded, bravely determined.

"Ladies want to scream aloud upon having their orifices filled by a colossal cock. A prick standing proud and erect from the bulging balls of a gargantuan footman. Rather than the tickle of a drooped appendage from an aged husband."

He expected shock, but remained undecided if her expression revealed horror, intrigue, or arousal. He wanted her to turn tail and scamper away.

"Even though women partake of quick screws bent over settees three nights a week with well-used rakes, these oh-so-proper-ladies crave the thrill of savoring all three of those men at their leisure. Without worrying if the library door is locked." He gave a growl of disgust. "Or if their innocent daughter sees Mama with her skirts tossed over her head and her pussy being ploughed by Papa's younger brother—"

"Enough!" She held up a hand. "It's easy to envisage how being surrounded by depravity disillusions even the most hardened rake. Still, it fails to explain why you stopped."

He waved a negligent hand. "Simple. I no longer needed the money. More importantly, I no longer enjoyed it. The women look the same. With and without clothes. Plus there is my hard-and-fast rule." He grinned. "There. Are. No. Watchers. Not at all."

Her golden brown eyes opened wide again, like glowing full moons. "No-no-no watchers."

Her high-pitched voice made him smile, even while his breathing quickened and his mouth dried. "No, only participants. Even if I was willing to open the house, you'd need to participate in the group romps."

"Gr-gr-group romps?" She faltered over the words, sounding unsure, quivery.

"Orgies! If you comprehend Greek or Latin terms better."

She squeaked again. He hid his smile. He rather liked her tiny mousey noises. Idly, he wondered if she made them in the throes of passion, as she was about to climax. Or would his little mouse become a full-throated screamer? A sudden desire to know wracked him.

His long dead appendage moved behind the placket of his pants. Twitched once, again, and again. Unbelievable. A whore's large bosoms had fallen into his lap and not a single jerk stirred his pants. Yet this dowdy woman stirred his cock into eagerness and demanded attention. Stunned, he glanced down, expecting his prick to be peeking out, eager to catch a glimpse of the femme fatale creating this phenomenon. In this position as he leaned over her, his groin was level with her face. Or more accurately, her mouth and soft pink lips. Did she know how to use them on a man's arousal to suck him into oblivion? Would she do it if he asked?

Dozens of other nameless women would jump at the chance. He didn't think she'd be one of them. Not yet. Perhaps she could be persuaded another time. No, he certainly wouldn't contemplate any other time. She would be dispatched tonight, before his mind went where it shouldn't, and his traitorous body followed.

She started to stand, but his arms trapped her. Her breasts bumped his chin. From his elevated angle, he peered down her gaping bodice, exposed when she leaned forward. His glimpse confirmed her breasts were indeed full and ripe, a woman's bountiful gifts.

Before he tempered his wayward tongue, he asked, "Do you have children?"

Pain flitted across her face. "No, I've never been blessed with them."

"Mmm. But you were married?"

"Yes, I'm a widow." "Recently?"

"Two years ago. Not that it matters to the business at hand." She peered up at him. "Why did you ask about children?"

"Because you've such magnificently lush breasts. They're made for suckling babies. And made for men's mouths."

"Oh!" She grabbed at her bodice to tug the sides together. "You're no gentleman to be peering at my bosom."

"You're quite correct." He shrugged. "I make no pretense to being a gentleman. And yes, my pretend prim princess, the flush on your cheeks tells me you're woman enough to be flattered because I think your breasts are so succulent that I long to draw them into my dry mouth. To take a long drink."

Whack!

"Ouch! That hurt." He rubbed the throb in his cheek where he was sure he carried the print of her hand. "Good," she snapped. "I intended it to."

"Why? If your husband didn't tell you every day of your married life that your breasts are magnificent, he was either blind or a fool." She slumped back into the chair, dropped her head, stared at the floor. A tense silence followed. "So," he probed with ruthless determination, "which was he? Blind or a fool?"

"His eyesight was perfect." "Ah, a perfect fool then. But now, it's truly time you departed. Before your reputation is compromised. Residents in my square resented my inheriting this house three years ago. Many still loathe me for residing here and lowering the tone of this exclusive area. They watch my house like hawks and report my comings and goings to the gossip sheets."

"Why would they bother?"

"Because I'm an upstart in the eyes of many. I didn't make my fortune in the time way of titled families, by inheriting it. My father left huge debts, whereas I've worked for every penny." He gave a disgusted snort. "The Pleasure House began it. Then, by using my

God given intelligence, I invested well and now reap the results. That doesn't sit well with men who've never lifted a finger to pour their own brandy." He gave a self- derogatory laugh. "Nor with women who treat people who perform any sort of task other than attending social events as of lower intelligence."

"I'm not bothered over my reputation. Few people know me in London. Even fewer are interested in my movements."

He studied her, frowned. "What about your family?"

"My family, such as it is, only cares about one thing." He raised a questioning brow. She shrugged, her feigned indifference not hiding her distress. "My money. And how quickly they may get their hands on it."

"Ah, I see." With his hand on the small of her back, he guided her to the door.

Before they reached Perkins, she halted and turned to him. "Please, call upon me tomorrow morning. At least meet my friends. Hear their stories."

"You haven't consented to give me your name."

She smiled, a real one at last. "From what I know of you, my lord, you intend having my carriage followed home. By morning, you'll know not only where I reside, but who I am." At his look of surprise, she added, "Do you deny it?"

He threw back his head and laughed. "Madam, you're a refreshing delight to a man's jaded palate. I mistook you for the normal spoiled bitch invading my privacy on a whim or a dare. However, you've beaten me at my own game. Yes, I'll have your carriage followed. And yes, by morning, I'll know everything about you."

Pretty white teeth worried her bottom lip, turning it the color of a ripe tomato, red and succulent. His neglected groin tingled, tightened. He needed to be careful around this particular lady, or she'd assuredly best him. In bed and out of it. Assuming she ended where he was already sure she was headed. Where he wanted her. Sliding undressed between his sheets.

"Then, Hawkesbury, I wish you goodnight."

"Pleasant dreams, my lady."

Bending, he intended kissing the fingers of her gloved hand but at the last second he changed his mind and tilted his head. His lips brushed her cheek. Soft as velvet and smelling of freshly picked garden violets. In surprise, she turned toward him.

Unable to resist the temptation, he brushed a butterfly-light caress over her lips and hovered, a scant breath away, before pulling back without succumbing to his raw need to taste her fully. The tension between them sizzled as heatedly as the air in a train driver 's cabin. He swallowed hard, fought for control. After several long moments, he stepped back and released her into Perkins's care.

He dallied in the anteroom after she departed, giving orders to Johnson to follow the lady's carriage. Her assumption was quite correct. He'd have done the same for any midnight visitor. However, he'd take special care to discover all her secrets. His black clad lady, the one bargaining with his family's future, resembled a multi-layered flower he yearned to unravel, one layer at a time, until the bud inside blossomed.

Ah, yes! Her auburn hair draped across his red silk sheets, across his naked body, would be incredible. A tightening in his groin made him reach down, check. Unbelievable! A hard-as-a-rock throbbing arousal greeted him.

His long dormant body had surged back to life.

3

Grosvenor Square ... West End of London

LADY CHRISSIE WELLSBY halted her pacing before the richly curtained bay window and groaned. Pulling aside the decorative swath of expensive peach fabric, she peered past her portico to where the square thronged with people and transportation of every sort. The noises she normally found soothing deafened her today.

She covered her ears to block out the ringing bell of the penny postman and the rattle of the wheels of the omnibus, but nothing helped. To her frustration, she couldn't sight a dark-haired viscount striding with his long-muscled legs toward her door so instead she muttered and fretted. Terrified he'd come, petrified he wouldn't.

"He's not coming," she said, speaking over her shoulder to her friends.

The two ladies, both beautiful, both very proper, both putting their uttermost faith in Chrissie's ability to solve their problems, observed her every movement.

"I prayed I'd be able to convince the viscount, but his mistrust of women runs deeper than I realized. Hawkesbury thinks I tried to cheat my way into his house, or into his bed. He believes I'm cut from the same cloth as all those other women who have fed him lies about his family in return for some sort of gratification." She nibbled on the corner of a fingernail. "And slapping his face mightn't have been prudent."

"No, possibly not the best way to gain his attention," Gillian said in a dry tone.

Her friends, and closest neighbors from the country, had followed her monotonous progress back and forth across the Westminster carpet for the past hour. All three of them suffered shredded nerves.

Giving a small squeal, Chrissie tightened the hand already constricting the curtain fabric and then announced, "Oh, merciful heavens, he's here. The notorious Viscount Hawkesbury is standing outside my door." She spun around to her friends, patted her already tidy hair, smoothed down the folds of her gown, wrung her hands. "Now, behave ... behave naturally. As if ... as if ... we engage a male sex instructor every day of the week. As if we're in total control of the situation."

"Even if we're terrified?" Anna's eyes were a wide-eyed plea.

Gillian, Countess of Eagleby, reached across to pat her friend's trembling knee. "Anna, all will go according to Chrissie's plan. Remember, we've discussed this. I know you're worried, but this man, this experienced viscount, is the only one who can help us. With his tutelage, we'll be well equipped to see to the physical needs of the men in our lives."

Lady Wellsby faced the double doors of her receiving room as her butler pushed them open. She swallowed, hard, as she realized the Virile Viscount lived up to his reputation. Heaven help them all. Despite the lateness of the hour when she'd departed his residence in the neighboring square, the man had looked fresh, and groomed to perfection. So strikingly male, so tall, so wide, and so commanding a presence, he stole the air out of her lungs, and out of the room.

She smoothed her sweaty palms down the sides of her morning

gown—a canary yellow to achieve a cheery mood—for a third time. She needed a chance to catch her breath and slow her racing heart. Her butler announced him in a slow and formal voice while she composed herself to step forward, to greet him without shaking. When Nichols withdrew, she performed the required introductions to her friends.

"May I present Miss Anna Smith, who is to be married to Captain Leonard Blythe of the Queen's Guards?" Anna dipped a curtsy and the viscount bowed from the waist.

"May I also present the Countess of Eagleby?"

"Ah, Eagleby and I were friends many years ago, as young bucks around town. I'd heard that he married. My felicitations." He dipped a formal bow before Gillian, whose face turned as white as a wash-day sheet, until Chrissie feared she'd faint.

When Hawkesbury studied her with the same intensity, her cheeks heated, excitement surged through her veins like heated steel, and she fought the urge to fan her face. The man's eyes were far too knowing, his gaze too searching, too delving.

"So, the mystery deepens." He turned to address Gillian. "Perhaps I was misled, but I believed Eagleby to be a happily married man. Yet, as a married woman and a new mother, you've joined your friends in their little misadventure. Might I ask why?"

Gillian looked up at him, wide-eyed. "When ... when I told Chrissie—"

"Chrissie?" He looked at her with one haughtily raised brow.

"We'd no chance to become properly introduced last evening. Nevertheless, I assumed your underlings scurried around in the middle of the night discovering everything about me."

His mouth opened an inch, pleasing Chrissie, as she imagined few people managed to surprise the shrewd viscount to the extent he displayed loss of control. He dipped his head and grinned, a dazzling transformation, until, with mounting horror, she watched her two friends twitter, smile, and fall under his spell. Oh, good heavens!

No wonder women spoke of him in awe-struck tones, or snuck into his house like thieves at every opportunity. Inwardly she groaned, knowing her behavior to be no better. She appeared as another lady of low morals, hounding him for his erotic experience.

Between the firelight and the distraction of a room full of half-naked women last night, Chrissie had noticed only that Hawkesbury's dark coloring of blue-black hair and midnight eyes gave him the same sultry look as that brazen gypsy dancer. Even in the light of a new day, the image of him sucking on that hussy's toes irritated her. His looks would send an eighty-year- old spinster head over heels. Blast the man.

"You're correct, Lady Wellsby. I discovered your location and title. It may take a little longer, perhaps the entire day," he said as he flashed his disarming smile, "to uncover all your secrets. Therefore, it'd be easier if you divulged your plans freely to me, rather than have m y underlings scurrying around seeking information."

Despite herself, Chrissie chuckled while her friends openly laughed. He'd already charmed them out of their country reserve. Shrewd, manipulative, absurdly handsome—damn! How did that thought creep in?

"I find myself intrigued by the three of you. Perhaps if you explain the drastic circumstances forcing you to approach me, I may offer some alternatives."

"But we want you—you're the best tutor in the sensual arts in England."

Under his darkly tanned cheeks, he flushed, appearing embarrassed. "Ladies, you labor under a misconception. When I opened the Pleasure Houses, I needed capital for my shipping ventures. I supplied everything. Venue. Entertainers. Footmen. But recently, I retired my title as the city's notorious lover. For several reasons, I've not participated in any actual ... ah—"

"Orgies?" Anna added with a child-like smile. "We know how you earned your well-deserved title as the Virile Viscount."

"No need for false modesty about your abilities," Gillian said. "We've asked women who've been entertained at your rituals, in your baths. They sing your praises."

"No, no, ladies. The depravity of some of the peers who participate in the ceremonies on my estate would be far too shocking for ladies of your sensibilities."

Chrissie smiled at him. "That's why we're employing you. England's most notorious, most experienced lover can introduce us to every erotic and exotic art. Teach us everything. Ensure that nothing will frighten us in the future."

His eyes widened, and for a second he looked almost ... terrified. Then he smirked.

"Ah, but before I'd agree to take my prick out of retirement and open the Pleasure House, or to perform my God of Sex ritual, I'd require a solemn promise from Lady Wellsby. Chrissie would need to agree to portray the sacrificial virgin I traditionally fuck on the altar."

Chrissie coughed, choked, spluttered, and then stared, stunned. She didn't know whether to laugh, cry, or scream. The wretched viscount had bested her after all, drawn her in with that single erotic image. She imagined him as her Sultan and herself as his slave, or one of those ladies he'd spoken of, her skirts tossed over her head as the Virile Viscount shared everything with her—lust, sex, and pleasure.

"My lord, last night I was a nuisance you couldn't be rid of fast enough. Yet today we're friends. Why such a sudden change of heart?"

"I find myself intrigued by the three of you. I can't fit you into the normal roles of women who've approached me over the years with various propositions."

"Is it so hard to believe we may simply be asking for your help, Justin?" Gillian asked.

"Yes," Anna said, sharing a shy and secretive smile. "We have it on good authority that you're the very best at what you do."

"And what is it you think I do so well?" Justin asked.

"Apart from providing a place for men, and women, to act out their fantasies, you teach the arts of seduction to inept gentlemen who need instruction in the bedchamber," Chrissie said.

"Or, in our case," Gillian said, "for women who need instruction on how to please a man in the bedroom."

"Although we spend a good part of the year at our country estates, we've friends in London,"

Anna said. "We know women who've been to your baths. To your various rooms."

"The ladies who've visited the baths did so in disguise. Some however, don't care. It's part of the excitement to unveil their faces in the dance of the seven veils."

"We've read of the things that happen in a harem," Anna said.

"So that we'd be well prepared for anything we saw," Gillian added in an excited rush, her face flushing red.

Justin shook his head. "I don't think you've any understanding of the sort of depravity some people are capable of when under the influence of drink."

Chrissie looked at her two friends and said, "Perhaps if I explained your situations to Justin alone, it may prove less ... ah ... embarrassing ... for both of you." Anna and Gillian both stood to take their leave. "Justin, I need to do this," Gillian implored him. "Please, let me come to the baths."

"I've also good reasons for needing the experience," Anna said, as she too departed.

Chrissie saw her friends to the door and then returned to take a seat across from Justin. He lounged on the sofa, his posture one of ease with one long booted leg crossed at the knee over the other. She'd have to be dead not to notice how the position tightened his breeches over his thighs so they clung to his muscled form like a wet leather glove. A frisson of sensual interest shivered down her spine as she surveyed him. What would it be like to have a man, a real man like the viscount in your bed?

Her late husband had been an inept and selfish lover, something she'd only understood later when she'd discovered that many women found pleasure, rather than embarrassment and pain in their marital bed. And that lower class women, maids and whores alike, romped with men not only for coin but for the enjoyment they gained from it.

The first time she'd inadvertently happened across a footman ploughing a maid in the stable, she'd mistaken the cause of the girl's moans and had been on the point of rushing to her aid. Then the girl had called out, "Oh yes, Dickey, like that. Do that again." Feeling like an eavesdropper but unable to contain her curiosity, she'd listened around the corner until a stirring of arousal had prompted her to peek. The pair had been so engrossed in each other, swimming in their own lust, they wouldn't have noticed her unless she'd dropped a bucket of water on their heads.

Several times after that, she'd wandered, quite deliberately, into darkened spots where she knew lovers met, in the hope of catching more couples in randy embraces. Somehow, enjoying a little of the overflow of their desires eased the distress in her own love life. Even when her husband was alive, he'd thought a quick coupling once a week after he rolled in drunk from a night with his cronies consti- tuted lovemaking. Later, when she knew he reserved any emotion or passion for a woman other than her, she'd been past caring. Her regret concerned never seeing her belly swell with his child, not his visits to the local widow when he was drunk.

She rarely saw her husband sober in the evenings, and knowing his distaste for coupling in daylight, she imagined the widow fared no better than she did. A quick grope under the sheets, port fumes breathed into her face, and the sound of his pig-like grunts had been all she'd received for Geoffrey. Then came the snores after he'd collapsed in an undignified heap across the bed.

Chrissie drew a deep breath before looking the viscount in the eye. It took great fortitude to stare at a face as heaven sent as his and not do what countless of other women had obviously done over the years— swoon at his feet.

"I suppose I should begin by telling you why it is so important that we all go to your house. Why we all want to learn from what we see there. And why we need to do it immediately."

He waved an elegant hand in a cream glove that looked so soft as to be made of butter. The viscount may have needed money three years ago, but his wealth now was reported to be one of the largest in the country. He could afford the best of everything.

She'd need a very convincing argument if she were to coerce him into opening the Pleasure House. But the future happiness of her two friends depended upon it. And hers too, she supposed, though there would be other avenues available to her later. Marriage was definitely not on her agenda any time soon.

Chrissie drew a deep breath before beginning. "Gillian thought her marriage was indeed very happy. But since her baby was born ten months ago, Edward has been spending a lot more time in London, coming home less. You need to understand that Gillian's mother is— oh, dear, how do I state this without sounding rude—the woman can be quite critical and stifling. She sheltered Gillian before her marriage, yet to my mind, it was more to the benefit of the older lady than the younger one."

"Ah, I see. Quite a common story. A mother who insists a daughter stays close at all times so she herself has someone to dote on her. Not the other way about."

"Exactly. And at present, she insists on spending long stretches of time with Gillian and pretending she does so to assist Gillian with the baby."

"But you don't think that is what happens?"

"Gillian's mother is far more concerned with living in the comfort of Edward's large house than anything to do with her new grandson. She convinced Gillian that it wasn't good for a husband to commence his attentions in the bedroom too soon after the baby is born."

The viscount studied her with his shrewd and intent gaze. "But once again you think that Gillian's mother has ulterior motives."

"I'm positive she does. She'd be happier if another baby didn't arrive for quite a long time. She enjoys playing lady of the manor so she deliberately keeps poor Edward from Gillian's bed. The unfortunate consequence has been that Gillian worries about Edward turning elsewhere for that sort of comfort, as many gentlemen do. Perhaps he has already."

"Gillian thinks her husband has taken a mistress?"

She nodded. "Yes. She confronted Edward when he was at home two weeks ago. He vehemently denied such a notion. But a week ago, he left again."

"So what does Gillian want from me? Surely she doesn't imagine taking a lover herself would solve those sort of problems in her marriage."

"No, no. Not that. Gillian loves Edward with all her heart. She believes ..." She broke off with a long sigh.

"Yes?" he encouraged. "She believes what?"

"Gillian has convinced herself, perhaps mistakenly ... I simply do not know enough about these things myself to counsel her. I'm out of my depth."

When she stopped speaking, he raised one dark eyebrow in question as if he was used to gaining all he needed from that one aristocratic and arrogant action. Evidently the man expected to have everything he desired fall into his lap. And it most likely did. He ignored her little put-upon huff and continued his silent wait for more explanation.

"Gillian believes that by visiting your Pleasure House and observing the happenings there, learning how gentlemen find their pleasure with courtesans, she'll entice Edward back into their marital bed. If he's happy at home, she hopes he'll not stray again. She blames herself and her self-esteem has suffered a terrible blow."

"And Anna? Does she also imagine she can watch but not participate?"

"None of us plan on becoming part of an orgy, but we'd like to observe what happens. When Anna was seventeen, she was left homeless and penniless by the death of her parents. Neighbors arranged her betrothal to their son in the army as a way of securing Anna's future, but they had only one night together before he left with his regiment. He is now returning. Unfortunately, we've heard a rumor that he has been ... courting the daughter of the commander ... while he was posted on the continent. Anna is nineteen but she's been sheltered all her life and knows nothing of life outside our area. She believes that under your tutelage she can learn how to please the captain and hold his attention during their marriage."

"I feel for Anna and Gillian. I really do. But I doubt their problems can be solved with a short visit to my estate. Besides, you haven't explained what you hope to gain by going there."

"Nothing. I'm doing this to help my friends. We agreed I was best positioned to secure your cooperation and arrange our days away from home as I have a house in London. Their families only know Gillian and Anna are accompanying me on a long overdue visit to the estate where I was raised."

"And that estate is close to mine?"

"Somewhat."

"Oh no, Chrissie. Before I make a decision about holding another event at the Pleasure House, I need total honesty. So far, you've not convinced me that you can help me locate my mother and sisters. Others have sworn they have proof of their whereabouts, but their evidence sent me down the wrong road. Time and again. How do I know your story won't also be a false start?"

"Your mother may not still be alive, Justin, I have to be honest about that. The last information I investigated was several months old before it reached me and when I searched, your family had already moved on. At that stage, your mother was ill."

Justin flinched. She knew her news upset him.

"Local people said she suffered from a persistent cough. Most likely caused by too many months in the damp accommodation they'd leased. Perhaps it's consumption. I don't know. I couldn't confirm it one way or another."

After searching for his family for three long years, Justin had obviously considered the possibility that he'd locate his family too late to save them. Disease and illness were a major part of daily life and poverty and starvation wore people down faster than anything.

"Justin, as there's no way of knowing your mother 's present condition, I can make no promises. But I do know your two sisters enjoyed good health when they lived in that village. They shifted when one of your sisters found employment in another village as a teacher. Unfortunately, the area named by my investigators consists of several schools spread over a large area, making it a slow process to discover which ones had hired teachers in the past year. But I've been promised news by next week. News that sounds very promising."

"So you're going to use this information to blackmail me into opening the Bath House?"

Chrissie threw back her head and laughed. "That is rich coming from you. I've heard that you've resorted to blackmail in your search for your family, my lord. Yet you balk at me hinting at it now."

"Touché, Chrissie. Very well. We'll talk terms. I'm desperate to find my family, especially if my mother is sick, and I'll do anything to locate them. I'd like to find my mother and bring her home before she ... before anything happens to her. I'm rich enough now that my sisters need never work again. I want to give them the life they should have lived if not for my father. He drove them out of their house. Forced them to take to the streets."

He turned to face the landscape on her wall but she'd already glimpsed the raw agony etched on his face. This man suffered. Suffered a deep and lasting cut to his heart. Even if she had no other motives for this quest, Chrissie would have been moved by his plight. That had always been her problem, according to her late husband. She gave herself, all of herself, to others. Geoffrey had complained constantly that she'd not enough time and energy left over for him and his needs.

At least, that had been the excuse he'd flouted, but by then she'd been past caring. There'd been too many months of excuses and too many times she'd forgiven his drunken state as he reeled into bed in the pre-dawn hours reeking of ale. And occasionally of the cheap perfume the widow used.

The ale she'd railed against, berating Geoffrey for wasting his life sleeping off the effects of his drinking and habitually leaving his estate for her to manage. Why had she also not railed against the infidelity he'd blamed on her? In the end, he'd not bothered to conceal his visits to the widow. Perhaps she'd stopped caring long before he passed.

She may have spent a lot of her time in the country after her marriage, but before that, when she was younger, she'd attended the grandest balls in London. She'd had her season. But her family's financial constraints had meant that she'd been pressured into accepting a proposal from the eligible Lord Wellsby at too young an age.

As fate had decreed it, her husband had been gifted with a wonderful estate, despite not being born as heir to the title and all the trappings that went with it. That had gone to his elder brother. But their great aunt had always held a fondness for Geoffrey, and his fake flattery, and after the earl inherited vast wealth in his own right, their aunt ensured Geoffrey would be comfortably set up for life by bequeathing him her own smaller, yet significant estates.

Upon Geoffrey's death, Chrissie had become independently wealthy. No one, least of all his disreputable brother, could touch her inheritance. Not only did Geoffrey's aunt appreciate his form of flattery, she also congratulated Geoffrey for having enough good sense to recognize that Chrissie made a far better estate manager than he did.

Great-aunt Imelda had seen to the legalities before her death in the event that Geoffrey ran true to family form and tried to squander the money. She'd informed Chrissie over tea one afternoon that in the event of Geoffrey's untimely death, Chrissie mustn't fret. Her future was assured. And she'd been correct. Chrissie was comfortably situated, more than comfortably.

So now, when the viscount asked why she'd chosen to aid her friends this way, Chrissie found it difficult to give him a suitable reason. She'd money enough to buy any sexual thrills she desired. She didn't need the Pleasure House in the same way her two friends did. She shook herself free of her mind's useless wanderings. Too much time had been spent revisiting her failed marriage and mulling over the wasted years of her life. Now was the time to move forward. To make more of her remaining years.

"Viscount ... Justin ..." He turned back to meet her gaze, his features once again schooled to reflect his customary reserve, and his self-control. "We can help each other and then move on, having gained all we need for our mutual satisfactions."

"Before I agree to your terms, my lady, we have another small problem. I don't know all the details of your own marriage, but I assume that any of the countess's bedroom antics were ... sedate. Uninspired. Under cover of darkness."

Chrissie gave a nod of agreement, not sure where this conversation was leading.

"And I also assume that as Anna has led a sheltered life with her prospective relatives, she has little knowledge of the more sordid side of sexual escapades."

Once again, Chrissie nodded, her apprehension rising.

"Then our main problem will be, my dear, that even if you're not anticipating an active role in the various entertainments at my house, many of the themed events take place during the day."

Chrissie gave him a blank stare.

The viscount sighed. "Broad daylight, Chrissie. You three ladies will be exposed, day and night, to the perversions around you. You'll not be able to escape. You'll not be able to squeeze your pretty little eyes shut and not look."

He grinned, a triumphant smug smile that irritated the hell out of her and put her back up. The arrogant viscount thought that by issuing that statement that he'd win, that she'd run away from the idea with her tail between her legs.

"We've no intention of keeping our eyes closed, my lord. That would defeat our purpose."

"Ah, but I'm afraid I must insist on at least testing that theory, and your fortitude, before I invite all and sundry to my estate. After all, the rituals may never take place. You may take fright before then and I'd look foolish before my acquaintances."

With that ludicrous statement, the viscount's self-satisfied smile became even more arrogantly pleased with himself. Chrissie frowned. She had no idea where this was leading but she'd no intention of allowing the viscount to win this battle. She may look like the country mouse he'd labeled her last night, but he was about to discover that even country mice could be cunning and devious. Especially when escaping from a stalking cat.

"Once I give my word on something, I do not renege. Ever. I'll surrender the information I've gathered and in return you shall open your estate, and the Bath House, for a week."

"If I agreed to this at all, it wouldn't be for a full week. Trust me on this, Chrissie. You, and your lady friends wouldn't survive a week of the house's excesses. One night, or day, will shock you so much that I predict you'll be scurrying, like the country mice you are, back to the safety of your hidey holes."

Chrissie tapped an impatient foot on the carpeted floor. The man tried her patience, to the extreme. Thankfully, after a week in his presence, they'd never have to meet again. She and the viscount rubbed sparks off each other's hide at every step. But for now, she'd pretend an equable acquaintance with the annoying man.

"I agree," she stated with a guileless smile.

Justin halted mid pace across the room, stopped with his mouth agape once more. She liked having that effect on the man. Enjoyed ruffling his demeanor.

"You agree to what? I haven't told you my terms yet."

"You just did. You said we wouldn't survive for an entire week and I agreed. Three days will be quite sufficient, thank you."

His eyes widened in shock. "I haven't agreed to any days yet, and you very well know it. You're putting words into my mouth."

Chrissie gave her sweetest and most insincere smile. "As you did to me? Perhaps you'd prefer we stayed for four days. To really absorb the atmosphere of your extravagances. Very well. I agree to your suggested extension of days." His lips twitched. At least the man possessed a good sense of humor. That was one thing in his favor.

"So, you think to outwit me? Let me assure you, Chrissie, I've been playing games of intrigue a lot longer than you. I've perfected the arts of confusion and diversion. You deliberately pretended to misunderstand the terms of our agreement. What I was about to say was that, in order to prepare you three ladies, I shall be escorting you to a very special place this evening."

Chrissie had a premonition of disaster. Hair on the back of her neck stood to attention. She had a bad feeling about his proposed outing. This man was sneaky and she needed to be on guard or he'd outwit her, despite the air of inconsequence he took pains to present to society.

No wonder the viscount was successful with investments. The man was shrewd, apart from being ridiculously handsome. Damnation! Why was she noticing the man's attractions? She knew better than to fall a gentleman's glib lines.

"I've a very bad feeling about what sort of special place you have in mind. Why do I sense that the most notorious viscount in the whole of London doesn't intend escorting us somewhere as inconsequential as the opera, or the theatre?"

"Perhaps because we're going somewhere a lot more exciting. Somewhere to test your mettle. You'll wear something flamboyant, perhaps in a vibrant red."

"Red?" She gave a small brittle laugh. "Are we going to a bawdy house?"

"Exactly!"

"What! No, no. I was jesting."

"Ah, but I wasn't. We shall attend the Sultan's Palace tonight. You will observe what happens in each of the special rooms, especially the red room."

"I don't think that's a good idea," she spat out in horror.

"Ah, but the point is, my dear, that I do."

Hawkesbury swept into a low, and probably ironic, bow. Before she could recover her thoughts, or her speech, he started toward the door.

He spoke over his shoulder to her as he walked. "Ten o'clock. Be ready. I'll call and collect all of you here."

After he'd departed, Chrissie sank into a chair, stunned he'd won their small battle after all. Few people vanquished her these days, and she didn't know whether to laugh or cry that it should be Justin, the Virile Viscount.

Perhaps she should scurry back to her country hidey hole after all.

4

Justin jogged down the steps from Lady Wellsby's house to the pavement, unable to keep the grin from his face. Reaching the street, he turned, looked up at her house, and laughed out loud. Even if Chrissie's information proved as useless as other leads he'd followed, the deep ennui weighing him down had already lightened while his mind accepted the challenges ahead with enthusiasm instead of dread. Three unusual women had renewed his interest in the opposite sex and stirred an interest in fucking that he'd thought long dead.

Two elderly ladies strolled by, arm in arm, their footman trailing behind carrying a bejeweled pug dog. The women stopped and stared at his strange behavior, heads bent close together as they discussed him in over-loud whispers.

"Ladies." He doffed his hat and dipped his head to them, hiding his amusement. "Beautiful morning, is it not?" He smiled, pointed upwards. "One can even glimpse the sun."

He put his hands to his hips, pushed back the tails of his morning coat, and laughed again, glancing between the ladies, encouraging them to join him on his short trip to insanity. Although how to deal with a gentleman's public laughter was most likely not covered in a ladies' book of polite behavior, these two ladies seemed to appreciate his light-hearted mood. In unison, they nodded, smiled, and tittered.

The one dressed in lavender patted his arm. "It's not the sun that does it, you know."

Her rose-clothed counterpart shook her head and said, "Oh no, indeed no."

He raised his brows, threw his arms wide. "Does what exactly?"

They glanced at each other and giggled like schoolgirls before Miss Lavender said, "Makes young gentlemen act strangely."

"It's love," Miss Rose said, giving an emphatic nod.

"L'amour, as the French call it." Miss Lavender nodded vigorously.

"Ladies, I am sorry to disappoint you, but I gave up believing in love many years ago."

This time it was Miss Rose who patted his arm. "That may have been true before, dear, but you are in love now. We know the signs."

Two plumed bonnets—one brilliant pink and one eye-straining purple—waved while both ladies studied him as if he was an interesting museum exhibit.

"So lovely to see a young gentleman so caught up in the excitement of his first days of a new love that he laughs aloud."

"And on a street." Miss Rose clapped her gloved hands. "Wonderful. Simply wonderful."

"Thank you, sir," Miss Lavender said, also clapping, "for brightening our morning."

The ladies giggled again, linked arms, and turned away to resume their stroll.

Justin stayed where he was, feet rooted to the pavement like one of the street-lining oak trees. Ridiculous. If he felt any stirring for the lady he'd just left—and, unless he mistook the twitching of a curtain at her window, the lady who still watched him—lust was first and foremost. Also ridiculous to lust after a woman totally out of his social sphere, and one he'd merely locked horns with the night before.

He faced the bowed window above him, once again doffed his hat, and dipped a bow, before striding down the path and whistling a tuneless ditty. Nothing unordinary about the fact that he felt light-hearted, light-headed. Nothing extraordinary at all. No, no, no, everything in his life was as it had been a mere day earlier. Except that today he noticed the sun shined a shade brighter, and the colors of the matchmaking ladies' gowns were shades more brilliant than any he'd seen recently. And Chrissie's hair shone far more than any ordinary brown.

He shook his head and cursed under his breath. This was a momentary madness that would be over this evening, as soon as he revealed to the three ladies the sordid underlay of society when he took them to his brothel. True, he remained too much of a gentleman to allow them to witness the most shocking undertakings there, but even a small taste, a brief glimpse through the peep holes would turn them into cowards. He was certain of it.

Rather, the reaction of Chrissie's two friends seemed predictable. With her, he admitted to more tumultuous thoughts and feelings as she'd proved her courage in facing up to him last evening. She'd not backed down even though he'd gone out of his way to taunt and torment her.

He hailed a hackney, threw himself onto the grubby seat, and prepared himself for a tiresome day trudging around the haunts in London a country earl would amuse himself in. This particular gentleman needed a quick insight into the adventures, or misadventures, his wife and her two friends sought in the city.

Because, in a very short time, with or without Justin's guidance, these three ladies were set to inveigle themselves in a bundle of trouble. And during his wild last three years he'd held many reputations, yet savior of the innocent hadn't been amongst them. Despite that, the situation tickled Justin's rather warped sense of humor and he wondered if his detractors could bring themselves to title him a Good Samaritan. Nevertheless, he owed it to his old acquaintanceship, or perhaps even friendship, with Edward, the husband of the countess, to at least track his movements, locate the man, and discover what he knew of the situation.

Several hours later, or rather, several frustrating hours and much wear and tear on his boot leather, and his patience, he discovered that the earl resided with a friend in Mayfair on his frequent visits to London. After questioning the butler at that residence, he ascertained Edward and his friend, another peer, habitually took lunch at a club on Regent Street after their bouts of wearing boxing gloves at Gentleman Jackson's.

Telling himself that if the earl weren't within this time he'd give up his quest, Justin stiffened his spine, climbed the steps, and waited admittance. The benefit of his reputation, and perhaps the only benefit of his title of viscount, was instant recognition amongst the clubs, gaming halls, and brothels. Few establishments dared refuse admittance to any viscount, and few wanted to confront the Viscount of Vice.

The maître de showed him to the room where Edward sat at a table with another gentleman enjoying a lunch of rare roast beef. Glasses of claret sat beside their plates, all indicating a lengthy sojourn. Edward's posture, slumped in a red leather chair, told the tale of a man who'd drunk more than a glass or two of claret this morning.

"Edward," Justin said, standing close to the table and speaking in a low voice. No need to give the over-inquisitive ton more gossip fodder. "You're a damnably hard man to track down."

The earl shoved a lock of hair from his face and looked up, eyes bloodshot, and squinted over the top of his half empty glass.

"Good Lord. Justin, is that you? Haven't seen you in a donkey's age. Heard you inherited. Felicitations and all of that."

Edward attempted to straighten his long body and succeeded in sliding lower in his padded chair. "What brings you t' London? Heard you engaged in some sort of—" Edward waved his hand, scattering drops of blood-red claret over the thick carpet. "A pleasure thingy at your estate. So do you—"

"Edward!" After wasting nearly a whole day trailing the earl, Justin was in no mood to listen to any drunken wanderings. "I've not spent a long tedious morning following you around London in order to discuss my life." He glanced over at Edward's companion, whom he vaguely recognized but couldn't place. "Perhaps we should discuss this in private."

Edward waved his hand again, accompanied by another splatter of wine droplets. A footman stepped behind Edward and plucked the fine crystal from his lax fingers before he caused more damage to the expensive floor covering. Justin nodded his gratitude to the footman.

"Sorry, old man," Edward said, his words slurred. "This is Percy. Percy's second son of Duke of ... damn. Who the hell is your Pater again, Percy?"

The other man, who appeared considerably more sober than Edward, struggled to his feet. With agonizing slowness, formal introductions took place until, finally losing patience, Justin clasped Edward's elbow and drew him to a secluded alcove.

"Edward, I want to discuss your wife." Edward stared at him, eyes vacant, no sign of recognition of the word forthcoming. Justin clenched his fists and said, "The countess. You do remember your countess, don't you?"

"Yes, yes, course I do. Lovely, lovely woman, my wife. Beautiful baby. Miss them both. Miss them dearly. In the country, you know." He gave a deep sigh, his eyelids drooping as he drifted into remembrances and he leaned on the wall behind him as his knees buckled a little. "Wish—wish I could be there. With them." Edward's eyes were like a cow's when it hadn't been milked on time—sad, mournful, pleading. "Miss them."

Edward nodded so much his supporting arm on the plush wall slipped and he slumped floor- wards. Justin grabbed his forearm and pushed him, without ceremony, into a nearby chair.

"If you miss them so much," Justin said, "why the hell did you abandon them in the country? Why tomcat all over London with young bachelors and get yourself into no end of trouble?"

Edward put his hands on the arm supports and pushed himself up straighter. "Who said I'm in trouble? Just a bit of fun, don't you know. Bit of drink. Cards." He shook his head, moaned, and then grasped it between both hands. "Bloody head hurts. Can't think why.

And anyway, not women for me. Wouldn't do that. No, no, no. Not right for a married man."

His head slumped to one side and his eyes took on the miserable, but resigned, expression of a street urchin not finding a bed to sleep in for the night.

"No matter how randy a man gets on lonely nights, not right, don't you think, to chase skirts? When man's not long married too."

"No, you drunk idiot, it isn't right. Which is why I cannot fathom your intentions, Edward. The only woman you should be bedding at this stage of your marriage is your wife."

"Percy says—"

"Edward, I can well imagine what Percy tells you, but he's a bachelor. Different rules for an unmarried man."

"Says it's time I stopped mooning over my wife. Go and visit a bawdy house. Going to do it. Going tonight in fact." Edward started nodding again, looking like an out-of-control hand puppet. "Percy says—"

"Stop. I don't want to hear any more of Percy's words of wisdom." Justin looked at Edward's expression, stunned and wounded, and guilt swamped him. Poor Edward's wit had always lacked something, yet they'd remained friends because Edward's good nature ensured people loved him, and he made no enemies. So now, unraveling where the marriage had veered off on the wrong track remained Justin's first and foremost task, albeit not an easy one. Then he'd direct poor susceptible Edward back onto the correct path, reunite him with his loving countess, and dispatch three far too inquisitive ladies back to their safe brocaded and ornamented parlors.

Justin smiled, the smirk of a smug do-gooder. He was confident that in three whisks of a cat's tail, his good deed for the week, indeed for the entire year, would be complete. Because as he and the entire world knew, he wasn't cut out for sainthood.

"Edward, you were explaining why you left your lovely wife in the country. Without you."

"Have you met my wife? She's a countess, you know. Married me."

"Yes, Edward, I met her. Very recently."

"So you've been in the country too?"

"No, I met her here. In London. This very morning."

Edward shook his head with vigor, then winced, his hands going up to clasp his head. One end of his shirttails hung over his trousers' waist, a button was missing from his waistcoat, and his boots would send any good valet into a fit of the vapors. Most likely the fool's head was in an advanced state of befuddlement in keeping with his advanced state of personal disarray. "No, no, no. Not possible. Wife's at my house. With her mother. Very determined woman, my mother-in-law. Told me in no uncertain terms to leave my wife alone. So I did."

"Ah," Justin muttered, nodding his head. Finally, the crux of the problem and the person upsetting the foundations of a decent marriage. He raised a questioning brow, yet feared he already knew the answer. "And why exactly did your mother-in-law tell you to leave your wife alone?"

" ... 'splained to me ... I didn't know, of course, being a man and all ... well, would you? Would any gentleman?"

"Would any gentleman know what?"

Edward regarded Justin with that same expectation of a quicker mind than his being able to explain it to him in a broken down and simpler form, as he'd done many times in their university days. He peered at Justin.

"Well, yes, bother it, maybe you do. With your experiences, with things you arrange and all. Games, nights. Things ... " He waved a hand vaguely in the air.

Justin understood his gesture to mean the Pleasure House and all that encompassed. He shouldn't be surprised that even Edward, honorable Edward, had heard word of what happened at his country estate since Edward's return to London and his frequenting of the lower class of clubs. Few people however, apart from his closest friends, knew of his close involvement with the Harem in the city.

Justin gave the other man an encouraging smile, hoping he would continue his confidences. "And what is it that I might possibly know, but that you did not?"

"Well, that gently bred women, like my dear wife, don't welcome the attentions of a husband, in the bedroom I mean, for at least... two long years ... after a woman carries a baby. Simply not done, apparently."

"So how did your knowledgeable mother-in-law explain the large number of titled families who've a string of children who are all a bare nine months apart in ages?"

Edward frowned. "I ... ah.

Damn! I've no idea. Perhaps those gentlemen force their attentions upon their spouses whether they're welcomed or not."

"Or perhaps those gentlemen don't have mother-in-laws who rule their households."

"Do you think that perhaps Gillian's mother was stretching the truth a little?"

"I am sure of it."

"It did occur to me that with me away in London, it was easier for her to assume control of my household."

"Then it is probably time, Edward, for you to assert yourself and let Gillian, and her mother, know who is the earl."

"You're right, my friend. And I do miss Gillian ... sooo much. I shall make a note to return home on the morrow."

"I need you to do something for me first. Something that I'm convinced will help save your marriage."

"Justin, my boy, I would do anything to regain Gillian's respect. The last time I returned home, I feared that she disliked me somehow, perhaps even hated me. And I didn't understand why."

"Christ, you ninny. She thinks you've a mistress in London."

"A mistress? Why on earth would she think that?"

Justin groaned in frustration. "Because, my friend," he said succinctly, "you haven't shared a bed with your wife since your child was born. Is that correct?"

"Well, there was one time. But ... very next day, Gillian's mother seemed to know all about it. Berated me in a sound manner ... like a schoolboy, and in front of Gillian ... and her own husband ... until I felt like the biggest cad in all of England."

"Because you've avoided her ever since, and because you run off to London constantly, Gillian thinks you have tired of her company. She thinks you have found another woman."

Suddenly, Edward's gaze narrowed on Justin. "How do you know this?"

"I told you, I spoke to Gillian this morning."

"No, no, she's in the country." Justin dropped his head into his hands and groaned again. "Saints preserve me from drunken country idiots." He thought for a moment, searching for a solution. "Fine, Edward. I see the best way to solve this is to show you what your wife has been driven to in her desperation to win you back."

"I don't understand. Win me back from what?"

"Your mistress."

"I don't have a mistress." "There's no point in telling me that. You need to convince Gillian of that truth. Tonight."

"Tonight," Edward parroted, like a child repeating a story he didn't comprehend.

"Yes, but first you're coming home with me. To bathe and shave. To clean yourself up. And then you're attending a brothel."

"Me? I can't go to a brothel. I'm a married man. Whatever would Gillian say if she found out?"

"Don't worry. This particular brothel encourages the wearing of masks. Nobody will recognize you. Although, you may recognize someone you know."

"Oh, and who is that?"

"Your countess."

Edward snorted. "No, no, impossible. She's at our country house, with my beautiful baby. And, her not-so-beautiful mother. Bit of a harpy, that one."

Justin groaned. Holding a sensible conversation with an inebriated man was impossible. Far easier to scoop Edward up, plunk him down in the carriage, and deliver him into Perkins's capable hands. At ten tonight, he'd hand him over to his wife and they could be tearfully reconciled.

And Justin's duty would be absolved. To one of the ladies, at least.

After a ridiculous amount of maneuvering, he managed to deliver Edward to his town house and, with a huge sigh of relief, leave him in the care of his staff.

Several hours later, Edward sauntered into Justin's dining room looking like a different man. A few hours sleep, the care of a good valet, and a day without guzzling liquor had returned his friend to his normal good humor.

Justin waved him to a chair and indicated to the waiting servant to serve the soup. He waited until Edward's belly was full of good food and his mood mellow before returning to the pressing subject of his wayward wife. He needed Edward to realize the urgency of the situation, yet he sympathized with Gillian. Her husband hadn't shown enough gumption to stand up to his mother-in-law, but had chosen the easy path and deserted her. Because of Edward's cowardice, well-meant or not, he wasn't inclined to let him off the hook lightly.

"Edward, do you recall our earlier conversation?"

"Yes, well, head a bit fuddled, don't you know, but I could've sworn we were discussing Gillian. My wife. Then, during my bath, which was just the ticket by the way, thank you for that, and thanks to your thoughtful staff. Well trained lot, they are."

"Christ, Edward, you're going off on another side track again. Please concentrate. What I need to talk to you about is important. Soon you and I are going to the Sultan's Palace."

"Oh, no, no, Justin. Couldn't do that. If you've a need to visit those sort of places, and I can understand, mind you, having been deprived of my own bed enough recently, to know how frustrating it can be, wanting a woman I mean, but for a man like me, a married man—"

"Stop!" Justin snapped, then instantly regretted it.

Poor harmless Edward didn't deserve to be yelled at, bless him, although his rambling chatter, which had worsened considerably since his marriage, would drive a man to drink. "Edward, when you're at home, do you talk this much?"

"Heavens, no." Edward seemed stunned at the idea. "Hard to get a word into any conversation of late." He heaved a deep sigh.

Justin's earlier sympathy for Gillian evaporated and his sympathy swung firmly back to Edward's side of the war. "Well, my friend, I may have a solution to your problem." As Edward opened his mouth, Justin held up a hand. "But you must do exactly as I say, no dispute, and no questions."

"But ... but how can I promise such a thing if you expect me to visit, to ... to indulge myself with women? A woman. At that place. I've heard of the Sultan's Palace and it's not my sort of ... Well, I couldn't do any of those things with a woman who isn't my wife."

Justin rolled his eyes. "That, you imbecile, is the point I've been trying to make all day long. Your wife will be there, at the Sultan's Palace."

"Ridiculous! As if my countess would visit a city brothel. Balls and musicals are much more her thing, don't you know?"

Smothering his groan of frustration, Justin spent the next half hour explaining to Edward why his countess wasn't in the country under the thumb of her dictatorial mother.

"So, tonight your wife and her two friends will attend the Sultan's Palace, in disguise, and accompanied by me. You shall be there wearing a costume."

"No, can't possibly allow such a thing. My Gillian will observe things far, far too shocking for a woman of her sensibilities."

Justin clenched his fists and pushed back his frustration. "Far from being shocked, I envision Gillian lapping up every sight and sound as hungrily as the stable cat with a dish of cream. You've underestimated your wife and consequently she's grown restless with her confinement." As he lectured Edward, he realized he sounded more like a father than a friend. "It was only a matter of time until she rebelled, so thank your lucky stars providence brought her to my door first. Before she decided to experiment with any of the young bucks around town, ones always willing to accommodate bored wives whose husbands spend their time and money on mistresses—"

"Haven't taken—"

"—or whose husbands abandon them in the country for long stretches, leaving them to imagine the worst."

A red flush crept up Edward's neck and spread over his pale face.

Ah. He mightn't have taken a mistress, or visited a brothel, but it would've only been a matter of time for Edward as well as Gillian. One of his naïve friend's new acquaintances would've dragged him along one night when he'd imbibed too much and tempted him with all sorts of new delights.

"Should I reveal myself to Gillian at the end of the night?"

"If she shows interest in sampling the wares at the Sultan's Palace, perhaps you should make yourself available to become her slave for the night."

"Me? Her slave? I thought the Sultan's Palace catered to men wanting women for slaves."

Justin shrugged. "It caters to all tastes, to every whim and fantasy known to man or woman. You'd have done better, Edward, to stay at home and ask your good wife what she'd like to see happen in your marital bedchamber. You might have been pleasantly surprised."

"Wouldn't mind if she did surprise me you know, old boy. One of the reasons I am forced to leave so often ... " The earl studied his boots and didn't look Justin in the eye. " ... is if I stay at home all the time ... I feel compelled by urges... and compelled often ... to drag my wife to the bedchamber." He swallowed and looked embarrassed. "To ... to ravage her. The way I did when we were first married. She seemed to enjoy it then, you know."

"Edward, this may come as a big shock to your sensibilities, but most women adore sex. As much of it as they can get. I think the countess is not sleep-deprived or in ill health so much as suffering a large dose of unfulfilled lust. And sick to death of waiting for you to do something about it."

"The mother-in-law, she told me, you know, that I have an heir. So it is the gentlemanly thing to do to wait a little before conceiving the spare."

Justin groaned and yelled at the ceiling once more. "Why me? Do I truly deserve this?"

While giving a few friendly thumps to Edward's broad shoulder, Justin searched for a way to phrase his information as best he could so his misguided friend didn't take offense.

"Edward, another shock awaits you. Men and women go to bed with each other for a lot more than conceiving. Women think about a lot more than offspring to carry on their husband's family names and titles."

Edward raised surprised eyes to his. "You mean ..." He swallowed. "Do you think high-

born women like my Gillian actually enjoy fickey-fick ... the way men do?"

Justin groaned and shook his head. "Not if you refer to sex by a greenhorn's term such as fickey- fick. And please don't say swiving. Or coupling." He thrust his hands into his already ruffled hair. "Women, women like your Gillian, they like to think of making love. Each and every time. Your mother-in-law may believe it nothing more than conjugal rites, but your Gillian needs passion. What names would you and the countess be comfortable with? Erotic congress? Bed sports? Or even a rollicking-good ploughing. But talk to your wife, woo her, seduce her."

Edward stared at him. "Is that how you do it, Hawkesbury? Rouse passion in all those women you collect like hen's eggs?"

"Huh. I needn't assert myself at all with those women who chase me, but sit back and go along for the cart ride."

"So isn't there anyone you'd like to woo, or to seduce, instead of ... ploughing?"

Chrissie's image popped into his mind. She'd been the only woman to arouse even the slightest interest in resuming his former life. And now he desperately wanted to plunge inside a woman's tight crevices and savor the heat, the smells, and the wet welcome women gave him. He nodded.

"There is one. Just one. Someone I've only just made the acquaintance of. Someone so far above me she wouldn't consider sharing my bed for any reason. Be it lust or passion or ... or love."

"What? You mean she possesses bluer blood than you? With all your new titles."

"No, I don't mean she's above me in that way. Rather, in her goodness, and the purity of her heart and thoughts." He gave a dry snort of laughter. "My presence in her life would sully every fine and decent thing about her."

He turned to leave the room and make plans for the forthcoming evening, then stopped and sighed. "No matter how much I wish it could be different. No, the noblest thing I can do for this magnificent lady is to stay away. Well, well away.

5

Later that evening, the Viscount of Hawkesbury drew up in his immaculate town carriage before the house of Lady Wellsby and he alighted with a quick step. He chuckled to himself, accepting this strange feeling, this lightness of spirit, as anticipation—something absent from his life for quite some time.

The forthcoming evening promised to be adventuresome, if nothing else. His friends, Bartholomew and Thomas, waited in the carriage, having been coerced into accompanying them to provide extra escort and protection for the ladies.

Before he could knock, the door swung open and the butler admitted him. The three ladies clustered together in the foyer covered in identical dark cloaks and, without saying a word, pulled up their hoods to cover their hair and accepted the masks the butler proffered.

Interesting. Obviously they'd plotted the best way to proceed for the night and had decided amongst themselves, rather than fight his decree, that they'd take the path of least resistance. And while treading that path, they'd ensure their identities were well protected behind cloaks and masks.

At the Sultan's Palace, Justin's driver drew around to the back lane where he habitually let Justin alight. By slipping in his normal back door entrance, the three men managed to smuggle the three ladies inside without being observed. Most of the illicit deeds took place in the front parlor where gentlemen, or ladies, were admitted and asked their preferences for the evening's entertainment.

"Ladies, if you will follow me. As I explained, we'll observe each of the separate rooms of the palace tonight to acquaint you with the style of entertainments I used to provide at the Pleasure House."

"The sort of entertainments you will again be providing during our visit, you mean," Chrissie said, her sweet smile belying the warning behind the words.

He dipped his head enough to hide his small smile at Chrissie's continued attempts to outwit him. "Perhaps we should reserve judgment until after this evening."

Chrissie chuckled, the rumbling sound in her throat sounding like the grateful purr of a well-fed kitchen cat and sending his thoughts straight back to silk sheets and the noises she would make when he laid her out upon them. When he pleasured her until she purred with gratitude. When she rolled toward him to beg for more, and more.

"If you still think to shock us into retreating, you grossly misjudge our fortitude." She waved toward the narrow hallway leading to steep dark steps. "Please, lead on. We are eager to begin."

Justin swallowed down his annoyance. Surely he'd not underestimated her. Surely this show of courage couldn't last much longer. He and the other men simply needed to stand strong, ruthless.

"You'll be able to see through holes cut into the walls of some rooms to watch what happens within. But be warned, when we reach the Bath House I'm afraid in order to view the performances, you must disrobe and wear a costume. The same as everyone else."

"I say," Thomas objected, "you cannot expect a gentle miss like Miss Anna to disrobe. 'Tis just not done."

Justin hid his smile. Thomas's eyes followed every move Miss Anna made, his fascination with the young lady already quite evident. Ah, yes! The two of them would suit nicely. Everything ran exactly to his plan. Well, everything except Chrissie's contrary attitude. Still, he'd been managing women for the past several years with ease.

How hard could it be to change the mind of one lady, one slightly difficult lady to be truthful, but still, merely one lady? For a man used to amusing and organizing six females at a time in his bed, one fully clothed lady would be walking out that door within the next hour.

After tonight, he'd be rid of all three ladies and their problems. He allowed a small smile to peep through, a smile of smug self- satisfaction at his own cleverness.

"What are you up to, my lord?" Chrissie whispered in his ear.

His body tensed, his eyes going wide, his pulse racing. No one ever read his intentions in his face. Normally, he was able to keep his expressions bland, his emotions well hidden from all and sundry. The only person who'd ever been able to easily discern his thoughts had been his mother. It was the reason he'd so easily fleeced gentlemen of their money at the gaming tables. His blanked face gave away nothing. So how the hell had Lady Wellsby read his mind?

He raised a brow and relaxed his clenched fingers. "Nothing, my lady. Nothing at all. Simply doing as you requested. Supplying you with a venue to explore the sensuous natures of men."

"Ah, but my wish is to explore them in seclusion on your estate. Not in one of London's most notorious brothels."

"The Sultan's Palace may be notorious, but it is also one of the safest in all of London for those of the higher echelons. Great care is taken to ensure that the staff is discreet and never reveal anything they hear or see. The palace is kept clean and free from disease, or at least as much as the owners are able."

At Anna's blank look, he added, "The French Pox. Syphilis. Gonorrhea."

Anna's eyes widened and she gave a little gasp, but held her tongue.

He turned back to Chrissie and frowned. "And how would a country mouse know which city brothels are the most notorious anyway?"

She gave an indifferent shrug. "I've spent far too many hours sitting outside either houses of ill repute or the houses of not quite respectable females, waiting to escort the drunken men in my family back home, to not understand about reputations. People talk. Gossip spreads. Men especially like to gossip about this house and that. Where they have visited and with whom they spent time. That is, after they'd finished spending all our money on card games, painted faced women and watered down drinks."

Justin bristled. "My drinks are—" He sucked in a breath.

She stared at him. "What were you going to say?"

"Nothing." He shook his head. "Let us move along before someone discovers us here. Ladies, I must insist you wear your masks from now on. All the clients expect uttermost discretion, and pay dearly for it, especially in the lower halls. When we reach some of the more exclusive upper levels, or should I say if you still want to climb that far—"

"Which we will," Chrissie said, a decided snap to her voice as she tugged her mask into place.

Even through the cut-out eye slits in the feathered mask, Justin could see the spark in her eyes, the flash of defiance she seemed determined to cling to. It mattered little though, as he was equally determined she would not progress past the lower floors tonight. The word tonight lingered in his mind. What was he thinking? Surely he wasn't mad enough to consider bringing her back again another night, without her two companions, so the two of them alone could sample the delights of one, or several, of his themed rooms. Which would suit her best?

After her quiet country existence, she'd undoubtedly relish the temptations of the Oriental room. And he'd enjoy demonstrating the many positions of the Kama Sutra, and the uses of his silver balls. He'd especially enjoy inserting the balls high up into Chrissie's soft, wet crevice and watching her experience the joy of her first climax with the magic balls inside her. He sucked in a breath.

Hell. His muscles were hard knots, his cock a pulsating baton. Stupid, stupid idea to imagine such things—and here, no less. Truly, he must be losing his sanity. He shook his head, turned back to the ladies, waved them down the first hidden corridor, and grappled for control of his wandering wits.

At the far end of the corridor, he arranged the three eager participants so they could see through the small peepholes spaced at discreet intervals along the dark wall. The men arranged themselves as guards between them.

Anna stepped up first to put her eye to the hole, curiosity of the young overcoming any modesty she might be suffering. Justin waited, tensed, for the inevitable. Hoping she was shocked, yet also hoping she decided to stay and witness the scene.

Stupid, he told himself yet again. All this was planned to force them to retreat with their tails between their legs, not linger and become excited, aroused, and stir the men's blood by association. Dammit. It would take so little to stir his blood tonight, as every few seconds his gaze drifted back to Chrissie. Back to the red dress hugging her curves and swirling with every step she took, her unconscious grace denoting her as an aristocrat as surely as his ownership of a brothel denoted him as a man of low worth. He closed his eyes, shut out the sight of her rounded woman's figure dressed as a courtesan. Another stupid mistake on his part. He'd imagined by dressing them in red, clothing them as whores, he and the other men would be able to think of them in that way. Treat them that way tonight—roughly, coarsely, and with brutal honesty.

Huh! So much for that plan. Even dressed in red and wearing fancy plumed masks, quality shone through. No one could ever mistake these three for anything but blue-blooded ladies, born and bred in good families, forever conscious of their stations in life, despite the squalid surroundings they'd agreed to immerse themselves in this evening.

Anna screeched as she took a hurried step back from the peep hole. Not a full-throated scream, more a choked gasp of noise that echoed her shock well enough. Ah, yes. Definitely shocked by the sights within the room but Justin needed her shocked enough to turn tail and run, taking her friends with her. Thomas stepped behind

Anna, rubbed his hands up and down her bare arms above her long red gloves. The gloves would have been purchased by Chrissie and her friends ordered to wear them in an act of defiance against Justin and his order that they don red gowns, a harlot's color.

In their silent battle, Chrissie was proving a formidable foe and he already doubted his ability to best her tonight. Seldom did he misjudge an adversary, yet he feared he'd vastly underestimated Chrissie's intelligence, and her stubbornness. He'd predicted her reactions and behavior based on his perceptions of pampered town ladies who hadn't a brain in their heads.

Justin's head reeled as he raced to plot another strategy, a plan to keep him ahead of Chrissie. He watched poor besotted Thomas lean around to face Anna, place his finger to her lips to indicate she should remain quiet. With great care, Thomas placed Anna's hand on his coat sleeve and folded his fingers over hers. Anna nodded up at Thomas, her pale blue eyes gleaming in the dim light. Her expression was one of pure trust, faith that Thomas would take care of her.

Justin glanced across at Chrissie and caught her watching her friend with the same bemused expression he was certain covered his own face. He nodded at her. "Amazing, isn't it?"

CHRISSIE AGREED with the viscount's assessment of the situation. She too felt a sense of amazement that her friend suddenly found comfort from a stranger. Although, she had to admit Thomas's face glowed with friendship, harmlessness, and a quaint innocence that made one trust him. His physique was round and pleasant and constant—jolly, even— exactly the sort of man Chrissie believed Anna should marry. Not a fibbing soldier of fortune who'd dally with the daughter of his colonel while abroad at the same time he was betrothed to a girl in England.

She dragged her gaze from her friend and turned back to the peephole, placing her eye over the hole and finding a comfortable position to stand and lean on the wall. At first glance, this room looked pleasant enough, unremarkable actually. She leaned closer to the wall and peered around the perimeter.

Decorated like the anteroom of a palace, fountains played in the center while marble benches flanked the colorfully draped walls. Men lounged on the benches, sipping their wine from brightly colored goblets while girls sashayed past them in a dazzling array of Arabian costumes. The girls wore sheer veils caught across their lower faces and as they walked, tiny bells tinkled around their ankles and wrists. Breasts were encased in meager swaths of silk, designed to accentuate their jiggling and bouncing as the dancers swayed their hips in movements she didn't recognize.

This dance was not performed in Almack's, nor in any of the elite salons of the ton. The movements were exotic, erotic, meant to draw the eyes to each swinging body part.

In one corner, a group of women with their faces covered and wearing long flowing Eastern clothing concealed their identities from the other men in the room. They giggled, chatted in high-pitched tones, sounded nervous and excited. Lined up beside them were a dozen strappingly built serving men with most of their bronzed bodies exposed to view. Leather vests ended inches above the flowing pants they wore low on their hips, as they offered the women platters of food and flasks of drinks.

As the ladies watched from outside, enthralled, the sounds of the dance increased. Drummers beat a rhythm on leather tightly pulled over drum bases and, by increasing the pace, whipped the dancers into a frenzied prance around the room's edge. Bare bellies thrust forward in tempting array close to the faces of the watching men.

To Chrissie's eyes, some of the men appeared to actually salivate with hunger. Then, to her stunned amazement, several of the ladies from the darker corner leaped to their feet and joined the dancers. Lack of expertise was no drawback, as their enthusiasm made up for all they lacked. When the drummers finally concluded with a crashing crescendo of noise, the line of serving girls wended their way to the men and slid onto the laps of the waiting men. With hoots of laughter and ribald yells of encouragement to acquaintances seated around the room, the men showed no shyness. Hands appeared like tentacles from a dozen octopuses, squeezed breasts, ran hands up and down over bare flesh. Strings at the waists of their loose harem pants were loosened, although by some magic feat, the harem girls managed to keep their lower garments more or less in place.

As Chrissie watched, the men pulled the girls down to kiss them, thoroughly, wetly, often two men taking turns to kiss a single girl who undulated back and forth between them. To her mind, the scene resembled an oceanic fantasy she'd read about—mermaids swimming through a waving sea of seaweed and encountering eager sailors whose hands continued to rove unchecked over every part of the dancers' bodies.

Often, their hands removed articles of clothing as they went, so in a short space of time, most girls were half-naked and squealing with delight. Then, some sort of arrangement had obviously been concluded with the madam who stood, arms folded, at the back door to the room. One by one, the men slid the girls they'd selected off their laps, or threw them bodily over their shoulder if they were sober enough, and strong enough, to carry them. They charged up the stairs, calling instructions to friends, teasing their conquests.

For several minutes, the scene became chaotic. Noise, people running, moving, jumping. The girls seemed as eager to go upstairs as the men. They giggled and chattered to their friends as they went, acted like children at playtime allowed to select a favorite toy. More women were escorted to their corners on the arms of the burly serving men, and they in turn slid onto the laps of the remaining men.

Everything was arranged with such precision, the whole interaction between male and female accomplished so seamlessly, Chrissie couldn't help but be impressed with the organization. All this was accomplished with a minimum of fuss and, she presumed, a maximum of expense for those paying. This was a high cost establishment, well run, well controlled, and more than likely, highly profitable.

She turned to look at Justin, gave him another accessing glance as the reality of it registered. He hovered at her elbow, not peering through a hole as they were, but watching her the entire time.

"Don't you want to look too, my lord?"

He shrugged. "No need. I've seen it all before."

"Ah, yes, of course. I assume you employ some of these same girls, and men, for your Pleasure House."

"I used to borrow some from the owner here, yes, when my Pleasure House was operating."

"Ah, I see. The invisible owner."

"Yes, unfortunately, he is unable to join us here tonight."

She stared at him. "I think, my lord, the owner is already with us tonight."

He blinked several times, but she gave him credit, he retained his gambler's blank face as he said, "Think what you may, madam, it makes little difference now, as the owner is selling anyway. Next week there will be a completely unknown person operating this wretched whorehou—" He stopped, coughed into his hand.

She gave him a small smile, waved her hand between them. "Oh, please. Go on. Do not spare my sensibilities now. Last night you teased me for being unused to coarse language. For blushing at your use of rude words. Why bother sparing my blushes now?" She pointed down the hallway toward a noisy sounding anteroom. "Or here."

He laughed, short, derisive. "I'm not sure why here, of all places, I find myself wanting to preserve your modesty. Bizarre, aren't I?"

She titles her head to one side, considered. "No, on the contrary, I think it makes you appear more real, more gentlemanly."

"Oh, there you are wrong. The last thing I can be accused of is being a gentleman. If I was, I would never have lost my family in the first place."

She put a hand on his arm and he flinched but didn't withdraw. "My understanding is if you hadn't left for the continent when you did, your father would have killed you." Under her hand, his arm muscles bunched and tightened like steel ropes. "Then you wouldn't be alive now, and able to seek your mother and sisters to try to bring them home. No, you did the right thing, the only thing you could do back then."

"How could you know that? Perhaps if I'd stayed they'd be here, living in the house in London, instead of running and hiding God knows where, across all of England."

"I'm sure you know that isn't true. If they'd stayed, if you'd stayed, your father would have murdered all of you. Believe me, I know only too well the atrocities drunken men are capable of committing when under the influence of drink." She patted his tense arm and waited for it to relax. "And I know you did the correct thing, because you are a man of honor."

"Look around you. You're assumptions are correct, you know." He leaned closer. "I do own this brothel, this high class whorehouse. At least, for another week I own it. I've bedded half the women in London. I've provided entertainments for men who follow the dress and acts of Lavenderism, for nymphomaniacs, and catered to more types of fetishes than there are pages in a book written about them. And do you know why I do it, these seedy chores?" He leaned in close to her face, his breath coming fast and furious upon her cheek. She shook her head, perversely sorry when he shifted back an inch and she no longer felt the hot puffs of his lungs as he panted out his anger. "I did it all for money. Pure, unadulterated greed."

"No, that money was not to satisfy some primitive urges of greed. The money was to buy you more time, more detectives, to seek your family. Every goal you'd had, all that you've achieved for the past three years, has been for a noble cause."

"Jesus!" He ran his fingers through his hair, standing it on end, yet the rakish air it gave him only made her want to reach out and hug him even more, to soothe his ruffled hair, his rumpled temper, his angry soul. "What does it take to convince you, I'm not a noble person. I'm not even a nice person. You shouldn't be near me, you or your innocent friends."

"I told you, we're not as innocent as you think."

His face thrust close to hers again, displaying his frustration, his raw fury, yet she knew she was safe with him. Knew instinctively he'd never harm her, no matter how much he disparaged his own.

"Compared to me, to my world, brown mouse," he said, breathing hard as if he'd run a mile, "to the sins I've seen written across the face of thousands of so-called good people, you're babes in the woods begging for a wolf to gobble you up."

She sighed. "I think, Justin, you provoke me deliberately still, as you did last evening, but I will tell you once more: I'm not a mouse and I'm not retreating. So, back to our previous conversation, when you open for us next week, I imagine you'll take some of the staff from here to ... to ... "

"To service you? Ah," he said, a smile—or was it a smirk—spreading across his face. "Did you perhaps view someone you liked, my lady?"

"No, no, no." She swallowed and took a step backwards. "I didn't mean that. I didn't notice anyone in particular."

There was enough light from the wall sconces to notice his raised brows, his wide grin. Irritating man, thinking he could throw this back at her when she managed to touch a raw spot on his emotions.

"Mouse, did you know your nose twitches when you tell a white lie?"

Her hand flew to her nose.

"What?"

"The adorable flush on your face gives you away also. Obviously you're fibbing." He leaned over, put his eye to the hole next to him.

"Ah!" He chuckled, and she spun around to check if any of their group had overheard. Thankfully, they were all engrossed on the antics inside the room, not outside it. "I see you're appreciating the assets of our most popular male entertainer."

She huffed, a show of nonchalance she failed to carry off. "I already said I didn't take particular notice of anyone."

Justin laughed. "Liar! The man you're staring at with such a keen eye is named Matthew Large, and yes, I can assure you, he's as big between his legs as he is everywhere else. Plus, his main asset to me as a performer is that he possesses the stamina of six randy stallions.

The giggling group of friends in the corner will be kept happy all night."

She swallowed again, cursing her suddenly dry throat. "All ... all of them?"

Justin winked. "Oh, yes. All of them. Matthew is large by name, and gigantic by appendage. Perhaps you'd enjoy being included in their group?"

Her eyes widened to the size of tea saucers. "Certainly not. I—we are only here to observe how your girls are trained to keep the men happy."

"Ah, but women must also be kept happy or else they too seek their entertainments in places like this. In disguise, under cover of darkness, and at enormous expense when that should be the role of a doting husband. Did your husband make you happy in your bed, Lady Wellsby? Or did you have a society marriage? A cold bed for you, and many warm beds for him."

She tried to back away another step but he'd her blocked in against the wall. "No. Unfortunately, no. Far from it. If my husband visited here, he may have learned the tricks the girls knew, although he most assuredly never carried them home with him. Never shared any of his superior knowledge with me."

"You sound bitter, and for that, I'm sorry. In my humble opinion, men who do nothing to please their wives are loathsome, self-centered creatures. They'll throw away their money having girls entertain them, cater to their every desire, yet they care not a whit for bringing any of that joy into the lives of the women who care for them every day in their own houses."

"You seem to be speaking from experience. Do you speak of someone you know?"

Justin grimaced. "My father. He was a bastard. He treated my mother in a sickening manner." He shook his head. "But we're not here to speak of the past. Come, we shall move on to another view."

Chrissie put aside her questions and moved behind him down the corridor to collect her two friends. She noticed, to her surprise, another man standing behind Gillian instead of Bartholomew. A man who wore a mask, as they did. From her view of his back, she failed to recognize him, yet something about the man, the way he held himself, reminded her of someone she knew.

Hawkesbury accept his presence without comment, as if he'd had a hand in arranging the man's presence here amongst them, yet she had no idea of his purpose in doing so.

Unable to resist her gnawing curiosity, she sidled forward to try to glimpse the man's face. Thomas stepped in front of her, blocked her view, and she was unsure whether the move had been deliberate or not. Poor Thomas's cherubic face wasn't made for keeping secrets, and she shifted closer to ascertain the truth from reading his rosy cheeks and blinking eyes.

Justin, however, interrupted her scrutiny. With a subtle touch on her arm, he drew her away, ushered them along the winding corridors to another part of the enormous old building.

"Ladies, I wanted to introduce you slowly to the wonders of the house, in the faint hope that you wouldn't find the scenes to be too shocking. In the dancing room, gentlemen merely gather to enjoy the benefits of an hour spent with one of our very supple and nimble girls. Girls who are practiced in the Eastern arts of sensuality."

"Which Eastern arts?" Gillian asked.

The masked man, who again stood close behind Gillian, gasped, dropped his head, shuffled his feet. Chrissie turned to see him better in the half-light, but he moved to stand directly behind Thomas.

"Justin, I don't think we've been introduced to one of your friends." She peered around Thomas's large body at the other man, then glanced between the others. "And where did Bartholomew disappear to?"

"Bart has ... ah ... gone ahead. To arrange for your participation in the tableau in the next room."

Chrissie gasped. "No, no, not participation. Remember—observation. No more."

Thomas patted Anna's hand. "Never fear, I shall remain at your side, Miss Anna. If you feel the slightest distress at what you see, I shall remove you at once. I would also be most happy to escort you home."

The group walked a few steps further along to where the corridor narrowed even more and the light dimmed. They ascended four wooden steps and crowded closer together until Chrissie became aware of Justin's body pressing against the length of her back. She knew by instinct that it was his hard body, his lean length molded against her, his lemon cologne tickling her nose. The hairs on the back of her neck stood on end as his mouth shifted closer to base of her ear, a hair's breadth away from nuzzling.

The man in the large black mask and covering cloak moved behind Gillian once again, stood familiarly close to her. Botheration —should she be worried or not? By contrast, Gillian stood relaxed, serene, perfectly at ease, as if a stranger didn't stand an indecent distance from her spine. She frowned. A strange situation.

Chrissie glanced at Anna, quiet and retiring Anna who'd been shielded from the harsh realities of life for several years. Anna, the young lady who now smiled freely at Thomas, who in turn beamed back at her. The entire evening proved to be a giant puzzle.

Justin reached past them, slid a velvet curtain along a rod to reveal an oblong cut out section at eye- level in the wall. From their slightly elevated position, they looked down into a long room, wherein roughly two dozen figures could be seen scattered around the room. Some lounged against walls, some bent and stretched, some talked in small groups.

She leaned forward, putting her face closer to the viewing hole. Roughly half of the people below looked to be women, dressed in the same eastern manner as those downstairs, except this group had arrived bare chested. Each of the women displayed their bosoms by strutting as proudly as peacocks, their breasts swinging in free abandon above their bared midriffs. All carried the same exotic look —the dark swinging hair and painted eyes the women parading in Justin's library had worn.

Hmm! The meaning of these similarities became clearer. When

she'd interrupted Justin and his friends last evening, they'd been auditioning women for employment here at the Sultan's Palace.

The Virile Viscount may tell people he no longer needed the money from the Pleasure House at his estate, but she felt certain he still gained money from his involvement with this establishment, this very high-class brothel in London that catered to the elite of society. She smiled, knowing she now had another way to blackmail the viscount into reopening the Bath House for their use. When she turned back to the window, she caught Justin's gaze fixed upon her, studying her, his expression intent and shrewd.

"What does that self-satisfied smile mean?" His voice was a murmur close to her ear, so close she jumped a little. "Ah, do I detect a guilty conscience behind the smile? Should I be worried?"

She thanked heaven for the dark depths of the corridor and prayed he'd be unable to detect her embarrassed flush in this dim light.

"I'm smiling in anticipation of the event about to take place."

She felt, rather than heard, his laugh as he shifted to stand behind her back, he pressed himself toward her, their bodies close, disconcertingly close. The muscles of his lean body shuddered, jerked, caused her own body to shiver, tremble, shimmy. Through the multiple layers of clothing separating them, intense heat radiated from his body and warmed hers, heating her inside and out. Something at her core, frozen for so many years, thawed a little. Moisture collected between her thighs, bewildering her.

Justin's rich male scent, his skin's unique aroma, permeated the air, made it hard to breathe without inhaling his essence into her body. Damn! She didn't need any more distractions.

Having someone so proudly male standing so close to her after all this time of physical drought sent her sensually starved body into an immediate tailspin. If her mind joined in the attention in the same way as her body had done, she'd be ready for Bedlam before they even reached his estate.

And a week of exposure to all manner of enticements would be an even worse form of torture. She'd long ago convinced herself she didn't need physical intimacy in her life after it proved to be a messy and unsatisfactory business in the past, one that didn't improve her existence in the least. Therefore, she'd embarked on this experiment merely to assist her friends. Plus, if she acknowledged the voice of her inner conscience, to perhaps understand completely what she was giving up, what she hadn't known. And that she hadn't been short-changed all her life.

"I hope you're still smiling in ten minutes."

Drat! She had a terrible feeling she'd made a fool of herself some-how, but before she could reflect upon it, the shocked gasps of her two friends reached her and she instinctively stepped toward the wall, eager to see whatever they'd seen.

"Good heavens," Anna said, sinking limply backwards into Thomas's arms. Once again, Thomas slipped his hands around Anna's waist, a gesture of support, of protection. Anna turned away from the spectacle in front of them and buried her face in Thomas's coat.

Chrissie peered further along to where Gillian stood. Unlike Anna, Gillian leaned forward, her nose pressed against the glass and her hands flattened on the wall. Whereas Anna had been shocked by the entertainment, her other friend viewed the tableau in the other room with open-mouthed enthrallment.

Although Gillian's mask disguised her features and her emotions, her awe-struck attitude showed intrigue and enjoyment rather than discomfort. The man in the mask, whose identity still teased at the outside of Chrissie's consciousness, appeared to be scowling. His face was contorted into a deep grimace, as if he suffered extreme pain. His attitude contrasted violently with Gillian's blatant rapture.

Chrissie touched the viscount's arm. "Who is that gentleman standing behind Gillian? He seems so familiar." The irritating man didn't glance down the passageway, yet the corners of his mouth turned up slightly at the edges, teasing a smile.

"Does he?"

Chrissie forgot her question as her attention snagged on the action unfolding in the room before them. She'd schooled herself not to show any shock before Justin, certain his intention was to frighten them into a hasty withdrawal. Retreating to the country would free the viscount of his commitment to them. But Chrissie held a slight advantage over her friends as she'd survived years of marriage to a man who'd made no effort to shield her womanly sensibilities. Not the way Gillian's Edward did.

"Edward."

The viscount leaned closer. "Pardon? What did you say?"

"You knew, you conniving man." She gave his arm a small punch. "You arranged it, didn't you?"

He leaned in, raised that damned arrogant brow again, and gave an excellent demonstration of feigned innocence. "What exactly is it that you think I've arranged?"

She scowled at him, pushed him aside, and peered at the masked man, the man she now recognized. "So why did you do it?"

"I ask again, what it is you think I've done?"

"Don't play games. You brought Gillian's husband here. In a mask."

He grinned, shrugged. "Despite the mask, I've a feeling your friends have recognized each other."

"But they haven't said anything."

He chuckled, a low rumble that rippled through her senses.

"No. I think they are both content to let the evening play out as I intended."

"You mean they want to view the entertainment together."

"I think Gillian wants to more than Edward, but he is prepared to for her," he said, and turned her gently back to the window. "Now, watch. And learn. There'll be a test later."

She shook her head but said nothing.

Twelve women wove backwards and forwards across the room, arms raised above their heads, in a rhythmic dance similar to the one they'd viewed being performed below. But here, the movements performed were more sensuous, as pairs of bared breasts swayed to the throb of strange music, its high notes piercing the silence and setting her nerves tingling.

Only now did Chrissie realize the other twelve in the room with them were men, who were seated in a row on straight-backed chairs. Candlelight picked up and highlighted the rainbow of colors glowing from satin cushions strewn across the floor in front of the chairs.

As she watched, nose pressed to the glass as Gillian's was, the women wiggled their naked bellies closer to the men and halted a step away from them. She'd expected this to be the famed Dance of the Seven Veils she'd read about in tales from Arabian travelers, yet these women had entered partially unclothed, as if not wanting to waste time with clothing removal.

The gentlemen had already thrown off their civilized skins and were yelling comments to each other, and to the women, urging them to hurry. Their impatience obvious, the tension in the room grew rapidly, so quickly in fact that for their audience, it was almost palpable.

Chrissie swallowed, her own senses stirred to life by the sensual display and by the rising looks of excitement and lust on the men's faces. Their eyes followed the sway of unbound breasts before them with hypnotized eyes, mesmerized by temptation dangled only inches from their faces. A few of the more daring reached out a hand, but the large men, garbed as palace guards, growled from their corners in warning. Obviously this part of the act didn't include participation by the paying guests.

"Anticipation increases the men's enjoyment," Justin said, reading another of her unspoken questions. "So we have a no hands rule." He slid his palms around her waist, his fingers sliding through the red folds of her gown, rubbing down along the dip toward her hips, and stilling her slender body when she gave a small jump. "Any man who breaks the rule will have his hands bound behind his back."

"It sounds a little extreme."

He laughed. "On the contrary, some gentlemen touch because they wish to be bound and gagged. Hands, feet, mouths. Having roles reversed arouses them. Slaves take control and subjugate the masters. Most patrons who role play as submissive to dominators do so in private rooms." He shrugged, pointed. "But some prefer the theatrics, and an audience."

One harem girl at a time dropped to her knees before one of the men, and then each in turn bent her head to wait until the others in the row followed, copying her movements, a performance of dance and ritual executed with the same finesse as Chrissie used to step and twirl up and down the length of ballrooms when she'd visited London before she married.

The women below moved as if they'd practiced this dance hundreds of times, and performed the ritual as one body. When she finally lowered her gaze to the row of waiting men, Chrissie realized every one of them had unfastened their breeches. Their trouser flaps lay open upon their thighs, though they'd made no move to expose themselves. They, too, had slowed every action to prolong the anticipation of what was about to happen.

They glanced up and down the line between each other, as each man had a woman drop to her knees in worshipful fashion before him. A ripple of laughter started at one end and rumbled down the line until the last man to be chosen for adoration threw back his head and bellowed. His roar sounded a cross between laughter and exultation.

"Oh, my good Lord." One man's comment drifted up to them. "This is even better than you told me it would be, Worthington. Why have I never been here before?"

"Because this place has just reopened all its Arabian rooms. While the Virile Viscount was running the Pleasure House outside of London, we had no need to risk venturing into this sort of establishment so often in London."

They raised glasses of wine in a toast to each other, one turning his face toward the light as he spoke to his seated friends. "I'm taking a great risk being here, you know. My wife will commit murder if she ever finds out."

At the mention of the gentleman's wife, Chrissie looked again, stared harder. She knew him, knew the voice that sounded like chips struck from a gravel pit, recognized him as one of their neighbors from their area.

"Oh, good heavens above," Anna said, her voice high-pitched and tremulous. She stood before the opening again, pointing down.

"That's Lord Mitchell!"

"Oh, my goodness." Gillian's voice came from further down, echoing Anna's shocked sentiments. "Bloody hell," Edward said, leaning forward and clutching the wall either side of the opening for support. "Gillian, turn away. You mustn't look at him. Not him."

Justin laughed. "Let me guess. You all recognize the gentleman, the one sitting the third from the left."

Chrissie's couldn't drag her gaze from the sight below her, not wanting to look at their neighbor displayed in this setting, yet unable to force herself to look away and miss something. Like her friends, she felt shocked into silence. She met Justin's gaze.

"He's a neighbor, in our county." She put her hands to her mouth but couldn't contain her giggle. "Our very devout, very conservative neighbor."

"One overly fond of criticism," Gillian said. "He and his interfering wife arrive at our house far too often to deliver a scold to me on what I'm doing wrong. Especially with regard to my marriage."

A shocked gasp came from Edward and he turned Gillian to face him, ripping off his mask with one hand. "My love, I'm so sorry. I didn't realize. Is it because of me? Because I was pushing my attentions upon you?"

"Heavens, no," Gillian said, all pretense of not recognizing the man standing behind her as her husband finished. "Quite the opposite, in fact. Lady Mitchell took me to task numerous times for failing to keep you by my side in our marriage bed."

"What?" Edward grasped Gillian's hands.

"She informed me it's my duty to lie back and think of England. And to let you do whatever you must upon my body to keep you happy. She said that's how she keeps her own husband so happily attached to her that he never wanders. Not the way so many other men do."

As one, the group turned their eyes back to the scene slowly unfolding in the exotic setting before them. The men slid to the carpeted floor and reclined on plump tasseled cushions, while the girls stretched their bodies fully over them.

The movements to the dance commenced again to the beat of a musician in the corner, as the girls performed an intricate pattern of weaving and wiggling movements, in sequence, up and down the men's bodies. The men, of course, thoroughly enjoyed themselves. Heads were thrown back in ecstasy, loud groans emitted.

"Gillian," Edward said, his voice pleading, "you shouldn't watch this. Especially not Mitchell. It's disgusting."

Chrissie could no longer contain her mirth. It bubbled up, and over, and she started to giggle. Her giggle became a laugh, then erupted into full-blown mirth, until she doubled over, clutched her stomach. Along the passageway, similar sounds emitted as both Anna and Gillian suffered identical reactions. The incongruity of the situation struck them so hard they were helpless to do anything but laugh. Chrissie knew by the tortured look on poor Edward's face that he didn't know whether to laugh or cry. Thomas's mouth dropped open in a soundless protest at Anna's reaction

Justin's reaction was a little more subdued, as, after all, his title of the notorious viscount meant he'd seen it all before, many times. Yet still he laughed, as amused by the entire episode as he would be by a Drury Lane drama. He took hold of Chrissie's arm for support, as she bent double again, her entire body wracked by violent shudders of amusement. Without speaking, he waited until she gained control of herself.

"Oh, look now," Anna said, pointing at the glass.

The dancers, in unison and in a rhythmic action, opened the plackets of the men's trousers and drew out their genitals, exposing them to the air. The three ladies watching from above gave a collective gasp, but Justin noticed their noses pressed even harder against the pane and their bodies leaned further forward. Using their hands, the entertainers commenced an up-and-down motion on the men's phalluses, until one by one, all along the line, each man's shaft snapped to attention, stood tall and erect. Some extended longer and straighter than others, while some were shorter but needed a girl's entire hand to encompass its girth.

Justin was fascinated to see Chrissie's head swivel backwards and forwards like a wind-up toy as she absorbed the scene. She ripped off her mask and her wide-eyed gaze fixed on the bobbing penises, jaw dropped as she studied different shapes and sizes.

"Oh, my goodness gracious," she said, her tone one of awe. "I never, ever imagined."

Standing close behind her so he could hear her gasps and catch every astounded utterance, Justin chuckled. He placed his hands around her waist so he could lean forward and glimpse the performance for himself, but his own pleasure came from seeing, first-hand, Chrissie's uninhibited reactions to the antics, rather than from watching acts he'd long since stopped viewing.

Chrissie remained so absorbed in the erotic scene before her, she failed to notice his grasp of her person. Failed to reprimand him, as she normally did.

"I imagine," Justin murmured, letting his lips linger beside her ear as he spoke, "you've never seen so many men's prize possessions displayed for your comparison before."

Her head moved from side to side, slowly. "I've only ever seen... one."

Anna turned toward them and in a breathless rush of words said, "I've never seen even one before."

"Dammit. You shouldn't be seeing any," Thomas growled out.

"I've only seen one, as well," Gillian murmured.

"Just as well," Edward muttered harshly. "And a married lady shouldn't be gaping at these either."

"Edward, I love you dearly, but there nothing in this world will drag me from this sight tonight. I came to London to broaden my education. I've no intention of leaving this establishment until I've accomplished my goal."

Edward groaned. "But, Gillian, you don't need to broaden anything. You know enough to enthrall me forever."

"And yet you left my bed. What is more, you're here." Her voice increased in stridency with every sentence, her chest moving up and down in small, agitated jerks. "At a brothel. Seeking other women." She swiped at her eyes with a red-gloved fist.

"No, no, you misunderstand.

Hawkesbury told me you'd be in attendance. Naturally, I didn't believe him, but he insisted I come and see for myself. He told me you thought I'd taken a mistress. I left because I thought my constant desire for you became an embarrassment."

"What?"

"When your mother informed me of all the ungentlemanly acts I was committing, well, naturally, I felt like a complete heel. Better to leave while I could."

"Oh, Edward." Gillian touched her husband's face, gently, with all her love shining from her eyes.

Chrissie dropped her gaze, unable to bear looking any longer at the pure happiness and love between this married couple. Not something she'd been lucky enough to experience. She glanced up, caught the same look on Hawkesbury's face as she was sure was on hers. She bit her lip, praying he didn't also see the raw envy that stabbed at her, or sense the nagging ache in her heart. Though she was happy for her friend, nothing could stop her feeling a sharp sense of loss for what might have been in her own marriage.

The poignancy of the moment fractured when Anna gave another shocked gasp, the sound a mixture of dismay, horror, yet titillation. A sound that already seemed normal for this evening. Each time Chrissie glanced at Anna's face, she didn't see repulsion so much as attraction and fascination.

"I cannot understand what those women are doing to the men. Or why. Doesn't it hurt them?"

Anna's tone sounded so indignant on behalf of the gentlemen she assumed suffered some sort of physical torture, the three men snorted.

"But they look as if they're about to ... to eat—" Anna's hands flew to her cheeks, as she gasped again. "Are they ... can they ... "

"Yes, Anna. Eating them. Well, sucking really." Justin pushed off the wall where he'd lounged after Chrissie gained control of her laughter and her wobbly legs.

"About to gobble them up and swallow them with their beautiful, wide mouths. So, as you ladies are about to be shocked into swooning, I suggest you depart now. And quickly." He glanced at Chrissie, his expression smug, arrogant, knowing. "Before any of you faint dead away, and need to be carried out in full view of all the gentlemen in the anteroom."

"Oh, I don't think so, Hawkesbury," Chrissie said, hands planted on her hips as she faced him. "I, for one, came to see everything. And I'll not depart until you've shown us all the themed rooms."

"And me," Gillian added.

"Me also," Anna piped up, her voice laced with determination.

"Anna," Thomas said, frowning, shaking her hands lightly in his, "no one will think less of you if you leave now. I'm positive you've seen more enough to comprehend the decadent manner of things happening here."

Anna placed a hand on Thomas's sleeve, looked up at him with big eyes, and pleaded. "But, my wonderfully concerned friend, if I'm to attract my dearly beloved when he returns home, there is so much more I need to learn. I'm not such an innocent I haven't heard talk of camp followers. I do understand men, perhaps even my betrothed, find women to comfort them along their travels, but as he has always been such a gentle soul—"

Justin made a strangled sound, while Thomas spluttered.

"What is the matter?" Chrissie studied their expressions, her eyes widening as realization dawned. "What do you two know of Anna's betrothed?"

Thomas's round cheeks pinked, and sweat droplets beaded his brow. He looked at Justin, a question in his eyes.

"Well, do you know my fiancé?" Anna repeated the question.

Justin sighed and replied, "Bart can explain more later. When we're away from here. But he did discover today—"

Chrissie grasped his forearm, forced him to address her. "You tracked down Edward, and then you investigated Captain Martin. Did you also spend your day investigating my circumstances?"

"No need."

She sighed and relaxed her grip on his arm.

"If you recall, I attended to that matter after you departed from my home last evening." He grinned, the unrepentant cad. "So my footmen had already collected more than enough information on you."

"I see."

He patted her hand where her fingers dug into his coat sleeve. She hoped she'd dug hard enough to leave permanent marks in his flesh. The odious man deserved an injury, being entirely too smug, and too conceited, in all his actions.

"Lady Wellsby, I do recall you doing the same. Before you came to me, you had me thoroughly investigated. I know, as I checked."

She bristled at his tone. "That was different."

He laughed. "No, it wasn't. You're just insulted I can have people investigated faster than you can. I know it took you several weeks, and several hundred pounds paid out, to find out about me. So, I assume you now have your money's worth and we can leave."

"No," three females voices said in unison.

Justin and the other men looked taken aback at the force of their responses, but Chrissie knew they all felt the same. This sample, dangled in front of their noses by Hawkesbury in order to frighten them, merely whetted their appetites.

"For someone with such intimate knowledge of women, Hawkesbury, you know so little of how their minds work." Chrissie spun back to the window in time to see the girls bend their heads and slide their mouths over the lengths of the men's phalluses.

Behind her she heard Thomas chortle. "The lady has you there, Justin. Bart and I know far more about women than you do, despite being called the Virile Viscount."

"I've never needed to know more than how to satisfy their bodies and take their money," Justin said. "Because all women are the same, Thomas—eager to throw money my way without me having to exert myself to make any sort of emotional connection with them. Most women are shallow creatures."

Chrissie didn't need to see his face to know the remark was directed at her and her friends. She squinted at the faces of the men below. Lord Mitchell lounged on a cushion in full light so he'd been easy to distinguish, but now she peered at the other faces, wondering if she also knew them.

She watched in silence for several minutes, as did her two friends, then she gasped and pointed. "At the end. Isn't that ... isn't that man ...
"

Justin leaned over her shoulder, his voice close behind her ear sounded amused, but unconcerned. "Bart. Hum, yes, it is. He's maneuvered himself into the line-up for Magdalene's first performance."

"Magdalene? Ah, I see. The one at your house."

"Yes, one of the women who were—"

"Servicing you and your friends?"

He snorted. "Not servicing. Well, not last night, anyway. Auditioning. For their employment here."

"And Bart is such a dedicated friend to you," Chrissie said, dripping sarcasm. "So kind of him to sacrifice himself, to place himself on view down there, to test you've the best women to entertain your clients."

Justin placed his hand over his heart in a theatrical gesture. "A truly dedicated friend." He peered past Chrissie's shoulder to where Bart's arms were flung back on the cushions, his back arched up, lower legs supported by his booted feet widespread and planted on the carpet, his trousers hanging forgotten around his ankles.

He pointed toward Magdalene, and to her profile clearly outlined as her head dipped across Bart's long lean body. She was on one knee with the other leg crooked, harem pants split open along her bare thighs, revealing her thatch of dark hair. Bart reached down, slid his fingers along her thigh and they disappeared into the depths of her sheath. As Chrissie watched, Magdalene's shoulder shook with laughter, her enjoyment of Bart's unexpected move evident.

"Does Bart have his limbs bound for disobedience?"

"Only if one of the palace eunuchs catches him."

"He's certainly a sly one."

She turned back in time to see Bart's body go rigid, as the movements of Magdalene's head grew faster, up and down, as she sucked him toward completion. His body bowed and bucked, his hands twisted in the tassels of the cushions, and he shouted out. In the final throes of his orgasm, his hands threaded through the long dark tresses dangling and tangling around Magdalene's shoulders and he tugged, holding her head down close to his shaft.

When he'd given his last jerk and buck, the dark-headed enchantress lifted her head, gazed at Bart, and slowly licked her lips. They could see Bart's wide-eyed stare fixed on his slave, and Chrissie realized Magdalene, indeed all these women, wielded incredible power in those moments. In her own marriage, she'd ruled the household, the estate, yet never the bedroom. Had never known the ability to hold sway over her husband's emotions or his mind existed.

Until the moment that she'd observed Bart's eyes, the pure admiration, adoration even, for the woman who brought him to such ecstasy, she'd not comprehended a woman could do that. Could hold a man in the palm of her hand. Could make him her slave, despite Magdalene wearing the slave costume here tonight and Bart supposedly the master.

Justin's breath tickled her neck as he whispered to her, "Any woman who can bring such pleasure to a man is to be truly admired, don't you think?"

She swallowed down the lump in her throat. "I ... I wouldn't know."

"Did you never service your husband in that way? Did you never suck his swollen penis into your mouth until he spurted his hot seed down your throat in a rush of pleasure?"

She tensed, unable to catch her next breath. "No, no," she said, a rush of words between panted breaths. "He never wanted that sort of thing from me. Gentlemen don't expect ... " She searched for a word.

"A wife to pop his cork, to ring his bell, using their mouth? Or their pretty little white teeth."

"Teeth?" She was intrigued despite herself. "I simply cannot envisage most husbands expecting their wives to do those things to their bodies."

"Huh, don't tell me. Your husband groped you furtively under the covers with the lights off, did he? How the hell did you manage to even see one penis?"

The lump in her throat rose up again, threatened to choke her, yet she refused to back down from his taunts. "I saw it often. When I undressed him when he came home drunk, filthy, and reeling of cheap perfume. There. Does that knowledge give you an advantage over me? Make you feel superior to me? Enjoy your victory."

She spun away toward the stairs, intending to descend, but Justin strode after her, grasped her shoulder, spun her into his body.

"Bloody hell. I'm sorry. I'm a complete bastard to taunt you, but sometimes I don't seem to know any better." He released her to run his fingers through his thick hair, the gesture of frustration she'd already come to recognize. "God knows what I'll do or say if my mother and sisters do come home. I'll embarrass them every step of the way."

Just like that, her own anger and frustration deflated like a hot air balloon leaking gas. The man, and his sudden changes of temperament, was a menace to her own equilibrium. He rocked her moral core as an over-eager boy rocked a rowing boat on a lake.

She laid her hands on both his sleeves to halt his obsessive combing of his hair with rough fingers. "No. When you bring your family back to live with you, you'll know exactly the right thing to say and do to comfort and support them, because that is the sort of gentleman you remain at your heart, no matter what has transpired during your last three desperate years."

"And you try to read too much good in people, where none exists." "Not everyone. I'm afraid in the end, try as I might, I found nothing good left in my husband. The man I married no longer existed in the stranger who slept off his drunk in our house each day and awoke demanding, belligerent, hopeless." She glanced down into the room again. "And yet even he never expected me to do that to him, or for him. Why? Don't all men enjoy it?"

He sighed. "I cannot explain to you your husband's thinking. But look down there." He pointed to the other end of the passageway.

"Edward quite obviously does, and Gillian's smiling at her husband." Chrissie looked where he indicated. Edward stood watching the performance, enthralled, as was Thomas. Chrissie could see that most of the men had climaxed, spent themselves into the eager mouths of their partners. Once finished, the girls reassumed their roles of slaves and carefully washed their master's spent organs using silken cloths dipped in steaming basins of soapy water.

For some of the men, the act of being washed, stroked, cleansed by such caring hands seemed to bring them another sort of pleasure. Perhaps nearly as much as their previous pleasure. Edward and Thomas looked as if they might leap through the glass and join Bart and the other men and find their own pleasure, while Gillian and Anna glanced alternately between the room and the faces of the men standing beside them.

Gillian laid her hand on her husband's arm and he jumped. "Edward. Are you all right?"

He leaned away from Gillian, rested his hands flat on the wall beside the viewing oblong, his chest heaving. "No, I'm not all right." They heard him along the passageway, his words practically a shout. "We need to leave now."

"Yes," Thomas said, speaking to Justin. "Now. We must leave now."

Justin straightened and with what seemed like reluctance, released his hold on Chrissie. He waved his hand at the doorway leading back to the street, indicated the way to their conveyance. Their exit from his house of debauchery.

"After you, my dear ladies," he said.

She studied the expressions on the faces of the three men. Two were contorted with agitation, one portrayed absolute calm. In fact, Justin's face held that same half smile of smug amusement and self-satisfaction that had irritated Chrissie the entire night. She looked toward her friends, brows raised in silent questioning. And then as one, she, Anna, and Gillian faced the men and shook their heads. One word dropped into the tense silence from all their lips.

"No!"

6

———

"**N**o?" Justin tensed. "What do you mean by 'no'?"

Edward and Thomas scowled at him, while the three women smiled as if they were about to partake of a formal afternoon tea in his parlor.

"How—" Edward held his wife's arms, stuttered over his words. "How can you say—say no?"

"I should think it's obvious, dearest." Gillian patted his hand as if he were a two-year-old. "We ladies aren't finished here. If you wish to depart, I'll understand completely. A brothel isn't the sort of place you feel comfortable in, is it?" She smiled, her sickly sweet sincerity making Justin's teeth ache.

Edward ran his hands through his hair, making it stand up in brown spikes. Poor man looked like an agitated porcupine. "What the hell is a man supposed to answer to that? If I say I've never visited a brothel, I sound like an untried greenhorn who doesn't know how to satisfy his own wife in the bedroom. But if I say yes, you'll accuse me once again of keeping a mistress. Or two."

Poor Edward spun away and paced across the confined corridor, oblivious to the others listening. Chrissie pretended to block her ears to what should be a private conversation by half-turning away from the quarreling couple, yet Justin knew she listened as intently as the rest of them.

"If you listened to your interfering mama, you probably think I'm randy enough to service three, or even four, women at a time." Edward held Gillian's forearms and gave them a slight shake. "Is that it? Is that what you think?"

"No, dearest, on the contrary. It's me who cannot satisfy even one man." A solitary tear ran down each of her pink cheeks. "You, Edward. I want to satisfy you."

"Oh, Gillian. And all I want is you in my bed."

"But when I see these women," his wife said, "what they do to men, for men, I realize I know nothing about seducing a man. Mama said good girls lifted their nightdresses and let husbands do what they must to beget children." She swiped at her freely flowing tears. "But those ridiculous ideas aren't effective. Not for me, nor my friends."

She waved at Chrissie and Anna, who stood arm in arm, nodding agreement and encouragement. "We've discussed this at length," Gillian continued. "As intelligent women, we'll not be treated like field animals any longer." Hands fisted on her hips, she faced the men. "Gentlemen, either you accompany us, or we shall proceed by ourselves. But be warned, we intend viewing every themed room and every debauched nook and cranny in this establishment."

Justin sucked in a deep breath, stunned into silence, while the others glared at him, accusation on their faces. By contrast, the women's demeanor appeared calm, determined, and more than a little triumphant.

"Botheration, Justin," Thomas said, his face as red as a ripe tomato. "Look what you've embroiled us in. Your masterly plan turned into a disaster."

Justin groaned, rapidly considered options of escape from this dilemma, and wondered what the hell he'd been thinking trying to outsmart three quick-witted ladies. Tonight proved to him he'd been too long away from the company of tasteful ladies, ladies who thought beyond their next fucking. Ladies eager to use knowledge to enhance their lives instead of using their bodies for a few minutes of gratification.

Hell, how was he meant to fix this?

Bart wandered into view at the end of corridor, a satisfied grin splitting his face from ear to ear. Even if the women hadn't observed him being well and truly serviced by Magdalene, his look of utter satisfaction would have relayed what he'd experienced. And how much he'd reveled in it. The women stared in fascination, and Bart's mouth twitched at their attention, but he addressed his question to Justin.

"Do I detect a slight hiccough in the smooth running of your cunning plot for the evening, my conniving friend?" With his normal bewitching smile for the ladies, he said, "I admit to being a little disconcerted when I looked up to see you ladies watching Magdalene service me so adequately. Though I've no problem displaying my naked member—"

As one, the ladies dropped their gaze to Bart's trousers.

"Bloody hell, Bart. You're not helping matters."

Bart ignored him. "— the idea of conservative ladies surveying my private parts felt rather titillating for my part. Justin accuses me often of being an exhibitionist. And I know he envisaged shock sending you fleeing for the country after the first half hour in this depraved house."

Justin narrowed his eyes at his friend's taunts. "Yes, that was my intention. But it seems the ladies, and I now use the term in a looser fashion, have other ideas."

Bart took Anna's hand, raised her fingers to his mouth, kissed the backs, and ignored Thomas pushing his large body between them.

"See here, Bart—"

"Anna," Bart said with a naughty smile, "if you saw anything below you'd like me to explain, or you'd like to try, consider me a willing participant for any of your experiments."

"And naturally," Anna said, "you let Magdalene practice her arts on your body as a kindness to her. To allow her to audition for Justin."

Bart threw back his head and laughed. "I like you. And I truly believe your disreputable captain isn't fit to kiss the ground you walk on."

"My captain? What have you heard of him?"

Bart raised his eyes to Justin who gave a small nod of permission. "When Justin asked me to trace your captain, it seemed a wild goose chase. Though, as it happened, I easily picked up his trail. The black-guard has cavorted in every hell hole in London."

"No, no, it's impossible. If the captain were already in London, he'd have written to me."

"I can assure you, your esteemed fiancé is a lot more dissipated than he has led you, or his family, to think."

"No, no."

Anna shook her head, curls bouncing in wild disarray from under the string of her mask, an occurrence that seemed to fascinate Thomas. He reached out to touch her hair and smoothed the fly-away strands.

"I refuse to listen to such lies. If he is indeed here, there'll be a very good reason he's not notified me."

"You're mistaken," Bart said, his voice laced with sympathy. "The captain has kicked up his heels alongside other reprobate ex-soldiers, for several weeks. They've racked up large gaming bills, and have spent freely at several of the bawdy houses."

When Anna slumped against the railing, Thomas placed his hands on her waist to support her. "I don't understand. Unless ... unless his friends insisted he have a bachelor's fling before we marry."

She appealed to Chrissie and Gillian, who both looked away and appeared more than a little embarrassed. "Don't you think?"

Justin guessed both women knew more of the comings and goings of Anna's esteemed captain than they'd revealed. Damn! The real reason they'd dragged Anna on this journey of discovery became evident. Nothing like a little city adventure to open someone's eyes to the narrowness of a gossipy rural village.

While Gillian tried to comfort Anna, Justin pulled Chrissie aside. "You knew, didn't you?"

She faced him squarely. "We suspected, yes. We agreed to remove Anna from his family before word reached his home and she discovered his perfidy that way."

"Thus the urgency you mentioned."

"For Anna to live with them, be dependent upon them, when she discovered their son had feet of clay would be humiliating. As would discovering the captain had no intention of honoring his promises and marrying Anna."

"She appears far too genuine a person to be misled by such a bastard." They looked toward Anna, where Thomas and Bart hovered over her.

"Anna is one of the kindest people to ever walk upon this earth. How do I dissuade her from ideas of marrying the wretched captain?"

Justin reached out a finger and smoothed the frown lines between her winged brows. "You care a great deal for your friends."

She shrugged. "They've been my salvation for many years. I'd do anything for them."

He raised a brow. "Anything covers a multitude of sins." He gave her a predatory smile, and she frowned. Good! She should be disquieted in his presence. "Perhaps I may put that to the test one day soon."

If every other lady in London went crazy and displayed wild swings of emotion and eroticism in the presence of the notorious Hawkesbury, this too calm lady should show some sort of reaction as well. Why it was important he didn't care to analyze. He didn't wish to stir the fearful looks debutante chits gave him, the terror of taint that caused them to back away from him on the streets. Nor did he want to invoke the titillation experienced women of the ton chased him for.

With Chrissie, he wanted something different. He wanted her to see beneath the façade to the real Viscount Hawkesbury. A ridiculous whimsy on his part. A desire lodged deep in the heart of the person most considered to be lacking a heart.

The stream of mistresses he'd rejected over the last three years would laugh in their beds if they read his thoughts now. He stood on the wrong side of his own pleasure room, thinking virtuous thoughts about three women. Wondering what he could do for them, all without removing their clothing.

Damn. Amend that thought. About two of them, he thought heroic and non-salacious things. Even a scourge of society as he was drew the line at bedding friend's wives, and hell, only a complete cad would touch someone as innocent and sweet as Miss Anna.

By contrast, each time he looked at Chrissie's rather ordinary features, looks that wouldn't garner attention from the ton's gallants, he felt flutters. Stupid, childish flutters in his stomach, his chest. Somehow, for him at least, her plainer appearance concealed mystery, more than the open beauty of golden ringlets and blue eyes of the prettiest debutante.

He cleared his throat, attracted the attention of the others who still huddled in a group around Anna. "It seems, ladies, I underestimated your determination. I imagined when you saw the anteroom and realized why all those gentlemen paid their money, you'd run away. I was wrong. We all were."

He looked at the other men for confirmation.

Bart grinned. "Not me. From the minute Lady Wellsby entered your library last evening, I knew you'd met your match." He bowed deeply before Chrissie. "May I commend you, my lady. It's not often someone out-wickeds the most sinful Viscount in England."

The ladies laughed, while Justin groaned.

"Thank you, Bart. If you ladies are still determined, we may proceed to another window. But I warn you, this may cause you to swoon."

Chrissie looked him squarely in the eye and asked, "Why? Do you intend on joining Bart in partaking of the entertainment?"

"I will if you will," he countered with a grin.

He was pleased to note a tinge of red on her cheeks, knowing at last something made her blush, because he didn't want to believe she was as brazen, or as unconcerned, about what she observed her as she pretended. Yet once again, she out bluffed him.

Her nose lifted. "We'll see when we get there, my lord. It may only be suitable for gentlemen to obtain their pleasure, like the last room."

"Oh, I assure you, many, many women enjoy drawing men's large penises as deeply into their throats as they can manage. Bart, do you think Magdalene enjoyed sucking your cock, rolling her tongue around your head, swallowing your hot seed?"

He knew he went too far in his attempt to shock her, but something goaded him, made him push her to the edge. Bart smirked, and Justin knew he'd play along. They'd been doing these sorts of games for years. "Magdalene told me last night she wanted her first experience to only be with me. From the taste of my kisses last evening, she said she knew my sperm would slide down her throat as sweetly as the best liquor. She promised to suck me until I was as dry as a desert, to lick every last drop from my head."

"Christ!" Justin groaned, as the pain in his suddenly swelling groin stopped him in his tracks.

Edward and Thomas also halted and rearranged their trouser flaps.

"You did that deliberately," Chrissie said to Bart.

He grinned, totally unrepentant. "I did. Justin thought it amusing that you ladies recognize me, watch me, when I was having what is called here, the sucking of a camel's mouth. Though, knowing you watched made it more exciting for me."

"Really?" Gillian asked. "So men like being sucked and watched."

Edward groaned, glared at Bart. "Did you really need to mention that? God knows what she'll want to try next."

Bart laughed. "Lucky you if your gorgeous wife agrees to watch while someone else performs a camel's mouth on you, Edward."

"Oh, no," Gillian said. "But someone could watch my performance while I did it to Edward. Someone like Magdalene. Someone who could tell me if I performed it correctly."

"Trust me, Gillian. What you do is already correct."

Gillian's cheeks flushed. Chrissie looked closely at her friend. "I think perhaps, Gillian, you knew a few more secrets than you might have shared with Anna and me."

Gillian shrugged. "Perhaps, with Edwards help, I've learned a little. Just not enough."

Justin gained enough control of his unruly erection to stand erect again. He waved at the far end of the corridor. "Onwards and upwards' is a most apt expression for what you're about to see. We're about to be entertained by Matthew Large." He grinned. "I'm sure Chrissie will be especially enthralled with what one man can accomplish in a short time.

Although, I do ask you to remain quiet during his performance as we don't want the ladies with him to realize they're being observed."

"Ladies." Anna's voice was a squeak. "More than one." Thomas started to speak but she stopped him with a firm hand. "No, Thomas. I will remain, no matter what."

Justin drew a deep breath, cursed himself for plotting the most ill-fated excursion in history, but couldn't see any way to progress but forward. If these obstinate females demanded more, he'd out- stubborn them by showing them things to make their hair stand on end. He looked forward to Chrissie's reaction to watching Matthew's seduction techniques. Ah, yes, that amusement could make up for a lot.

Stopping in another corridor, he waited for the group behind him to catch up and cluster around. A small opening cut high on one wall of the room provided the usual viewing point for them to look down upon the three people already there. Justin glanced down, assured himself the scene was set, and stepped back.

"Please, be my guests."

In their eagerness to reach the viewing point, the ladies almost knocked him over while behind him, Edward groaned. He felt a flash of sympathy for the Earl, forced out of his own house, roaming London in misery under the misconception he helped his marriage. Poor misguided man now discovered how badly he'd blundered. Added to which his wife's out of character behavior bewildered Edward, panicked him.

Blame, Justin knew, would be laid squarely at his door whether he deserved it or not, although deep inside, he accepted blame for some of it. If not for his sordid reputation, one he'd spent three years cultivating, Chrissie and her friends wouldn't have sought him out.

Down below, Matthew showed himself to his best. By the chorus of female gasps, Matthew's most prominent part had sprung into view, displayed like a butcher's sausage to the two ladies in the room below with him, and also to the three women up above, open mouthed with awe.

Edward leaned forward. "Christ almighty, the man's hung like a stallion."

"He fucks like one too," Bart said with a grin, peering over shoulders like the best of voyeurs.

"Very soon, those two mares will squeal loudly enough to blow the roof off."

Thomas studied the participants below them. "Isn't that woman—"

"Which one?" Bart asked.

"We can only see one face. The one on her back, facing up, with that enormous black collar around her neck. It looks like ... No, no, it can't be."

Justin chuckled. "Yes, it can. The extremely rich one wearing the jewel encrusted slave collar and with the big smile on her face—and presently being held in place by Matthew's very large fingers between her legs—is the Duke of Brinkley's wife, Margaret. And without seeing her face, I can identify our other generous patron, the one being ploughed by Matthew's enormous cock."

"Who is it?" Gillian demanded with a girlish eagerness.

"That pair of luscious buttocks that Matthew is so intently thrusting between belongs to Margaret's best friend, Cynthia."

"Cynthia?" Thomas echoed. "Lady Cynthia Abernathy, the wife of our esteemed Member of Parliament, holder of several titles? That Cynthia?"

"The very same," Justin remarked drily.

"And how is it, my lord," Chrissie demanded of Justin, "that you're able to recognize Lady Abernathy from a quick glance at her ..." She waved her hand in small circles as she searched for a suitable word.

"Arse?" Justin offered with a grin.

She snorted. "You seem to have an intimate knowledge of both ladies' bodies."

He chuckled. "Do I detect a touch of jealousy, my lady?"

"Jealousy? Certainly not. What would I have to be jealous of? I barely know you."

He leaned closer to Chrissie's ear so as not to be overheard. "No, but you want to know me better, and soon I'll allow you to do that."

Her eyes widened and she gasped but before she could reply, he held a finger to his lips to signal for quiet. "We don't want to alert them to our presence. If I know Matthew's routine, any moment he'll finish off Cynthia and you'll hear her scream. Then he'll attend to Margaret, although Cynthia will help with her too."

"You mean—" Chrissie swallowed, tried to appear cool and sophisticated. "You mean they do things ... to each other?"

"Oh, yes. Most definitely. That's the part they enjoy the most."

"Oh, my goodness. I never knew women could do ... " Anna said, in a small voice from in front of them. "That. Any of that."

"Anna," Justin said, compassion in his voice. "There are many things occurring here a well- bred young lady should never under-stand." She glared at his dismissive tone until he gave a resigned sigh and leaned back against the wall. "Some women enjoy other women, Anna. The two down there come here twice a week. They use Matthew to give them physical release. The emotional closeness they crave, they get from each other. Did you notice what Margaret is doing while Matthew's fingers are busy working other parts for her?"

"Doing?" Anna echoed, as she turned back to the room. "Oh, my goodness. She seems to be—"

"Sucking on Cynthia's breasts!" Bart announced, after peering through the aperture. "She always enjoys that part of the evening. Anna, wait until you see Cynthia return the favor in a moment."

"Cynthia must have strong teeth because Margaret always screams. When Matthew is inside Margaret and Cynthia latches on to her nipple, you'd be wise to step away from the opening," Justin remarked in an offhand way. "Margaret's screeches pierce your ear drum."

"And you let them do this? Every week?" Chrissie asked.

"Me? It's naught to do with me."

"Oh, come, come. You are the owner of this establishment."

Justin smiled. "So, I don't suppose there is any possibility of taking you ladies home now, is there?"

Once again the women looked at each other in search of an answer, but once again three heads shook in a row.

Justin groaned before looking to the other men for assistance. He raised his hands in application. "I assume you gentlemen blame me for this."

Edward glared, and his words sounded as an angry hiss. "Who else should we blame?"

Gillian placed a hand on her husband's arm. "Edward, please." She looked at Justin and smiled. "The next window, my lord. What do you have in store for us there?"

He moaned. "There'll be an elderly gentleman in the next room who may be recognizable to you. Once again, I'd ask for discretion." At their puzzled looks, he explained, "On his weekly visits, he receives special attention from one of our larger and stronger ladies." He looked toward Bart, who shrugged and laughed. "Don't expect me to explain his particular fetish. I may indulge in some of the other treats on offer here, but I detest pain."

Justin rolled his eyes. "This gentleman dresses in one of our silk slave costumes—" At their continuing looks of incomprehension, he said, "He enjoys the feel of female slave clothing against his skin, and being whipped on his bottom through it by a woman who pretends to be the wife of an Arab sheik."

"Oooh," Anna said, screwing her nose up in distaste.

Justin shrugged. "He's quite harmless and he pays well for the privilege of kissing her feet and debasing himself before her. In the Sultan's Place our policy is not to condemn but to provide for each member's particular needs."

"And then accept a lot of money for providing it," Bart said in irony.

Justin ignored him. "To save you future embarrassment, I'll share the gentleman's name now. It's Lord Mannerly."

"Bloody hell," Edward exclaimed. "That pompous bore gave me a lecture last week on the rights and wrongs of well-mannered behavior of a gentleman. And he cavorts in a brothel every week dressed like a female?"

Justin chuckled. "We prefer calling it a house of pleasure rather than a brothel, which always sounds so ... low class."

Bart snorted his laughter and even Thomas grinned. Chrissie's mouth turned up at the ends as if she tried not to laugh. Feeling slightly more relaxed, Justin linked Chrissie's arm through his and waved to the next corridor.

"Onward, ladies. To the next entertainment."

From within the next room grunts and moans, pleasure intermingled with pain, interspersed with squeals of pleasure. Squeals sounding suspiciously girlish, yet manly. Chrissie jumped back after one particularly loud groan from Lord Mannerly.

"Steady," Justin said in her ear. He ran his hands up and down her sides from her hips to under her breasts, but stopped short of the soft mounds quivering above his fingers. Holding his hands still, he beat down the urge to continue his explorations a few inches higher. With the slightest upward movement of his fingers, those lush breasts would fill his palms and her nipples would rise up in greeting.

Her body tensed, poised for his next movement. Up or down? His body clamored for hers, but others stood near them, too close to risk arousing either of them further. His unruly erection, refusing to play dead again, prodded against her back, pushed against her buttocks. If he wiggled or gave the slightest forward thrust, his yearning penis would press in the right position to slide home. His fingers itched to slide the eye-catching red gown upwards, over her ankles, past her knees, to expose her thighs. They'd be white, smooth, and incredibly tempting.

Hell, get a grip. If he wanted sex, he owned a houseful of willing prostitutes. Yet for months, he'd not felt a twinge of arousal, his mind and body deadened from overuse and overexposure. Only Bart knew the truth, because his reputation as the Virile Viscount had provided a necessary protection in many situations. Thank God matchmaking mamas and timid virginal daughters avoided him like the plague.

Chrissie leaned back to speak to him and pressed her curves harder along his already taut length. Damn her! Didn't she understand how dangerous it was? Or perhaps she knew, but did it to punish him. As he tried to puzzle out her motives, he nearly missed her whispered words.

"I feel so terribly sorry for Lord Mannerly."

Justin leaned around to read her eyes, looking for a hint of her thinking. He prided himself on being able to outwit women, all women. Nevertheless, when it came to Lady Chrissie Wellsby, he floundered like a green youth struggling to make sense of his first love. An unfeasible task.

"Why would you pity him? Listen. He revels in every lash of the leather on his bare arse. Comes back for more, time after time."

"But to suffer such debasement in order to feel manly, it seems somehow ... pitiable. A lonely existence. Doesn't the pitiful man have anyone in who cares enough to keep him out of a house of debauchery such as this?"

He gave her a wry smile. "Describing my establishment in such contemptuous terms is not the way to endear yourself to me. I'm more likely to refuse to help you and your friends." She bit her bottom lip, clamping down her escaping giggle, but it did no good. He heard it. "You find my distress amusing?"

"I doubt my mild descriptions of your establishment discomfort you in any way at all. With your reputation, you're well used to being talked about."

He raised a brow. "Gossiped about, yes, insulted, no. No man enjoys being affronted by a beautiful woman he's trying to impress."

"Nonsense." She turned to the spectacle before her and effectively dismissed him.

"N-nonsense? Why is my regard for your beauty or my avid desire to please you nonsense?"

"Hawkesbury, practiced flattery may work on susceptible ton ladies, ones enthralled by your insincere words, and I imagine, swept up and into your bed. I am not one of them."

He studied her for a minute. "Ah, now I see." He gave her a smug smile, knowing it'd annoy her.

She pivoted, so close to his body she stood on his boot. He smothered his grin. To unravel this sparrow's secrets, he needed to ruffle her plain brown feathers, expose the passionate female hidden beneath her dispassionate exterior.

She scowled. "What? What is it you imagine you see?"

"You're unable to accept flattery for one of two reasons. Either you're unused to it, as we did establish your husband was a blind fool who didn't notice your beauty... "

"Or?"

"Or he used flattery insincerely, and in the way most husbands resort to in marriage."

One shod foot commenced a tapping rhythm under her skirt, and the frothy red flounce around the hem rose and fell like a sparrow's puffing chest.

"Oh, pray, do enlighten me. Although as you're not married—" She inhaled, sharp and hissing. "Oh, dear. I simply assumed you're not." She stared at him and then shook her head. "No, no, of course you aren't."

He lifted a brow in question. "Why so certain?"

"Apart from my investigator describing your situation, it stands to reason you've no wife. If you did, you'd not freely cavort with actresses in your own house."

"Many men have no such qualms in their spouse's absence. They entertain courtesans in their houses, under the noses of household staff."

"Yes, but you wish to return your mother and your sisters to their rightful home. You'd not cause scandal at your residence if you already had a family to protect."

"Ah, yet I auditioned the women there. And they demonstrated all their tricks to us, before you rudely interrupted."

"No, no. You cannot convince me your morals are lacking to that extent. But please, do continue with your fascinating lecture on the mind of a married man."

He frowned. Should he feel complimented or insulted? She'd barely made his acquaintance, yet read every thought in his head without effort. Bloody irritating. His turn to seize back control of the situation.

"A man offers false flattery to his wife when he's sinned outrageously and is desperate to crawl back into a woman's bed. Any woman." He shrugged. "A wife being the quickest and easiest to gull into surrendering her wet, warm sheath, a husband appeals to her."

"Your theory doesn't always hold water. My husband never cared enough about his sins to beg my forgiveness by flattering me, nor did he care if he crawled into my bed or not. I failed, miserably, to hold his attention, sensually and sexually, and thereby forced him to seek other women to ease his suffering."

"Good Lord above! Did the bastard fill your head with those lies?" She winced, so he gentled his tone. "Why would you believe him?"

She sighed, but raised her eyes to meet his gaze. Damn, he admired her bravery. "Because I know my limitations. I know I don't appeal in ... in a bedroom way ... to men."

"Bollocks." Ignoring her startled gasp, he lifted the back of her gown, hooked it over his elbows, and pressed his body down the length of hers. "You appeal in and out of a bedroom. Your fucking cad of a husband went to great pains to kill any esteem you held for your skills, therefore enabling him to do whatever he liked and to never apologize for his behavior." He pushed against her back, once, twice, three times. "Trust me, I've more experience with judging female flesh than your husband, and I say yours is very enticing."

Her spine stiffened. "Now I know you are funning me. I've neither the petite physique not the coloring of the popular ladies. Even during three seasons in town, I didn't come close to being considered an original. Not even striking enough to be interesting."

He trailed his fingers over as much of her bare skin as he could reach, gratified to feel her chest movements become quicker, more irregular, the catches in her breathing audible. She swiveled her head to check the position of her friends but didn't pull away, a sign the sexual delights she'd viewed this evening had an effect upon her libido.

God knew watching her view the erotic acts had affected his. Put paid to his belief he was doomed to permanent impotency. He could laugh about it now, although in the small hours of morning, on cold miserable nights, he'd privately lamented he'd never share his large inherited oak bed with a warm and willing woman. The forever kind, not the paid by the hour sort.

He continued his exploration of her hidden treasures, primitively and arrogantly pleased to be the first after her husband to touch her. She'd not needed to tell him that, as her reactions gave her away as an innocent, despite her widow's status.

No gloves disguised the roughness of his hands, his callused fingers, the signs of a working man and not a pretend gentleman. But she hadn't pulled away from his aroused body, and she didn't pull away now. Breath seized in her chest, her inhalation suspended, her breasts no longer rising and falling.

"Breathe," he murmured. "Just breathe. I promise I'll not harm you."

He looked toward the others. Bart's long body slumped in the corner, his eyes closed, hardly surprising after the little sleep they'd managed. Thomas hovered behind Anna, whose attention had drifted from the performance below as she listened to whatever story Thomas regaled her with.

In the darkest corner, the shadowy forms of Gillian and Edward could be seen locked together—the recognizable sounds and smells of animals on heat filtered out. If their interlude grew any more intimate, the curtains surrounding them would ignite. Gillian's groans filtered through the corridor 's silence like the screeches of a cat in mating season.

Justin chuckled. "Your friends are too busy to notice anything we do." He applied himself to his task, or rather, to the pleasure of touching her thighs, running his hands over the tops of her stockings and letting his fingers wander in a slow circular pattern. "Soft." He spoke near her ear, his voice raspy and raw with arousal as he caressed the bare skin of her inner thighs. "Soft with excitement. It seems being a voyeur stimulates you."

"I-I'm sure I don't know what you mean," she said, then gasped when his fingers crept higher.

"Liar. Ah, I've discovered another of your secrets, my not-so prim-lady."

"Wh-what secrets?"

"You've forgone the wearing of pantaloons. Perhaps in anticipation of what might happen here in one of the rooms. Was that it? Did you expect to undress for someone? With someone. Perhaps for me."

"No! I did not. I refused to undress for you last night, and I'd refuse again if you asked me."

He touched one finger to the nest of curls between her legs and although she clenched her thighs against the intrusion, he kept his finger in place, resting in her damp thatch. "I think, Chrissie, you're not telling the truth. You enjoy the feel of a man's hand upon you there." He moved his finger a little and she hissed in a breath. "But I think you'd prefer my hand there now. If I'm correct, nod."

A long moment passed when neither of them moved so much as a muscle. She moved her head in a slow motion that became a faster, more emphatic, nod. He released the breath he hadn't known he'd held. Relief flooded him, though why her permission mattered so much he couldn't say, simply knew it did. He ached, and needed her to suffer the same pain.

He waited, and though it took longer than he liked, she relaxed her taut muscles, unclenched her thighs, allowed him access to her most alluring place. Her crevice, scalding hot and dripping wet, felt so good only rigid control prevented him from thrusting his entire fist up and inside her tight passage. Like a pirate, Justin yearned to pillage and plunder his captive princess. Like a salivating sheik, he dreamed of initiating his young bride into the erotic tricks experienced in his harem.

Leaning forward, he nuzzled below her ear and dragged the tip of his tongue across the scented skin of her neck. Violets would forever be his favorite flower. She shivered, not a ladylike shimmer but a full bodied tremble that shook her from head to toes, and started a mirror movement in his own tightly held muscles. For a few moments, he savored the feel of her response as it rippled over them both, then flicked his tongue around the inside shell of her ear. Her limbs loosened, knees sagged.

Keeping one hand snugly fixed in her groin, he draped his other arm across her body. "Lean back against me. I've got hold of you." "What ... what are you doing to me?" Her voice sounded dreamy, floating, and her body rested against his in supplication. Nothing had felt so good, no one had been so physically and emotionally close to him for so long, a lump rose up in his throat.

"Pleasure," he said, swallowing down the jolt of emotion threatening to weaken his knees as well. "I'm delivering pleasure. Can you remember what it feels like now?"

He slipped two fingers higher still, slid through her sodden passage, shifted and wiggled inside her until she squirmed and writhed.

"Shush, shush." For his own part, he was barely able to murmur the soothing sounds, yet knew she'd be mortified if she screeched aloud and he did nothing to prevent it.

The placket of his trousers stretched so tautly across his shaft it rubbed and chaffed with every movement he made, yet even torture was better than no relief. Veins carrying blood to his penis throbbed in time with his finger 's strokes inside Chrissie, his engorged head screamed to be let free of its confinement.

He'd not known such torture since he was a gawky youth and the milkmaid had bargained a glimpse of her quim in exchange for a half- sovereign. For a full sovereign, she'd let him touch it while baring her breasts. His costly first sexual experience had lasted precisely one minute and the maid had laughed so hard when he'd creamed his trousers her cap had fallen down to catch between her pendulous bosom.

Fighting back the agony of his fully aroused lust, he swirled his thumb over her swollen and protruding clit, circled, while with two fingers, he kept up a relentless motion, in and out, up and down. Her folds swelled under the tip of his thumb and she gave small soft moans which increased in pace and volume at every touch.

She swayed from side to side, eager to increase the pressure between her legs on her most sensitive places. Bending her head sideways, she buried her mouth into her shoulder to muffle her excited whimpers and grunts.

Then it came. Her release burst free in jolts and jars, while the outside evidence trickled over his bare fingers and down his hand. Moisture continued to gush even as her inner muscles clenched as tight as a welder 's clamp over his fingers. He flicked his thumb over the tip of her clitoris with the lightest touch, again and again, prolonging her lengthy climax.

He waited until the last twitch of her vagina ceased before he extricated himself in a slow, reluctant withdrawal. She moaned over his withdrawal from her body and he groaned over the loss of his sanity. Taking a half step back, he dropped her skirts to the floor. Her head dropped to her chest and she wobbled on unsteady legs, yet he didn't dare touch her again. The temptation to scoop her up and carry her away to the nearest empty room ate at him.

If he did that, gave into the raw lust riding him he wouldn't stop until he'd sated himself in her lush warmth. Sated? How many times would it take? Once, twice, a lifetime's worth of climaxes, both hers and his? Instead he strode away, sought to drag up his usual inner calm by putting a generous distance between them.

From the room below, the performance continued. By Lord Mannerly's cries, his evening's ritual timetable had progressed to the part where his dominatrix commanded him to find his release using his fist, while she berated him in a loud cruel voice for tugging his prick and finding release the way green youths did in their beds at night. He hoped Chrissie and the others would be enthralled for the next few minutes at the agony and ecstasy his lordship endured.

Justin sat on the darkened stairs, slumped against the wall, dropped his head to his knees and covered his face in his hands. Stupid, stupid! He berated himself. Had he not learned his lesson over the past years? Giving in to lust every time the urge struck him had entangled him in this mess in the first place. If he'd been at home when his family needed him, not as far away from his disgusting father as possible and rutting his brains out with some nameless French mistress, he'd know the hiding place of his mother and sisters.

By now, they'd be safely ensconced in his family home, his inheritance, the mausoleum he'd never wanted. The pile of stone hanging like a noose around his neck. An enormous cross he was forced to bear through nothing but his own folly, his inability to keep his breeches fastened when he was younger.

Back then, in his wilder younger years, he'd thought it a vast joke to seduce his father's latest mistress. To fuck her every way he'd learned, and by then, he'd learned plenty. In his last defiant act, he'd plowed her on every piece of furniture in the house his father bought for her using the estate's income. Considered it retribution for his mother and sisters doing without new gowns and fripperies so his father could pay for his own extravagances.

Justin's chosen method of revenge had appeared intelligent to an angry and vigorous young man whose father chose the rest of the world over his own family. Back then, his good looks were maturing, his virility peaking, and he'd only to lift a finger and women fought for the right to invite him to bed.

Despite the long line of conquests awaiting him, he'd stalked and chosen the high-flyer paid for by the man who'd spawned him, then neglected him. Maria had been an easy mark. So easy even he, a titled gentleman known to harbor no conscience and no heart, had felt twinges of guilt at using her with such ruthlessness.

As fleeting as his revenge had been against his father, Maria's suffering had been the opposite. More prolonged, as had his mother's when she'd learned of what he'd done from London's gossips. It'd seemed merciful when Maria died soon after, though Justin's guilt had increased threefold when he learned later that a miscarriage had caused her deathbed fever. Sickened by the thought of Maria dying because two ruthless men had used her without thought to consequences, he'd been too disgusted with himself to leave his house.

For weeks he'd been too ashamed to speak with his mother as she'd read in his face the dishonorable part he'd played and her humiliation would be increased. Finally his compulsion to discover the truth about Maria drove him out onto London's streets, where he freely spent coin to locate Maria's staff—her footmen and at last, her personal maid.

"Tell me, Betsy," he'd said, trying not to frighten her with his desperation. Though he'd dressed, he'd long since given up his usual care with his appearance and she looked about to turn and run. "I need ... I must know. Was the babe mine?" He groaned, remembering the quake in his voice as he'd asked. "Or was it my father's?"

By that stage, he'd been so angry, so crazed, the poor maid backed away, terrified of whom he'd become. Ruthlessly reining in his temper, he'd offered more money than she'd earn in a year for her truthful answer.

"The babe weren't yours, my lord. My lady already carried the child before you—"

"Before I wormed my way into her bed, the bed paid for by my devoted pater." Betsy had nodded. "So why didn't Maria tell me? Why let me suffer this torment later?"

Betsy hadn't been able to meet his eyes, but the lure of gold coins loosened her tongue. "Me mistress afeared when your father found out he'd filled 'er belly with a babe 'ed toss her out. But she 'oped you'd not leave 'er, no matter who planted the seed."

"Humph! Your mistress's belief in me was misplaced. I seduced her to strike out at my father, nothing else."

"Oh, sir, she knew it, she did. But it made no matter. You treated 'er right. Your father ... " She'd gulped, swallowed, stared at the ground. "'e never was a kind man."

"My father mistreated her?" Betsy had confirmed Justin's suspicions about the true cause of his mother's anti-social behavior. Like all his foolish and self- obsessed peers, he'd shut his eyes to the truth and let a woman, his own mother, protect his sisters from their father 's wrath. Time and again when they were all children, she'd put herself in harm's way to save them from his cruelty.

Yet, in his youthful arrogance, he'd turned every fight with his father into his personal affront, never giving a thought to the women in his family when he'd stormed out. He'd left London that last time in the belief that he did what was best for everyone, yet he'd failed to ask his mother her preferences. For her, or for his sisters. He'd failed them then, and now, after three years back in London, he'd still failed to locate them.

A gentle hand touched his back, and Chrissie lowered herself onto the step beside him. "Are you well, my lord?"

He gave a snort of laughter. "My dear lady, very recently my fingers were inside your body. So I think you should address me less formally. My name is Justin. Say it."

"Justin ...are you well?" She peered at his face, her brown brows dipping together as she frowned.

"Sweetheart, it should be I enquiring as to your well-being. After all, I'm the notorious Virile Viscount and you're a discreet lady. You should slap my face for taking such liberties."

"My lord ... Justin ... I'd be a hypocrite to attack you for something I allowed."

He shook his head. No matter what he threw at this amazing lady, she retained her composure—with the exception perhaps of those minutes in the corridor when she was mindless to everything bar her own rapture. Her golden eyes had spun to meet his gaze as she climaxed and he'd felt their heat burn through to his cold heart. Felt the ice around it crack a little.

Good God! Like a love-sick fool he rhapsodized poetical about her attributes. He held one of her gloved hands in his bare hand and squeezed with fingers still carrying the lingering musky scent of feminine arousal. Would she be shocked if he licked them, sucked the sweet and salty taste of her into his mouth? Ignorant of his lecherous thoughts, she flashed him a rueful glance.

"And to answer your question, yes, I found comfort in my husband's arms when he visited my bedchamber. For the first few weeks of my marriage anyway."

"Comfort? What about pleasure?"

"My willingness, or rather my eagerness, to couple more than once a week shocked my husband. Though he knew I was eager to conceive our child. After he chastised me for my ill-bred behavior, I feared he may cease our conjugal visits altogether. I'd lose my chance of becoming a mother. I learned to hide my emotions and appear as dispassionate as my husband." She glanced sideways at him through her long thick lashes. "Necessity forced me into a meeker role, but I wanted to become enceinte. So I took the cowardly road."

He snorted. "Despite me labeling you a mouse, you're no coward. Anyone who beards a panther in his den in the dead of night unguarded and unchaperoned cannot be deemed a coward."

With his teeth, he tugged the fingertips of her glove until the soft satin slipped off her hand. Despite it being every rake's well-practiced move of seduction, Chrissie gave an incredibly sweet and surprised little gasp, alerting him to her rapidly rising level of arousal. After only one day, he recognized it and delighted in it.

"If I'm no longer a coward, I shouldn't be so afraid to ask you for what I need. Wouldn't fear being thought brazen."

Justin smiled his amusement. "I hardly think that I, or my friends, will look at the prim and proper Lady Wellsby and think her brazen."

She glanced down at herself. Their cloaks had been left downstairs and her mask had been abandoned. Her low cut gown stretched taut across the bodice of her red gown, purchased by a maid that afternoon from a shop that catered to ladies of the night. Soft mounds of pink flesh pushed up, an enticing feast for a man's eyes, but he refrained from pointing that out and increasing her embarrassment.

"Those women, the ones who sell their wares on the streets, must be less well-endowed than me," she said, making a futile attempt to push her breasts into her bodice.

Justin was unable to prevent his mirth escaping. She frowned.

"Sweetheart, any whore blessed with breasts as large as yours would bow down and thank their Lord for providing a way to make pots of money."

She glared at him. "You're ridiculing me."

He bit his lip to smother more laughter. Bringing her hand to his mouth, he flicked his tongue along the bare skin exposed above her glove.

"I swear I'm telling the truth. You're beautiful. From the curls on your head to those rather large feet that you insist on stomping when I annoy you."

"I do not—" She shook her head. "I may have stomped. Once."

He grinned, shook his head, waited.

"Perhaps twice. But only because you are an extremely annoying man."

"I know." He smiled again. "But please, ask away. What is your question?"

"Question?"

He squeezed her hand. "Do you repeat things that everyone says, or is it my charming presence that makes you so flustered?"

"Oooh!" Her leg twitched, and he placed a firm hand on her knee. She narrowed her eyes at him, opened her mouth to say something, closed it again. Her leg jiggled again, a restless little motion under his hand, and he allowed her to see his amusement.

"Bloody hard to stomp when seated, isn't it?"

"You, you ... No, you'll not irritate me. Rousing my temper is merely another ploy to goad me into retreating. I'm made of sterner stuff."

"Good. I detest spineless women." He kissed the back of the hand he still held. She frowned down at it, seemingly puzzled by its presence. "Now, what did you want to know?"

She sighed, a long expulsion of breath and a sag of her shoulders.

"It hardly seems to matter now. I was concerned about you, your welfare."

He stared, open-mouthed. A lady, a truly gracious lady, who'd suffered and lived a small, unfulfilled life worried about him. Unaware she'd rendered him speechless, she continued to speak in a hesitant voice. "I-I wondered if you needed ... if-if I should ... "

"Should what?"

She glanced at his groin where his erection tented his trousers. "Should help you." She used her head to point. "With that."

He looked down, shifted on the step, and with his free hand attempted to readjust his flap. "Let me understand, you're offering to relieve my hard on?"

She swallowed, nodded. "My husband preferred me to do it that way."

"Jesus Christ almighty." He sucked in a breath. "How? Your hand?"

"Mmm. My hand and a cloth inside his drawers." Her words came out in a rush. "He said it was faster, less messy. Easier for us both. Especially when it became apparent I was barren."

"Bastard. I wish to God your husband still lived, because I'd like to kill him. Slowly. Several times."

"He did it for me," she said, her tone snappy, defensive. "So I didn't suffer soiled nightdresses or sheets by continuing our couplings." He knew he looked ridiculous with his mouth open like an imbecile, but he couldn't seem to recover from his shock enough to close it, or to speak. He'd never in his life heard such a cartload of horse shit—and to think that a clever woman like her had fallen for it stunned him. Horrified him.

"Until now, I thought I'd seen and heard every low trick in the world. Married men use tricks and lies all the time to either entice a woman into their beds, or to keep them out of it. But never, never in my entire life have I heard of a man who demands his wife tug his dick to save dirtying the bed linen. Didn't you employ a laundress?"

"Yes. Geoffrey, however, thought it distasteful to have such intimate tasks performed by a servant. He preferred me to see to our personal linen."

"Fuck me! My father was a prick of the highest order, but your husband and his subtle cruelties outclassed him by a mile. He eroded your self-confidence. In ways you couldn't fight, ways that freed him from any guilt over his liaisons and visits to brothels."

"No, no. It wasn't like that." He rubbed his thumb over the back of her hand, longing to rub some warmth back into her sterile life. The indescribable tortures women suffered at the hands of their male relatives disgusted him.

"Yes it was, and it's time you knew. Your sainted husband lied. Apparently about everything. Wellsby spent many nights at my houses and believe me, nothing he did was to save you from washing extra laundry."

"Geoffrey went to your Pleasure House? To the Bath House?"

He nodded, stroked her hand, and ached for her pain.

"I don't understand. Geoffrey explained that he used the services of a ... a woman. Occasionally. Because seeing to his physical relief every week wasn't something he believed a wife, or a lady, should be asked to do, especially after it became obvious I was barren. But he visited a woman, an older widow who needed money."

"Christ! The selfish bastard." "Why you are angry at Geoffrey? Though he wasn't the most attentive of husbands, he didn't treat me any worse than any other gentleman. My expectations for our marriage started out being very high, unreasonably so."

He snorted. "So saintly Geoffrey pointed out you expected too much from him. Said you drove him to other women."

She frowned. "Well, yes. But only one woman."

"And you believed him? Hell. For an intelligent woman, you allowed Wellsby do you a lot of harm. Didn't it disturb you knowing your husband fucked another woman?"

"I'm ashamed to admit it, but when he visited the widow again, I was relieved. Not that I hadn't enjoyed those times when my husband touched my body. Those few moments before he completed his business. Because I did."

"A few moments." Justin rolled his eyes. "Go on. Tell me the worst."

"It was the next part that I didn't enjoy. Not when it hurt so much."

"And I'll bet Geoffrey made sure you gained no pleasure from your couplings, as you called them. Made sex so vile that you encouraged him to seek it elsewhere and expunged his guilt over his sexual escapades. Though I doubt he suffered any remorse." He threw back his head and groaned aloud. "What did you do, pack his valise when he went roving? Sent a cake to his hostess like a good little wife."

She leapt to her feet, her face crumpling into creases and tears. "You're despicable. I offered to help because you looked to be in pain and you're repaying me with cruel taunts and untruths."

He stood to face her, their noses almost touching. "I am in pain. Life's cruel and bastards like Geoffrey, and my father, have caused us both pain. And yet naïve believers in good, like you, would still lie down and allow someone to walk over you. To crush your hopes and dreams."

He rubbed his nose across hers, gently, and wished he could as easily rub salve onto her inner wounds. Her hands came up, grasped his forearms, either to push him away or pull him closer. He hoped for the latter. Wanted her to lean into him, lean on him.

At that moment, Lord Mannerly gave his loudest squeal as his dominatrix completed the last act of chastisement in his lordship's ritual. Along the corridor, the others stirred. Gillian appeared flustered and Edward smiled, the smug look of a man who'd enjoyed an unexpected bout of sex. Thomas gripped Anna's elbow and tired his best to look unaffected as Anna chattered like an overexcited monkey about the red streaks now marring Lord Mannerly's fat white bottom. Bart awoke, stood, and ambled toward Anna like a disjointed puppy scenting a new bone.

Thomas towed Anna toward the stairs and as he passed Justin he muttered, "Are we finished for the evening? Or do you have more torture to inflict upon us?"

Obviously he and Thomas suffered a similar frustration.

"No, I think we've suffered enough for one night."

He led the group outside to the waiting carriages, using back corridors and avoiding front parlor members. Decadent noises erupted— high-pitched giggles from his girls, squeals and moans of pleasure from his guests. To Justin, the noises were simply a qualifier as to how busy his house was for the evening and how much coin the girls were earning. The three ladies, however, moved at an annoyingly slow pace along the maze of corridors and at every room or window they halted, faces alert, and listened to every emitted grunt and groan.

He'd seriously misjudged them, as nothing upset their composure. He also owed Bart a crown. They'd wagered on how long the women would last and Justin's overly optimistic assumption of less than half an hour seemed ridiculous considering that more than two hours later he couldn't coerce them back to the carriages. Plus, more dallying meant more risk of recognition as the women had discarded their disguises.

Ironically it was Edward who, although furious with Justin earlier, grasped his hand in a shake hard enough to pull his arm out of its socket. "Thank you, Hawkesbury. I can't tell you what this evening has meant to me." He pulled Gillian closer, his arm firmly around her waist, and kissed the top of her head. "To us, and our marriage."

Gillian stretched up on her toes and kissed Justin's cheek. "You're a wonderful man and I'm grateful you brought us here."

He ran his fingers through his hair and gave a quiet groan. "My intention, as you probably guessed, was to shock you into running away."

Gillian patted his cheek as a nanny does to an errant infant. "We knew. But we'd spoken of it before we approached you and decided we'd not allow ourselves to be upset. After all, we'd taken a great deal of care, and time, with our research."

"Research." His mouth dropped open again.

Anna stopped beside Gillian and smiled—or was she smirking? "Oh, hell," Justin said. "I've a feeling I've been outsmarted. By three country women."

Anna spoke up. "Mm hm. We made a pact before we left that nothing would deter us. Chrissie knew I'd be most easily shocked, so we studied before we came to London."

"Studied," Thomas said, his wide-eyed gaze fixed on Anna's face.

She smiled again. "Oh, yes, Thomas. Many books carry detailed illustrations, if one knows where to purchase the right books."

"And from these books you learned what you'd see here," Justin said. He bowed from the waist. "Ladies, I take my hat off to you for your ingenuity. You've outwitted me well and truly."

Chrissie dipped a quick curtsy and a cheeky grin. "You didn't really believe we were so naïve that you'd frighten us away after one night, did you, my lord?"

"I did have high hopes for that, yes," he told them wryly. "So, what is the next step in your devious plans, my dears? Seats in Parliament? Investing in the Exchange?"

The three women looked at each other and did something that sent another chill down Justin's spine. They giggled. Even Chrissie. Prim, sensible seeming Lady Wellsby gave a girlish sound of delight at having flummoxed the men, especially him.

"Next, Lord Hawkesbury, we are off to your estate. To the Pleasure House. To the Bath House. Friday will suit us best for our arrival as we need to spend the next few days making arrangements here in London before our departure."

"No, that's impossible. I cannot arrange a Bath House occasion in such a short time."

"Ah, but I think you can. I think you will. I didn't mention this earlier as it may have spoiled your evening, or caused you to cancel ours, but I've received new information on your mother and sister. Time is now of the essence."

Edward gaped at Gillian. "You cannot mean to still accompany the other two. Please, Gillian. Return home with me. You've proved your point. I'll no longer leave you alone with your mother."

Gillian patted her husband's arm and looked at him with

sorrowful eyes. "But Edward, do you not want to participate in some more adventures with me?"

"You want us to go together?" "Yes, I do. I certainly never intended to become involved with any other man, Edward. I merely intended to watch. But with you by my side, perhaps the viscount could arrange for us to have a little adventure. Together."

The look she gave Edward was pure sexual enticement, one no normal man could resist. Especially not a husband starved of his wife's affection and robbed of the enjoyment of her bed for so long by a manipulative mother-in-law. Edward turned pleading eyes to Justin. His future would be far different if he allowed his wife a week of experimentation.

Anna placed a gentle hand on Justin's arm and added her plea to the needs of her friend's. "Please, my lord. I also need what only you can give me. Knowledge. Experience. Confidence. I know you think my fiancé is a bad person, but I'm certain he loves me. I am his betrothed. As a gentleman, he'd never hurt me, or his family. I need to learn how to be a good wife for him."

Thomas looked horrified. "No, Anna. Your captain is not good enough for you. There's no need for you to change anything about yourself. You're perfect just—"

"Hell, Thomas," Bart interrupted in disgust. "Leave Anna be. She's discovered courage for what sounds to be the first time in her sheltered life. She escaped the suffocating conservatism of the captain's family. From what I've learned today, that bastard of a fiancé—"

Anna gasped. "Bartholomew!" "Well, Anna, he is, as you will soon discover. In the meantime, love, you should enjoy yourself. Whatever happens in your future, you'll have at least experienced one week of pleasure."

Bart took both of Anna's hands in his and caressed the backs of them, making Thomas clear his throat loudly in annoyance. Bart grinned and ignored him. "And I can assure you, sweetheart, Justin's house delivers endless hours of pleasure to those who want it." He looked at Chrissie. "You especially, Lady Wellsby, will love it."

Chrissie raised her eyebrow at him. "Why me particularly?"

"Because I couldn't help but overhear your conversation with Justin—"

"Christ, you were eavesdropping again, weren't you?" Justin said. "I thought you were asleep."

"I was until the conversation became too interesting to miss. It seems, Lady Wellsby, you've even more reason than your friends for wanting to experience the joys of the Pleasure House. By the sound of it, Geoffrey was a self-centered bastard who took no interest in your pleasure. Any man who denies his wife his presence in their marital bed yet expects—no, demands—that she service him by hand, or allows him to act like a bull entitled to pick any cow in a field—"

"It wasn't like that!" Chrissie interrupted.

"That's exactly how it was. It's time you stopped deceiving yourself about your dearly departed's motives, Chrissie. The man was a perverted and lying scum. Let Justin show you how good it can be between a man and a woman. He's the expert when it comes to women with unleashed passions."

Justin groaned and ran his hands through his already tousled hair. "Dammit! Why am I being put in this position? If I refuse to reopen the House, the only person who'll be happy is Thomas. The other five, all staring at me so intently, will hate me. And if I refuse," he sucked in a deep breath and watched Chrissie, "I'm not going to obtain Chrissie's information on finding my family."

Chrissie swallowed hard and bowed her head slightly as she answered in a subdued voice, "I'm sorry. Honestly, I am. My actions may seem like heartless blackmail, but I was desperate to get you to agree."

Justin gave a harsh laugh. "Well, it seems the Pleasure House is back in business. London's bored upper crust will be thrilled." He glared at each of the people gathered around him in turn. "However, let's be clear. Viscount Hawkesbury is opening his estate for three days, no more, and only because he's been ... requested ... to do so for one last time."

He glowered at them. "And I'm considerably less than thrilled about the prospect. Now, please go home and leave me in peace."

7

L ady Wellsby presided over her breakfast table the next morning surrounded by her friends when her butler entered. "My lady." He offered a note on a silver salver. "This arrived by messenger, and he awaits a reply."

She opened the missive and read. "Oh, my goodness."

"What is it?" Anna asked. "Not bad news I hope."

Chrissie looked around the table and shook her head. "It's from Hawkesbury. He's asked me to drive in the park with him this morning."

"Just the two of you?" Gillian asked.

Edward frowned. "Is that wise? Hawkesbury can be charming, but he has an unsavory reputation. Apart from the Sultan's Palace, he's well acquainted with... females of all sorts."

"Really? Is he what's known as a rake?" Anna asked.

Edward's face turned the same shade of red as the raspberry preserves Chrissie had spread on her toast. "I can't claim close acquaintance with him in recent years, but he's sought out and fought over wherever he goes."

"So," Chrissie said, "he doesn't need to exert himself as a rake, because the women throw themselves at his feet."

Edward nodded. "I understand that's the case, yes."

"If women are so ridiculous as to do such things, then he cannot be held totally accountable."

Edward thrummed his fingers on the table, rattling the silverware. "As you're not conversant with the immorality of the ton, you should still take care."

All three women stared at him and then burst into laughter. Gillian patted her husband's arm. "Dearest, after seeing Lord Mannerly and other supporters of conservatism romping naked at the Sultan's Palace last evening, we've a good idea of the debauchery of our peers and politicians."

"And with whom they cavort," Chrissie added. "Edward, your concern for me is sweet, but a drive in the park will hardly ruin my reputation. Besides which, Hawkesbury also requested we join him in his box at the theatre this evening."

Anna squealed, clapped her hands. "The theatre. Oh, how wonderful."

"I imagine," Edward said with a sigh, "that if we all attend it will be acceptable. Gillian and I shall take our little Georgie to visit some of my family today as they haven't seen him since he was a babe."

Chrissie's heart squeezed with a pang of envy over her friend's strengthened marriage and their being blessed with a beautiful baby boy. Anna's face showed the same look. The biggest disappointment in Chrissie's marriage was never conceiving a baby. Her deepest longing was to hold a child in her arms. Last evening, both Justin and Bart had ridiculed her lack of sexual pleasure in her marriage, but until she'd leaned back against the hard muscled heat of Justin's body and climaxed at his hands, she'd not understood how much she lacked.

Today though, her groin ached and itched and she yearned for more of that tiny glimpse of heaven. A shimmer of excitement rippled through her at the thought of driving with Hawkesbury, of seeing him again so soon. With only three days to organize the Pleasure House, she'd thought his time would be stretched to the limit. Now, she was elated.

Anna smiled a faraway, dreamy smile. "I wonder if Thomas will also attend tonight. And of course, Bart."

The others shared knowing looks.

"It seems we're to be a complete party, yes," Chrissie said. "The viscount's carriage will call for us at eight. I shall return in time for luncheon. We've the afternoon for leisurely preparation, to bathe and dress before we dine."

Chrissie excused herself from the table, resisting the urge to rush upstairs and change her gown. She told herself it was normal to want to look her best for a drive in the park and had nothing to do with the man she was accompanying. However, that did not explain the quickening of her heart and the catch of breath in her chest as she tried not to run to the door.

"Chrissie," Gillian said, "you haven't finished your eggs. I thought you were hungry this morning."

Chrissie felt her face heat. "I... I'm finished. I need to prepare for the viscount."

When her friends exchanged knowing glances, Chrissie groaned and hurried from the room, not daring to say any more. An hour later she waited in the parlor, trying not to appear either anxious or over-eager. The smirks that Anna flashed her way warned her that her ploys were not succeeding. She'd pricked her finger so many times in the five minutes she'd attempted her mending that she'd laid it aside, hoping Anna's eagle eyes wouldn't notice.

Anna giggled, a small sound she tried to smother when Chrissie scowled at her and picked up a book, upside down. Surreptitiously, Chrissie tried to turn the boring tome on the exploration of Greek mythology and give the appearance of one engrossed in classical study. Anna giggled again.

Chrissie dropped the book to the couch beside her and muttered, "All right, I give up. If I'm amusing you anyway, I may as well pace before the window like an excited debutante."

When Anna threw back her head and laughed, Chrissie's breath caught in her chest. She was struck by the change in her friend in the scant days they'd been in the capital. Already, Anna's good nature had blossomed into a wider appreciation of the lighter side of life. Her reserved friend had laughed out loud, something frowned upon in the strict household of the captain's family.

Smiling at her friend, Chrissie said, "It's wonderful to see you so happy, Anna. I must admit, I worried whether bringing you here with Gillian and me was the best thing to do. Your life has been so sheltered until now."

"Chrissie, our visit to the city has been the most amazing thing to ever happen to me."

"Even last night?" Chrissie blurted out.

"Oh, especially last night," her friend replied, a dreamy expression on her face. "If I'd not come to London, I'd never have encountered Thomas or Bart."

Chrissie frowned, uncertain how to broach this subject. "Anna, it wouldn't be good to attach too much importance to the interest shown by either Thomas or Bart. They're both gentlemen of the world."

"Like your viscount."

"Justin is not my—" She broke off when she saw the teasing grin on Anna's face. "Oooh! He's not my anything. I'm using what he can provide for us and in exchange I'll tell him all I can about his family. After that, I'll never see him again."

"We'll see," Anna said with a shrewd look and a knowing nod. The front knocker rapped. "Ah, and here is the viscount, the one who is not yours."

"You're being impossible." Chrissie readied herself for the butler's admittance of her visitor by pulling on her gloves and bonnet.

But she spoke to thin air. Anna had dashed past her into the foyer to greet Hawkesbury in a warm voice. Chrissie ground her teeth. Although she'd no idea why it annoyed her to watch her friend blossom in the company of a handsome man.

Anna's pretty charm would flatter any man who had her attention focused upon them, as was evident from the appreciative smile Justin flashed her. Chrissie cleared her throat as she stepped into the hallway from the parlor, but to her vexation, neither Anna nor Justin noticed her.

Their gazes locked as Justin drew Anna's bare knuckles to his mouth for a kiss. Chrissie hissed out a breath loud enough to cause Anna to jump a little. Justin carried on uninterrupted, and lingered over Anna's fingers with his mouth until Chrissie thought she may scream.

"Hawkesbury," she snapped. "Perhaps we should depart. I've much to do to prepare before we attend the theatre this evening."

Justin raised his head with maddening lethargy and fixed Anna with a seductive smile. "I look forward to the pleasure of your company in my box this evening. Every gentleman present will desire an introduction to such a beautiful young woman."

Anna tittered. Chrissie snickered. Justin looked at her with one dark eyebrow raised in question and a grin on his face.

"Did you say something, my lady? Perhaps you're concerned such a gentle lady from the country will find herself disconcerted by the rush of male attention."

"No, no, it's not that which worries me." Chrissie felt her cheeks heat as Anna and Justin awaited her explanation. "Anna, I'd be delighted if you widened your acquaintance with gentlemen in London. Your views on men have been restricted to your captain."

"Oh, not you too, Chrissie. I'll not believe the worst of my captain. I'm certain that if he is already in England, there'll be some reasonable explanation for why he hasn't contacted me or his family." Chrissie smiled, accepting the futility of trying to convince Anna of her fiancé's foibles.

With a last smile for Anna, she and Justin left, descending to the street below where he assisted her into his barouche. The groom leaped on behind and they were off, hurtling through the streets at a fast pace. She grasped the brass bars at the side of her and hung on for dear life.

"If you are trying to frighten me, you'll not succeed. I am made of sterner stuff."

Justin looked across at her, surprise on his face, then pulled back on the reins to slow his horses to a more dignified pace. "Sorry. I like to go fast. Speed makes me feel alive and not many things do that for me anymore."

"Not even taking a woman to your bed?"

He closed his eyes, a look of pain on his face. "Not even that anymore. Once you've bedded as many women as I have, the canvas paints itself with the same strokes, over and over. Each face flushes with the same tint. Each woman's title becomes lost in row upon row of canvases stacked one upon the other until they become one enormous blur and are then discarded without thought."

"Goodness gracious. You are in the mood to wax lyrical, although the subject of bedding women is not one that I thought would have brought you to such levels of boredom that you are reduced to describing it as a dirge."

Keeping a tight control on the leather running through his gloved hands, Justin nevertheless managed to loosen his whole posture enough to give a deep chuckling laugh that rippled through his entire body. He shook with it from his beaver hat to his long hessians, throwing his head back while still watching the road ahead for obstacles.

"I do like you, Lady Wellsby. You've an unusual and refreshing candor that's been lost in a city where people lie to each other as often as they take tea. With you, there's no false modesty."

She squirmed on her seat, feeling her face heat to a glowing red, and she fiddled with her spread skirts. "That is because I have no great beauty to pretend to be modest about."

"Oh, but you do. Yours is not prettiness like Anna's."

His lips twitched up in another smile at her irritation at the mention of her friend. She wasn't jealous he thought Anna pretty, as it was only natural. Her friend was younger and prettier than Chrissie by a great length.

Wrapped up in her self- examination, she almost missed his next words.

"Yours is a far deeper beauty. It shines through from the inside out.

An inner radiance lights up your features and entrances a man so he cannot look away. Tonight, every man in that theatre will be struck by the same thing I am. They'll surround you like birds to the flowers or bees to the honey, seeking your warmth, your intrinsic goodness."

She sat open-mouthed in shock, clutching the railings against the sway of the vehicle. Finally, she managed to utter, "You're mistaken, my lord."

"You seem intent on continually correcting me, but I assure you, if there's one thing I know, it's women. And despite the pains you go to hiding your feminine assets, you are most assuredly a woman. A warm and sensuous woman."

She gave a snort of laughter. "Nobody has ever considered me sensuous."

"I do."

Robbed of speech, Chrissie held on and enjoyed the trip through the bustling streets with an expert driver steering his cattle. They turned into the park and he settled the horses into a steady clip.

Justin broke their contented silence to say, "I've remembered who you are."

She jumped, surprised, as she'd imagined him far too self-involved to have ever noticed, much less remembered, a country miss like herself.

"Yes. I remember you from when we were children. Our families were neighbors and we played together, did we not?"

She gave a small resigned nod. "I had no idea you'd recollect any of that."

He shot her that half amused grin again. "Because you assumed that a notoriously decadent lord with interests in not only an estate built for pleasurable pursuits but also with an involvement in a city brothel, would have nothing on his mind but reveling in decadence."

She laughed. "Yes, I'm afraid you've caught me out. By your reputation, I didn't consider that you might also have any sort of intelligence as well as—"

"As well as what?"

She glanced sideways at him. "If I finish that thought, I'd only pander to your already enormous conceit."

He laughed. "Then please continue. My conceit knows no bounds."

"You're incorrigible. And, as I'm certain many women have told you, you're also a very handsome man. The way you treat others shows you are compassionate. You've recovered enough of the family fortune to be able to restore your estate and close the Bath House to others. That shows your intelligence and skill. I've found very few titled gentlemen whose character encompasses all those traits. So many of them are shallow."

"Many call me shallow." With effortless skill, he negotiated the walking paths and pulled his team to a stop at the side of the lake. "Yet I do recall my happier hours spent as a child and as a young man on my estate. Before my fights with my father drove me to the continent. I asked you out driving with me today so we could talk about that."

A stab of disappointment went through Chrissie. Of course a man of his ilk wouldn't want to spend time in her company without another purpose. "Oh, I see."

"I want a chance to get to know you again," Justin continued, unaware of her disappointment. "And to talk about what has happened in the district while I've been gone. I've missed out on so much and with my family gone, there is no one to tell me."

He dipped his head to see her face beneath her bonnet brim and lifted her chin with one cupped hand to meet his eyes. "What is it? What did I say to make you so sad?"

"I'm not sad," she lied. "Yes, you are, though I don't understand why." He studied her face, and frowned. "A moment ago, you thought I had another reason for asking you to come with me today. What was it?"

"There could be no other reason. I'm hardly your normal sort of flirt."

"Ah, I see." The damn man's knowing smirk irritated her

immensely. "Naturally, I also wanted a chance to spend more time in the company of a fascinating woman."

Oh, ho. The man thought he was so clever but Chrissie was too old to fall for his tricks. "Please take me home, my lord. I've more to do than sit here and listen to a practiced rake hone his glib range of falsehoods."

He gave a much put-upon sigh but instead of taking up the reins once more, he took her face between his two hands and bent his head to her lips. His pressed against hers in a soft questing motion, asking her forgiveness, seeking her consent. Despite her will, her lips parted.

On a small sigh of enjoyment and relief, she opened her mouth to allow the entrance of the tip of his tongue. He ran it around the inside of her mouth, explored in a gentle sweeping motion that sent her stomach swirling in a matching twirl of butterflies fluttering deeply within her. She pressed a hand to her middle to still the sensation and he drew back slightly to look down.

"Chrissie?"

"You make my stomach tumble. My mind whirl."

He held his hands cupped around her hot cheeks and whispered into her face, "Good. It's only fair that you feel it too."

She gasped. "You feel that?" He nodded, grimaced. "Yes, I do. However, you mustn't tell anyone or my reputation as a hard- hearted breaker of hearts will be shattered. If women imagine I'm soft as custard inside, as soft as you make me feel, I'll become a laughing stock around London. My bedroom will be overrun by women wanting to test the new theory."

She pulled back. "Can you never be serious?"

"Oh, but I am. Completely serious."

He bent again and his kiss this time wasn't soft and gentle, but so full of hunger and passion it left her reeling. When he lifted his head, she grasped the back of it, sliding her fingers through his silky dark hair and brought his head back to hers.

This time, she took control of the melding of their mouths. All the yearning she felt at his touch was released from containment and the only way to ease the ache was to have more of him, more of her body pressed to him, his mouth on hers. For long minutes, they remained that way, locked together. He slid one hand down her body to press her hips against the lower part of him and moved so his erection was more prominent, so she felt it, a long and hard rod, prodding her midsection. She purred like a kitten, then felt him chuckle. Ever so slowly, they pulled apart. She gasped and looked around. She'd lost track of everything. Where they were. Who might be watching.

All the rules of propriety flew out the window whenever he came near. From the loud gasps for breath coming from him, she suspected that he was as rattled as she was by their embrace, although he had much more experience with these sorts of encounters. It was gratifying to know that she could at least upset his equilibrium to some extent. He groaned and squeezed his eyes shut. "My lady. Chrissie!" He touched her hand. "It isn't a good idea to take anything I do too seriously. My life is a mess. I don't want anyone else to be caught up in it as I try to unravel my family problems."

The hurt she felt was excruciating. She wanted to pretend for a few more minutes the kiss that had devastated her meant something to him. But already he pulled back, erected his habitual shield.

Never mind. She also knew how to erect defensive shields.

"Take me home. Please."

With a nod, he pulled his team out onto the path once more and in a short time stopped outside her home. She ignored his outstretched hand and took instead that of the groom to jump down to the footpath. Picking up her skirts, Chrissie fled up the steps and through her entrance when her butler opened her door for her, not stopping to say goodbye to Justin. Not waiting to be embarrassed any longer.

Justin left Lady Wellsby's house cursing his own stupidity. One minute he'd kissed those luscious lips, enjoyed the feel of a woman more than he had in many months, and the next he warned her to stay away from him. Idiot!

He cursed himself for the tenth time. What was wrong with him? Chrissie was the best thing to walk into his life since his return to England, and he'd deliberately wielded his rudeness, his habitual sardonic streak to drive a wedge between them before she stepped closer. He'd treated her as if she was one of the others, one of the many shallow women of the ton whose bodies he'd remorselessly used and left.

At his house, he spent three hours making arrangements to have the Pleasure House opened and the rooms set up. There was a lot to do. Each room had a theme and the lavish drapes and furnishings needed to be brought out of storage and aired. The Bath Houses must be filled with water from the hot springs running through the estate.

He sent the servants he normally used ahead to prepare the lavish spreads of food and wine that set the mood for the wealthiest of the ton who came and were prepared to spend a the coin, but the extra people were necessary to provide obscurity for the principle players to hide behind. The more people who wore masks, veils, and other concealing costumes, the less chance the three women would be discovered and their identities uncovered. After his tasks were finished and his servants organized things to his satisfaction, Justin slumped back into his desk chair. Memories of the conversation he'd had with Chrissie that morning haunted him. He'd made such a mess of things. He needed to fix it. To take away the hurt he'd caused.

Calling for his butler, he ordered his curricle brought around. Impatient to get to her, Justin leapt down the steps and into the seat, barely waiting for his tiger to jump into position before he took off at speed. Upon reaching the mews behind her town house, he gave the reins to the groom and circled around to look for a way in. In the end, it was easier than he imagined.

The laundress walked out the back door with a large basket of washing, leaving it ajar. A peek inside showed the kitchen staff were occupied preparing the dinner and nobody looked in his direction as he slipped up the servants' staircase.

If he was caught, he had no story prepared, though he was used to thinking on his feet after the number of times he'd leaped out of bedroom windows to escape husbands who'd returned home at an inopportune moment. Making no sound, he slipped up the narrow stairs to the next landing. Which bedroom belonged to Chrissie was a guess but he went with instinct, remembering what she'd said about Geoffrey's great- aunt leaving them the house.

Geoffrey sounded like such an arrogant prick that he would have demanded the best of everything, therefore the best room in the house. The front room over the street would have the best outlook and by the dimensions probably the largest area.

It was the end room on the corridor and he quietly walked down the carpeted hallway, hoping no one opened a door and discovered him. At the end door he halted, an ear pressed to the wood to listen. Water splashed as someone bathed. He prayed to God it was Chrissie and not one of the others. He'd no desire to walk in on a naked Anna, no matter how much he'd teased Chrissie over her friend's pretty looks. Anna was a true innocent, and therefore the sort of female he took care to avoid. They carried with them the threat of entrapment, marriage, and forever. Things he had no intention of embroiling himself in at this stage of his life.

Turning the knob, he cracked the door a scant inch and peeked inside. Steam rose in curling tendrils above a tin bath but all he could see were the clawed feet at the bottom as a screen covered the top half, preventing him from identifying the occupant.

He sucked in a deep breath, terrified of whom he'd discover. If Edward arrived home and discovered him ogling his wife, he'd demand pistols at dawn. If it were Anna, what remained of his gentleman's honor would oblige him to offer marriage. The risk was enormous, yet the urge to glimpse Chrissie's body—naked, slippery, and soft—rising from the water proved greater than any risks. Opening the door a little wider, he slipped inside and closed the door behind him, clipping the lock as he did so. He took the necessary steps to bring him beside the screen and closed his eyes, waiting.

"Is that you, Mary?" Chrissie's voice called.

The breath he'd been holding expelled and he relaxed. It was her.

The right room, the right woman. And the thought that she was naked a step away from him brought his erection leaping to life, tightening his trousers. He'd been in perpetual pain since she'd entered his room days earlier and now he was in her room and in even worse pain.

Stepping sideways, he stood beside the bath but out of her eyesight, a little behind her head. He picked up the soap from the dish at her fingertips and plucked the cloth from her dangling hand. She gave a start of surprise and jolted upright, splashing water over the edge, but Justin barely noticed as her nipples arose from the sudsy water to stand at attention before his eyes. His hiss of lusty admiration drew her attention and she swiveled in the bath to face him, her mouth dropping open in shock.

"You!"

She flung her hand up to cover her breasts but not before he was treated to a full view of them bouncing and bobbing as they rose from the water in all their unrestrained glory.

"Christ," he said, his gaze fixed on her chest. His hands reached out without thinking to cup her full globes. "They're magnificent."

She followed his eyes down to where her hands quivered over her breasts, trying to hide them from his view. He touched a finger to one hand and waited. "Please. Let me look. You're so beautiful."

"I've told you, I'm not beautiful."

He nodded. "Yes. You are. So beautiful, you rob me of breath."

With gentle persistence, he tugged on her hands until she dropped the shields she held before her full breasts to expose them to his hungry eyes. He wanted to devour her visually, and orally. Her breasts were full and round and when he cupped them, weighed them, treasured them, they filled his hands like ripe fruit. Leaning forward, he touched his tongue to one pouting tip and inhaled sharply when it budded instantly, tightening into a red puckered bud. He looked up at her, begged with his eyes for permission to proceed, and was overjoyed when she sketched a tiny nod of approval.

Knowing he needed to move slowly, he covered one nipple with his lips and sucked in light pulling motions that drew the nipple between his teeth until he heard her breath catch. Her fists unclenched from her sides and came up to rest on his head. His teeth bit down lightly on the end of the nipple and she groaned and wriggled, sliding her fingers through his hair to hold him tightly against her breast. Using his teeth, he drew the nipple in slow elongating motions over and over out to the end to nibble delicately on the sensitive tip.

She shivered, writhed, and clenched his hair even tighter until he winced.

"Ouch!"

She let go suddenly and jerked backwards, releasing him. "Sorry," she cried, her hands coming up to cover her mouth. "I didn't mean to hurt you."

He chuckled and reached for her again, pulling her warm body against his. "That should be my line, if I was a gentleman. But as I'm known to have no morals, you may kiss it better."

"Kiss it? Where, your head?" "You may kiss any part of my body you wish. I assure you I'll not jump away from your mouth." She glanced down to his groin and he groaned. "Especially not there."

"I've been thinking about it, about what Magdalene did to Bart last evening. What all the women did."

"Yes?"

"Do all men like it?"

"Oh, yes. I can assure you they do."

"So you wouldn't object if I wanted to try it with you?"

Justin gulped, hard and fast. Words failed him. He stared at her with his eyes popping and his mouth working soundlessly as he scrambled for the right words. If he were a civilized man, he'd reject the very idea that a decent woman, a lady like Chrissie, would go down on her knees before him. His mind swirled with the image of such an exquisite woman sucking on his aching arousal until his climax took him and he spurted in hot jets into the coaxing cavity of her mouth.

However, his reputation wasn't for decency, but for depravity. The fact it was a mostly false reputation didn't matter. What mattered was he should be strong enough to say no to such a bad idea. No, he thought. No, he told himself. Yes, he nodded. Nodded like an imbecile.

Her hands dropped to the flap of his trousers and fumbled there until he moved his own over hers to assist with the buttons. Pulling aside the flap, he grasped his shaft in one hand and lifted it clear of the cloth while she watched with a transfixed gaze.

Her small hand, still damp from her bath, reached out and moved his aside so she could wrap hers around his engorged flesh. The second she touched him, he heated and swelled, throbbed under the tiny pressure she exerted. He covered her hand with his large one and showed her how to move up and down in a slow rhythm upon him and immediately his knees weakened. No other woman had ever affected him in this profound and overwhelming way. Courtesans, wives, widows, and whores had performed the same act over the years and none had brought him to his knees. Yet now, he felt on the brink of collapse.

As one hand continued to stroke him, her other came up to touch his chest where his heart pounded so hard his ribcage shook. She stroked him there as well and murmured, "Shush. Let yourself relax for once."

He opened his mouth to reply, to inform her of his noted calm and tranquility. Then he understood. Through her perceptiveness, she understood him. Knew he rarely allowed himself to slip into a tranquil state for fear of what might happen. Normally, he remained fully alert for the next disaster in his life. With his family, the estate's finances, or the ownership of his properties. Only his closest friends realized the prince of pleasure rarely let himself be sucked into the whirlpool of pleasurable pursuits that he provided for so many others.

Letting himself go to that degree wasn't something he was comfortable with. He'd learned early in life the only way to survive his father 's wrath and fits of extreme temper was to retain control at all times. To know where he was, how much money he had, who he was with, friend or foe.

As he tried to use what remained of his rational mind to decide, she thwarted his plan once again by dropping to her knees in front of him. In a quick movement and before he could stop her, she engulfed him with her whole mouth. No tentative touch of her tongue to his throbbing cock, but a full- throated assault that robbed him of breath and of any semblance of reason.

"Jesus! Oh, Christ, that is unbelievably good."

His body shook like a bough in the wind but he couldn't control it, all he could do was clutch at her head. Not to pull it away but to keep it in that divine place between his thighs where her tongue slid up and down from the coarse hairs at the base to the tip where he oozed fluid. And not drops either. Like a green boy, he seeped hot liquid into her mouth with every suck on his length and he wanted to apologize, explain, something. The words froze in his throat. Her tongue flicked over the slit in his prick, around and around, until his head spun in a dizzy fashion and he was sure he would faint. Then she changed the motion and sucked, drawing him through her sharp little teeth like an expert courtesan anxious to finish with her customer. And be paid.

He had no idea how Chrissie knew all these tricks but some feminine instinct had seized her. She was treating his cock to the tastiest licking he'd ever had. Looking down at Chrissie's flushed face and the ecstasy there as she edged him closer and closer to climax, it was difficult to decide into which category he should slot her. Seductress, temptress, or sedate widow.

Right now, kneeling before him as if she were indeed his concubine, she was as far from a sedate anything as she could be. He threw back his head as his thoughts scattered and the end surged upon him in a rush that he'd been unable or unwilling to hold back.

Thrusting clumsily into her mouth, he gripped her head to anchor it firmly in place and not allow any retreat as he felt the pulsing of his muscles and the tightening of his balls. His dick stiffened for the final assault and with a loud moan of release, he thrust deeply into the back of her throat and spilled his seed in an almighty gush that seemed endless.

A couple of smaller, less urgent thrusts wrung him out and drained the last drops. She swallowed deeply, gulping at the volume he'd inflicted upon her. His body shook and he dropped to his knees before her, head bowed on her neck, and waited for the trembles to cease. She lifted her arms and engulfed his quaking form, hugged him, and held him until he came back to himself. Until he came back to her.

Nuzzling her neck, he licked at the taste of her soap-washed neck, the delicious scent of lemon tickling his senses. Every time he inhaled the scent of citrus, he'd remember this. And he'd think of her. Fresh and enticing. Too sweet and wholesome to be sullied by a man like him. Sucking in a deep breath, he drew back a little, keeping his hands on her shoulders.

"I shouldn't have done that. I tried to stop. I swear I tried."

He picked up the wet cloth and carefully wiped her mouth and face, removing all trace of himself and his clinging climax.

"I wanted it, Justin. I did it."

He shook his head. "I mean I should never have let myself empty into your mouth in that way. It's unseemly for a lady of good breeding to know of such things, let alone be forced to endure it."

She looked at him in surprise, and then she laughed, dropping her head to his shoulder in her mirth.

"Why is that so amusing?" He felt irritated his attempt at consideration and conservatism was met with such hilarity.

"Because ... " she gasped, still laughing, "because last night we watched a row of a dozen women swallow the results from sucking on the organs of a dozen men. And it was your idea to show us. You who took us there to shock us. Now, today, you're worried about my good breeding. Doesn't your concern seem a little misplaced?"

He gave a halfhearted grin and shrugged. "It does make me something of a hypocrite."

"Justin, you didn't force me to do anything I didn't want. You've made me hungry to try things I didn't know about in my marriage.

The excitement Geoffrey denied me. Now I've realized how much I missed, I want it. All of it."

With a gentle hand, he brushed the damp hair back from her face. Her skin glowed. She looked flushed, excited, and triumphant. He drew her to her feet and moved to position her as he wanted her to repay her by giving her the same sort of pleasure she'd freely given to him.

"Put your leg up on the stool, here." He raised her leg and placed it on the stool next to the soap dish. Her eyes went wide with realization and she dropped her hands to her exposed groin, attempting to cover herself with widespread fingers.

"No," he said, dropping a light kiss on her full lips. "Let me look. I want to see all of you." He nudged her hands aside and with one finger rubbed through her silky curls. He kept his eyes fixed on hers. "Do you play with yourself here?"

Her mouth dropped open as a denial sprang to her lips, but he shook his head.

"Tell me the truth because I'll know if you lie to me."

"How?"

"Because already you're wet and soft to my touch. So I know that you've done this before. Your body is readying itself for what's about to happen. And I very much doubt that your dearest Geoffrey spent any time preparing your body, making you so slick and hot your passage screamed out for a man to fill it. To slide inside with his swollen cock and rub against every place you need the ache to be soothed."

"How ... " She gasped again, as his finger continued to stroke through her wet folds in a slow and steady motion. "How do you know what my body wants?"

"Because all women's bodies are made to take a man inside them. To procreate, and to create the ultimate in pleasure. Am I giving you pleasure now, Chrissie?"

Her head jerked in several shaky nod while her legs trembled as he continued his relentless stroking, probing deeper and deeper between her puffy folds.

"Do you want even more? Do you want me to give you an orgasm — the same way you did to me?" This time her eyes grew as wide as saucers, and her mouth formed a small pouting oval as she tried to imagine the action required. Her brows furrowed into a frown, and he knew he'd confused her.

She opened her mouth to answer, but no sound issued. Her pink tongue darted out to sweep over her lips, dampened them, and made them pulse blood red.

Justin groaned. He'd just exploded into the welcoming cavern of this beautiful lady's mouth, yet when she licked her lips his knees shook with the force of his renewed desire. With his free hand, he ran his fingers over her plump lips and dipped inside her mouth. Her teeth parted as he entered.

"Can you feel me inside you here?"

He twirled his finger around the roof of her mouth and slowly withdrew. The suction of her mouth released his digit with a loud pop.

"And in here?" With his other finger, he swirled the swollen bud of her clitoris where it proudly protruded. Thank the good Lord she felt the strong pull between them as intensely as he did. Hell, he felt it as never before.

Minutes after his last climax, his body was tensed and ready. His growing erection pressed against her hip, prodded her, a demonstration of how much he wanted her. Again, already, urgently.

She looked down at him, his penis standing long and straight against her side, and she gasped. "Again? I didn't know. I mean ... Geoffrey never ... "

The pink in her cheeks deepened and she dipped her head. He placed a finger under her chin to raise her to meet his gaze. He nodded.

"Generally, men require a much longer time to recuperate. Yet I only need to look at your body, so soft and pink and with so many curves, that my own body responds the only way it knows. By readying itself again." He sucked in a breath, inhaled the heady essence of aroused female, and in an instant he was more than ready. He was hungry again, ravenous for the smell and taste of her.

"Chrissie, believe me, I'm ready to take you, to have you. To drive myself deeply inside you and ride you. I'm ready now, I'll probably be ready again very soon. And then I'll more than likely want you again after that. One taste of you will never be enough."

Chrissie trembled in his arms, her breath came in loud pants, and her heart pounded against the wall of her chest. He felt an unprecedented urge to make this experience perfect for her, to show her a small part of the pleasure she'd given him. Dropping to his knees, he used both thumbs to part her folds. He swallowed, twice, needing a moment to compose himself after sighting her seductive pink coloring.

"So pretty. So pink and sweet."

He flicked his tongue from top to bottom along her creases, once, twice, and again. She moaned, squirmed, and he held her steady with his hands on her hips. He drew back for a moment to roll his tongue around the rim of his lips, savored her taste, and groaned aloud. He looked up at her so she could watch him enjoy her taste in his mouth.

Time and again he bent to his pleasurable task, swept his tongue around and over her swollen bud, up and through every crevice. He varied the movements in a relentless assault designed to drive her as insane as he felt. Around and around, up and down. Each time her orgasm crept closer and her tension escalated, he eased back. Nuzzled her thighs, licked behind her knees, until she unclenched her knees and relaxed. Over and over, she shifted, muttered, moaned, and shuffled her feet. She didn't move away from his marauding mouth, but showed him without words he tormented her beyond bearing.

He let her tension climb, build to the ultimate peak, bringing her closer and closer with every breath, every moist and intimate lick. As he used two fingers inside her hot passage to arouse her internally, he used his ever-moving mouth to arouse her externally.

His fingers curled inside her hot passageway at the peak of each upward thrust, touched her most sensitive spot, until she rose on her toes and writhed on his fingers. He held her in place by embedding his fingers in her womb, while she wriggled like a worm on a hook and all the while, his mouth drove her toward climax.

Her scream came so suddenly, so loudly, and with such a piercing note of exquisite pleasure, he feared the servants would come running. She dropped her head to her shoulder to muffle her noises.

Her thighs clamped hard over his forearm, and the walls of her vagina clenched like a vice on his fingers. She quivered on and on through an extended climax, as small aftershocks rippled through her body, while her knees buckled. He caught her as she slumped in a limp and lifeless heap and eased her to the floor.

He watched her face until, at last, her eyelids fluttered and her eyes opened, although unfocused at first. The look in her eyes was soft and drifting, her expression dreamy and satisfied, and she looked like a well-loved woman. He couldn't keep the smug self-satisfaction from his face, an expression he'd been careful to not reveal with any lover for a long time. In bedding women in exchange for money or business information, he felt duty bound to ensure they enjoyed the experience, though he never lingered long enough to see the aftermath. Never lingered to observe the after-effects sexual release had on a woman's disposition.

Usually, he was too busy making a discreet departure, or, in his early days, climbing out a window to escape irate husbands. Lingering was not part of the ritual he'd established and clung to as a form of self-protection. If it was a ritual, it became a piece of theatre like the performances he orchestrated at his estate. And a piece of theatre was merely acting, not something real. Not something that involved real people in a true lovemaking situation.

Now, however, he wanted to stay, to linger, to shed his actor 's cloak. Wanted to scoop up this intriguing woman and carry her naked body to the bed and join her there for the next week. To make love to her every way he knew, and every way she'd read about in those infernal books she'd bought. He wanted to be the one to teach her all the ways a man and woman could enjoy each other 's bodies, something her husband had neglected to do, and show her all the ways he wanted to be touched by her, the ways she could reduce him to a puddle of lust as she had before when she took him into her mouth.

Lazily, she reached up and ran her hand down his face, caressed his cheek, hovered near his mouth. He turned his head to suck a finger into his mouth in a searing caress, causing a spasm to ripple across her thighs. She clenched them, tightly. He followed her movement with his eyes and watched, intrigued, as her entire body flooded with a brilliant flush. "You don't have to be embarrassed." He ran one finger through her nest of hair, watched the next spasm ripple. "Christ, you're so sensitive. Your body is made for loving."

He slipped his finger past the silky protective hairs and she clenched even harder against the intrusion. "Shush, let me take care of you. Or else you'll be hot and aching the whole night at the theatre."

"Oh, no." Her face reddened even more. "The theatre. I'm supposed to be preparing." She shook her head. "I'll have to bathe again. My maid will wonder what is wrong with me."

"You could go without bathing. I'd be able to smell the scent of your arousal all evening."

By the little frown between her brows, Justin understood that she was considering that intriguing thought. "It wouldn't be proper."

He laughed. "Considering what you just did to me, and what you let me do to you, I don't think you need worry about what is proper. Although, on the other hand, Bart can sniff out an aroused woman a mile away."

She gave a little jump and her brows knitted again. He smoothed away the worry line with a finger and then, unable to resist, leaned forward and kissed the spot.

"He can deduce, simply by smell, when a woman is aroused."

Her head tilted to the side as she considered the idea. The small smile on her face irritated him. He didn't want her thinking about Bart in the same context as her own newly aroused sensualities. Now that he'd introduced her to desire, to experimentation, he felt entitled to a slight possessiveness where she was concerned. It wouldn't last. It never did. But for now, her body and all its unfolding secrets belonged to him.

"If you keep smiling when you think of Bart sniffing around your skirts," he announced rudely, "I'll imagine you want to indulge in an afternoon's delight with him tomorrow." Ignoring her shock, he continued, "Is that it? Do you want me to invite him to join us?

Perhaps, that will become to your newly acquired taste. To have two men attend to your body."

"No. No, I wasn't thinking anything of the sort."

He raised a brow. "Chrissie, I told you, you cannot lie to me. I saw your eyes light up when Magdalene had Bart in her mouth. He looked up at you and you were practically drooling down the glass. You wanted to leap down there and knock Magdalene aside and take over."

Thwack!

Once again, his face tingled where she had slapped his cheek. He groaned and spun away. What a stupid rude brute he was. There was no way a woman like her deserved his crude mouth sounding off at her. First, he invaded her bedroom, her bath, and then he invaded her body.

Now, not happy with that much intrusion in her life, he was insulting her into a fury. Without facing her, he spoke in a hushed voice that held a quiver of horror at his own disgraceful behavior. "I sincerely apologize. That was totally uncalled for."

He turned back to her and took her hands in his, willing her to accept his heartfelt apology.

"Please, let me take care of you and then I will leave."

"No, just go. I need to prepare for this evening." She glared at him and he winced at the anger in her look. "I will bathe very carefully before I greet Bart or any of your other guests. I would not want to embarrass any of the gentlemen with my overpowering feminine smells." "Damn, Chrissie! I've begged your forgiveness. I was being ridiculously possessive of your body. I hated the thought of Bart, or any other man, being close enough to touch you or smell you. It will not happen again." He gave a snort of laughter. "Believe me, that sort of possessive behavior is not normal with me. For some reason, sweetheart, you seem to have a strange effect on me."

She narrowed her eyes in a manner that could only be called menacing and he decided it would be best to stop trying to excuse his disgusting behavior, and depart while he had a shred of dignity left. She walked to the door and unlocked it, pulling it open a crack and stepping back so he could leave. Feeling like a cad, he checked that the corridor was empty he slipped outside. His body was barely clear of the opening when she slammed it shut, the noise reverberating against the wall beside him where he stood.

Retracing his steps through the servants' back staircase, he left the house in the same way he'd come. Well, physically at least. Emotionally, he was in a totally different place. His insides were twisted in a tight knot of some feeling he could not name, unused as he was to speaking of such female things as emotions.

All he knew was that he hated the feeling and what he'd said to get himself into this situation. Loathed it. Reviled himself.

8

Chrissie walked down the staircase in her evening gown to join the others. She waited for the viscount's carriage with trepidation in her heart and a knot in her stomach. After Justin departed her room that afternoon, she'd remained unsettled, disconcerted. The pleasures to be found under his experienced hands were exquisite and so enticing that to now do without them would be excruciating agony.

Nevertheless, she could not forgive his crude words, nor could she forgive him for diminishing what they had shared this afternoon with his disgusting remarks and jealous references to Bart and the previous evening. Watching the women service the men that way had been arousing, she would admit that in truth, but it was not Bart that aroused her. It was Justin. The thought of putting her mouth over his proud flesh and sucking him to completion, seeing the erotic pleasure echoed on his face was what she'd wanted. She looked up to realize her friends were all gathered at the foot of the stairs and staring up at her.

Anna stepped forward looking concerned. "Chrissie, dearest, are you speaking to someone?"

"Oh, no, just myself."

She gave them a watery smile to reassure them, disconcerted to realize she'd spoken aloud her worries about the viscount. Bedlam would welcome her with open arms before too much longer. Perhaps she would be ready to admit herself there.

"I think I hear the carriage now. The evening should be delightful."

As she sat in the carriage, she allowed the talk to drift over her as she braced herself for the coming evening. Delightful, she'd declared it. Secretly, she labeled it horrifying. The viscount was a man about town with a reputation for knowledge of women far surpassing most men's, and after her performance, he was, in all honesty, probably appalled. It would be a wonder if he didn't invent an excuse to avoid attending tonight.

That comforting illusion was shattered when the viscount's well-upholstered carriage rocked to a stop in front of the theatre and the viscount himself opened the door.

His hand came up to meet Anna's as she was the first to alight, but his eyes met Chrissie's. She felt a shiver of sensual awareness ripple through her entire body at his heated and hungry look. She'd been fooling herself. Nothing had changed between them and pretending the intense connection between them would dissipate because she willed it that way, because it frightened her, was stupid. And she'd never been a silly person.

In the village, people spoke of her sensibility, her knowing right from wrong and her strength of will to carry out the right course of action. Lady Wellsby was known to all and sundry as a person of great intelligence and fortitude, a person unflappable in emergencies.

But one glance from the notorious viscount, one sizzling perusal of her person, and her heart stuttered in her chest. Her breath caught, and she yearned for things she'd no right to want, and she'd no need of in her life. Yet, still, she wanted them. Wanted him. She sucked in a deep breath, and then did it a second time. No. Nothing helped.

Anna walked toward the theatre with Gillian and Edward and Justin's hand reached inside the carriage to take the last hand in the line, hers. She hesitated, certain that when she touched him again she would feel the jolt of it but unsure whether it would affect him in the same way. His hand stretched toward hers, his fingers long and strong like his body. Unthinkingly, she accepted his strength and took what he was proffering. He gripped her gloved hands firmly and helped her step to the pavement.

As she started forward, he wrapped her arm through his and kept it in place with his other hand on top of her gloved one. It felt good—comforting and nice. Together they walked inside behind her friends and Chrissie experienced a feeling of happiness that had eluded her recently.

His head bent closer to hers and his breath tickled her hair as he whispered in her ear, "Have you forgiven me yet?" He looked completely serious, worried, and fatigued.

The amount of work required to prepare the estate for their arrival must be enormous and she had pressured him into it, giving him no road for escape. If she did not forgive him, she would be pushing him into even more misery in his life than she already had by dangling her knowledge of his family over his head.

In all fairness, he did not deserve that. He may have the reputation of a rake and a rogue but all her reports on him recently showed a different sort of man. One who cared deeply for his family and friends. Inflicting more pain upon an already suffering man was not her way.

She inclined her head in a gracious nod. "Yes," she replied simply.

His deep sigh of relief made her profoundly glad she had said it. Glad she could relieve his torment in a small way. He patted her hand and smiled as he walked to his box, a new spring in his step. She also smiled.

Three hours later, the play finished and the group rose as one from their seats to thank the viscount for his hospitality. Chrissie hadn't stopped smiling during the entire performance and her thanks to Justin were the most profound and heartfelt. Going to the theatre was a treat that had been denied her for so long by her husband. Geoffrey had never understood Chrissie's fascination with performances and plays and books.

Edward addressed Justin. "Hawkesbury, I want to thank you for this evening. These three ravishing women are all mad for plays, but living in the country they get little opportunity to attend them." He smiled at his wife.

Gillian gave him a radiant look and then she added for Justin's benefit, "Chrissie misses plays the most."

Justin looked at her and smiled, that personal smile that spoke just to her, to her heart.

"I'm glad, Lady Wellsby, that you enjoyed it so much. I would be delighted if you could join me in my box on many more occasions." His smiling invitation encompassed the group. "All of you. Generally, women feign an interest in the theatre only so they may preen in a box and be seen by the ton in the latest fashions. It is refreshing to be in the company of those who really appreciate the arts." He dipped a small bow of his head in Chrissie's direction and she warmed under his praise.

"And for women, my lord, it is refreshing to find a gentleman who appreciates that we may have more on our minds than the latest style of gown or the latest on dit."

"Lady Wellsby, in the short time we have been acquainted, I have come to appreciate that your intelligence is far superior to mine in many matters."

Chrissie laughed at his teasing. "Now, my lord, you are being absurd. No man ever gives a woman credit for being more intelligent than any member of the male species."

"Even if I believe it to be true?" he enquired with a lift of his brow.

"Even then. Because I would know you are teasing me, enticing me like a spider into your web for some illicit purpose."

They walked slowly toward the doorway but by the crowd clustered there, it would be some time before their carriage could be brought around to them. Justin's hand came up to rest in the small of Chrissie's back and once again, that annoying tingle of awareness made her shiver. She glanced sideways at him and saw that he had indeed noticed it once more. Blast it. No matter how hard she tried to appear immune to his touch, he had only to place his hand upon her in a protective and asexual gesture and she was ready to melt in a puddle at his feet. He flicked those long lashes at her in his knowingly seductive way and she was ready to drop to her knees and rip his steely shaft from his breeches. To whip her tongue over it as fast as she could manage and be damned to all those watching.

This strange need to have and be had by him grew in intensity so rapidly that she floundered in her effort to control it. Soon it would overwhelm her, sweeping her along in the tide of feelings like a storm blew a leaf, blowing it in every direction until it landed somewhere out of its realm.

Justin's warm palm slid over her waist to bring her to a halt and he turned her slightly so the others couldn't overhear as he asked, "And what illicit purpose do you think I have in mind for such a beautiful—" He hissed in a breath. "Forgive me. I know how you object to being called that. What could I possibly have in mind for such a stickler for propriety such as yourself?"

The twinkle in his eyes belied the seriousness of his words and Chrissie had a sudden urge to stomp her foot. So, with a devious smile, she did just that. Gave in to her impulses for once and stomped down hard, right on his black evening shoes, and for good measure she ground her heel into the top of his foot.

He winced and his eyes watered but he remained a gentleman and said nothing to the others, which only served to make her feel like the heel she had used to inflict pain upon him.

She covered her mouth with her hands, feeling her face heat and flush. "I am so, so sorry. I don't know what came over me. I just, just gave into an impulse. A horrible one." She looked down. "Your poor foot. Is it all right? Have I done any damage? Oh dear, what I can I do to make amends?"

Far from appearing to be in agony, Justin ignored his injured foot and grinned at her. "You could kiss it better for me later, at your home. You could start at the toes and work your way up my leg until you reach—"

Chrissie stomped her foot again and only narrowly missed his toes. "Ooh, you are impossible."

"Ah, yes, but I am beginning to grow on you. Soon, you won't be able to go a whole day without thinking of me."

She opened her mouth to deny his arrogant assumption but the lie would not come. Already, she was unable to go a day without her thoughts skittering to him and where he was, how he was occupying his time, what he was preparing for them at his estate.

"Fiddlesticks," she declared, not meeting his eyes in case he could detect her fibbing.

"So you are already thinking of me as I think of you. Naked, and in bed."

"Certainly not!" she said, peering forward to the street to glimpse his carriage and wishing the queue would shorten in a hurry.

His voice came closer to her ear and caused her to jump. "Not a bed then. No, a bed is not adventurous enough for someone who revels in futtering as much as you do."

She gasped and looked around but her friends were deep in conversation with Bart and Thomas a few feet away and could not hear, although by the heat in her face, they would notice her embarrassment. Or was it arousal, as the viscount kept suggesting, that made her body feel hot and aching and had her squirming against her clothes whenever he whispered huskily in her ear. His breath smelled of the brandy Bart had smuggled into the box to mellow his mood and relieve his tedium during the performance.

"Being a voyeur of a dozen sultans being serviced by their harems slaves or standing with your leg raised high beside a tin bath is much more your style."

She swallowed and tried not to cry out when his words immediately stirred her to fever pitch and she was unable to remain still. Despite her best intentions to remain invulnerable to his seductive charm, she was far from resistant. Every word sent her good sense spiraling away like that leaf on the wind and her mind filled with the raunchy images he painted there with so little trouble.

"Don't try to speak or move. We are going to play a little game to pass the time while we wait."

Cold air touched bare skin on the backs of her thighs and she realized with a shock that this experienced rake had raised her skirts without her even noticing, much less objecting. What sort of wanton was she?

"Just nod when I guess the correct answer and you will be rewarded."

"But you should be—"

"No, not me," he said, with a low chuckle pressed close to her neck. "Trust you to want to play a game of seduction by the correct rules. In this game, I guess but you gain the reward. Later on though, I am happy for you to devise a game where I will be rewarded for my patience tonight."

His hands were now running in long caressing strokes across the roundest parts of her bottom and she wriggled against the feel of his fingers touching her there. Nobody but her maid or her dressmaker had ever done that before. The sensation when a man's large and calloused hands did it was decidedly interesting, tantalizing, mind-numbingly good. Momentarily, she lost her train of thought and had to search her memory to remember what they were discussing.

"Your patience?"

"Yes, my infinite patience as I sat behind you and smelled the lemon that I knew you had washed your hair in. The rose petals that were scattered in your bath water. And the musk of your arousal. And I knew."

"Knew," she gulped, pushing back against the fingers that caressed up and down the crease between the mounds of her bottom.

"Knew that you had not washed away the scent of your arousal after I left. You didn't wash it off knowing that I would smell you tonight. Knowing that Bart would also sniff out your lust and want to have you on the floor of the theatre box and how it would drive me to a fury of jealousy. My cock twitched all evening just thinking about how hot and wet you were under that gown. How your folds ran with sinful juices when you thought of all the men who wanted to lap at you like cats with a bowl of cream."

As he spoke in his compelling tone, his hands were at work in the dark under her skirts and between her thighs. They moved and caressed, prodded and poked, until she was trembling with excitement. His fingers dragged from the back of her crevice to the front and rubbed around her engorged bud twice. That was all it took. Her body spasmed in his arms and she bucked and swayed and her entire weight fell onto him. Her knees buckled and he wrapped a strong arm around her waist to keep her upright.

She was barely conscious of his whispered, "Christ! You're so responsive."

The sounds around her faded, her friends seemed far away, and only Justin and his strength provided an anchor. Turning, she laid her head on his chest and gulped in heaves of air and waited for her heart to slow enough to stand on her own feet. By the time she was able to straighten away from his hold, the group was staring in their direction.

Bart threw back his head and laughed. "In front of the theatre, Justin? Are you trying to win some bet I forgot we made?" When Justin glared at him, he laughed even harder, bending double to drop his hands to his knees. "Even I refrain from public displays of seduction." Thomas shot Bart a disbelieving look. "Well, with titled ladies, anyway."

Thomas rolled his eyes at Bart and then gave Justin a look of disgust. "Hawkesbury, it is not the done thing to be holding Lady Wellsby so tightly in a public place."

Justin released his grip a little and allowed Chrissie to regain her feet but she felt his hand still resting lightly against her back in case she tottered.

Straightening, she said, "The viscount kindly assisted me when I felt faint."

"Faint," Gillian echoed. "But you never feel faint. Chrissie, what is the matter? You are acting very strangely lately."

Bart spoke up again in his teasing voice, "Yes, perhaps Lady Wellsby is expecting a happy event."

Chrissie paled at his teasing words. Bart had no way of knowing how much his torment hurt but her friends did and they rounded on him now, especially Anna.

"How dare you joke of such a thing, Bartholomew. Chrissie longed for children in her marriage and Geoffrey blamed her when she did not carry any."

"As men always feel entitled to do," Gillian added, in a cross voice. She too faced Bart with a belligerent stare. "It is never considered to be the fault of the man, yet, in this case, we all knew that Geoffrey was only able to—" She broke off with a shocked gasp and clutched her mouth, her eyes wide with horror. "I am so sorry, Chrissie."

Chrissie stood before Gillian with a puzzled question in her eyes.

"What were you about to say, Gillian? Geoffrey was only able to what?"

Gillian turned her frightened gaze to her husband, an appeal in her eyes. Edward stepped forward to comfort her and reassure Chrissie at the same time.

"Nothing important, nothing important at all." He peered hopefully at the road. "Is the carriage coming yet?"

Chrissie was not going to be put off by Edward's obvious attempts to change the conversation but the cat had been let out of the bag and was not to be put back in.

"It must be something, or you would not be at pains to hide it from me." She turned to Anna. "Do you know Geoffrey's secret?"

Anna shook her head. "No, no."

"Well, Gillian, what is it?" Tears welled up in Gillian's eyes and she looked down at the ground as if willing it to rise up and swallow her whole. "No, Chrissie. Don't make me say any more. I cannot bear it." She buried her red and tear-streaked face in her husband's shoulder and he patted her awkwardly while looking at Chrissie with the same pain in his eyes.

Edward gulped and stuttered, "I ... I suppose you should know. We did not want to hurt you, you understand. It was Geoffrey's fault. For being such a ... for not telling you. For never explaining. It may have made things easier. For you."

Chrissie shook her head in confusion. "I don't understand. What was Geoffrey's fault? That I did not conceive? No. It was my fault entirely that he stopped coming to my bed. If I had been more receptive to his demands, the type of lovemaking he wanted, he would have continued to visit my bed and I would have conceived."

Edward and Gillian shared another glance but still gave no explanation. Finally, after a lengthy silence, Justin gave a groan and then cleared his throat. "I suppose it may as well fall to me as to your friends to explain this, but I would rather do it in privacy. Here is my carriage. Please, Lady Wellsby, let us leave." The trip to her house was excruciating for Chrissie as neither Edward nor Gillian would meet her eyes and, with Anna, disappeared to their rooms in a rush as soon as they arrived. Justin walked beside her to her small parlor and even he was subdued.

"Would you like a brandy?" she asked. "Please."

"Is it so bad that you need fortification?"

Justin shrugged. "Depends how you see Geoffrey's problem. In my business, I see many men who have similar problems."

Pushed beyond her limits, she stomped her foot on the thick carpet. "Dammit! Tell me what it is."

"Your husband stopped visiting your bed because he couldn't do so without assistance."

She looked at him without comprehension.

"He came to the Sultan's Palace because there he could pay for two or three escorts at once."

"He needed," she swallowed, "more than one woman in his bed?"

"Not always women. He often asked for men as well. Geoffrey was one of those men who, as time went on, could only get aroused if he could watch, and participate, with others having sex around him." Her mouth had dropped open in shock and she knew must've appeared to be an idiot to a man of his knowledge, but in her small world, people of taste did not speak of such things over the dinner table. Nor were they discussed by women at tea. Her mind raced trying to assimilate this information and what it had meant to her marriage.

He took her hands in his and she saw the pity in his eyes. "No!" She wrenched away. "No pity. Just explain it. Please. I know to you I must appear to be incredibly naïve but my mind cannot grasp the situation. The how and the why escape me."

He nodded. "Luckily, the facts of such relationships escape most people's notice. Unfortunately, I am in the business of catering to the obscurities of life. Whether I want to or not, I am forced to observe sex in all its deviant forms on a daily basis."

He had paced away but he stopped to look back over his shoulder at her, gauging how much she could take. "Your husband's proclivities were nowhere near the extremes that happen but his was probably the most extreme I allow in my establishments. The men, or women, who like to inflict pain, torture, and other indignities to women and children are not allowed anywhere near me. They disgust me."

"Geoffrey did not like pain."

She gave a snort of laughter. "In fact, it was a family joke that he would collapse at the sight of blood or at the slightest hurt to anyone around him."

"I know. He gave strict instructions that he would not tolerate being near the whipping chambers."

"So what did he want with these other ... escorts?"

"Watching women being fucked by one of the bigger men, like Matthew, aroused him. Seeing a man being poked by another man also did it for him, but only if there was a woman or women in the room. He liked groups doing it best. Liked to tug himself while he got excited watching them."

"Men can do those things to other men?"

He snorted a laugh. "Human beings are capable doing all sorts of things to each other that a woman of your upbringing is unable to imagine."

"So, did Geoffrey come to you often?"

"No, he didn't. He was one of those who tried to fight their nature, damp down the urges when they came to him. He told me once that he hated himself afterwards and that he would wait days, a week even, before he could go home to his wife because he was so horrified at himself. Of course, he was disguised at the time, as was I, so he did not realize who I was."

"But you knew him?"

"I made it my business to know everyone who visited my estate. I had to be careful. But if the patrons wanted anonymity, I gave it to them. Or pretended to at least. Most of them had families—families who would be horrified to learn what their loved ones were capable of when away from home. I have one large area at the Pleasure House that is for groups and on the nights that I open it and provide entertainment there, it is the most popular. You would be amazed at how many men, especially older lecherous ones, cannot get an erection at all. Yet, they still pay money, and a lot of it, to watch other people have sex. They like the sights, the sounds, the smells."

Chrissie sank onto a settee. "I'm beginning to comprehend how perverted our society has become." She dropped her head and considered all she'd just learned. A horrible notion filled her mind. She looked up at him, her gaze sharp.

"Gillian and Edward heard this in our district. Who else knew about the reason my marriage failed, I wonder."

"I suspect Edward discovered it from one of his acquaintances in London, not because he had firsthand experience. If it eases your mind, I shall ask him."

She shook her head. "No. I'll ask him. And Gillian. I need to know if anyone else, perhaps Geoffrey's family or the servants, was aware. Though perhaps they all knew. Perhaps they whispered behind my back of the mistress's stupidity in thinking she, and she alone, understood Geoffrey's needs. The stupidity that stopped me from questioning him more deeply."

"Why didn't you question him? You're not unintelligent. You must have suspected something was amiss with him, his attitudes, your marriage."

She winced at the accusation in his tone.

"Damn, I didn't mean to infer you should have taken more of a role in his life. I'm simply surprised a woman with your curiosity, with your thirst to learn, wasn't driven to ask more questions."

"I did. Ask Geoffrey, I mean. After I asked, he admitted he craved some adventure in the bedroom. Escapades ... " She waved her hand between them, hoping he wouldn't ask for explanations. "Adventures I wasn't providing. He said I was the reason he couldn't get ... "

"A hard prick when around just you."

She rolled her eyes. "I would not have put it quite so crudely, but yes, you are correct. And as you've pointed out more than once, my upbringing of narrow and staid conservatism prevented me from agreeing. After that, his visits to my bed ceased. Therefore, any chance I had of becoming enceinte also disappeared."

Justin gave her a shrewd look. "Who did he want to join you in your bed—or should I say, how many?"

She flushed, and even though the conversation with her husband had been five years earlier, she recalled every word as if it was yesterday. "He suggested several people, all friends. And the worst of it was, he expected me to extend the invitations. If the request came from me, his wife, he believed they wouldn't be shocked. Rather, they'd be flattered."

"I'd hazard a guess that Gillian, Edward, and Anna were on his suggested list."

"Top of his list. Naturally, I refused to affront my friends by asking if they'd care to join us in our bedromps. Provincial of me, wasn't it?"

He sat beside her and pulled her head to his shoulder, rubbed her back with one hand in comforting circles. "I'm sorry, for you, for not having children. But I'm glad the bastard's dead or I'd strangle him with my bare hands."

"Thank you," she said with a sigh.

"At least you now know nothing that happened in your marriage was your fault. Geoffrey is an example of the many indolent gentlemen who develop strange desires and demands and their wives should never be held responsible for their failures. Remember, Chrissie, there are men who will value all you have to offer."

"I'm not looking for another man in my life. I prefer my peaceful existence."

"You can either hide away in the country where nothing can hurt you again, or you can show real courage and face life. Live again."

"This whole adventure, finding you, coming to London, has

forced me to live. But I don't know how much more I'm capable of doing."

"You're capable of great things. I just ask one thing. When you come to the Pleasure House, let yourself enjoy. Don't simply come to accompany your friends. Come for you, to broaden your mind. Have an adventure with me. Will you do that?"

"An adventure? Like the one we had at the theatre tonight?"

"Yes, only better. More. Three full days of it."

"What will I have to do?" One shoulder came up in a gesture she was coming to understand meant he was considering his options.

"Nothing you don't want. Nothing that makes you uncomfortable." He smiled, then leaned over to kiss her cheek. "Or, we could seek every gratification we can in the time we are together."

"I promise I'll consider it. But as you know, I only ever intended...
"

He groaned, loudly. "I know. You intended going to my estate to observe. Nothing more. To support your friends." He stood up and bid her a polite farewell.

As Justin walked away, he wished he and Chrissie were going to the Pleasure House for entirely different reasons. He wished she was going to be with him, to sample the entertainments as his guest, his concubine, his love.

9

———————

Two days later, Justin had everything in place for the arrival of Chrissie and her friends. Sweat beaded his brow and his muscles ached from the surfeit of physical labor he'd subjected his body to—ostensibly to hasten the erection of the tents. In truth, it was to keep his body too exhausted for it to crave relief, to crave Chrissie. He glanced at the mantle clock for the tenth time in an hour and Bart laughed.

"My friend, they'll not arrive any sooner for your pacing. Chrissie certainly has you tied up in knots. I've never seen you in such a twist over a woman before."

"Nobody mentioned Lady Wellsby. There are thirty other guests coming."

"Yes, but only one to whom you gave an orgasm while standing outside the theatre."

"Damn! I hoped you'd forget having ever seen that."

Bart placed his hand over his heart. "I swear your little indiscretions will not be discussed by me."

"And in return?"

Bart grinned. "Would I ask for anything in return?"

Justin gave a snort of laughter. "Yes!"

"Ah, yes, well, you know me too well. If you were to grant me a tiny favor in return for my sealed lips, it would be that Magdalene could be allocated to my service for the next four days."

"One day."

"Three."

"Two."

"Agreed. Two days with Magdalene. But she'll not have time to be your exclusive slave, you know that."

Bart smiled. "I do know that, but I also know you require her for the groups and I'm more than happy to become a participant then, too."

Justin stared at him with dawning horror and then groaned.

"I forgot the groups. I forgot Chrissie would have to see what happens when men like her husband take part."

"You'll have to find other ways to distract her from morbid thoughts then, won't you?" Bart said with a smirk. "You know, join her in the romps with the other thirty guests."

Justin's ears pricked up when he heard the sound of carriage wheels. "God, they're here. What if she doesn't like it? What if she turns tail and runs?"

Bart slapped him on the back and strode to the door. "If it is them, you'd best hurry. Make sure they're in disguise before anyone else sees them. There are at least twenty people in the garden house already."

Justin's mouth opened, terror freezing his reply in his throat, but he recovered and raced to the door. He pushed past Bart, eager to ensure Chrissie was protected by disguise. Luckily, he reached the carriage in time and instructed the women to cover their faces with the veils he'd sent them beforehand. His glance flicked downwards over the rest of the costumes he could see exposed from under the hems of their coats.

Wide harem pants floated out on each of the women and more tapered pants covered Edward's legs. He stuck one out for Justin to observe and remarked, "I feel dreadfully foolish in this costume."

"You'll blend in. Everyone wears one to protect their identities. It's easier this way. Now, ladies, may I escort you to my notorious Pleasure House? The festivities have begun in the garden with entertainment provided by the dancing girls from Arabia, followed by a demonstration by the sword swallower."

Anna clapped her hands in excitement and leaped out of the carriage door. "Sword swallower. Wonderful."

"May I say, Miss Anna, you look wonderful," Bart's deep voice said from behind Justin.

Anna smiled at Bart, a full-blown smile of such sweet innocence that all the men watching groaned in unison. Her head spun between them.

"What is it? Thomas? Bart?" Justin debated throwing her back into the carriage and ordering the driver to take Anna straight back to her country house. And to lock Chrissie and Gillian in the dungeon with her.

Bart spoke first as Thomas seemed too flustered to answer. "Miss Anna, many of the men here tonight are known rakes. If you look at them with those baby blue eyes so full of innocent guile, they are going to gobble you up like monsters who eat children who wander into dark and evil places."

Thomas swallowed loudly and took Anna's hand. "Miss Anna, it's as I've been trying to convince you— you must leave here immediately, before you are seen."

"But gentlemen, nobody will recognize me. Who could possibly know me? Unlike Chrissie and Gillian, I've never even had a London season."

Edward, Gillian, and Chrissie stood beside the carriage.

Edward voiced the sentiment of the others. "You may as well save your breath. I've spent the entire journey from London trying to convince them to turn around and they've spent the entire journey ignoring my pleas and trying to coerce me into divulging what sort of sights they may encounter here. Bloody determined women will be the death of me," he muttered, glaring at his wife.

Justin placed his hand on Edward's tense arm. "Easy, my friend. I held no expectation that they would rescind their decision. Therefore, I made careful plans to ensure they blend with the other girls I employ only to serve food and beverages."

Chrissie swung toward him and narrowed her gaze. Her tone was angry, accusing. "You told me no watchers were allowed at the Gardens. Only participants."

"Obviously, I lied. I freely admit to attempting any ploy to divert you from your ridiculous plan." He planted his hands on his hips and spread his feet wide. "What did you expect me to do? Give in to your madcap scheme without protest?"

Chrissie's silence alerted Justin to the fact his words had fallen on deaf ears. He'd lost the attention of all three women. Their eyes had dropped to his lower body. He followed their direction to run a critical eye over his light trousers and black boots. His loose shirt hung past his knees, while his head was wrapped in the typical headwear of the men of the desert countries.

"Amazing," Chrissie muttered. "Staggering likeness," Gillian added.

Anna gasped, clasped her hands to her chest, and cried out, "Prince Zoltan."

Thomas threw his hands in the air and groaned. "Oh no, Justin. Now you've done it."

Justin was as taken aback as Thomas. He couldn't believe these ladies had discovered the name he'd assumed to play his theatrical role. He scowled at the women.

"How the hell did you hear that?" Anna spoke first. "We know the name because we've all read the book about your exploits." She gave a girlish giggle. "Several times. I think Chrissie wore out some of the pages."

"Damn!" Justin muttered, while Bart burst out laughing. He turned to his friend and sneered. "Bart, this is not amusing." Bart, however, couldn't contain his amusement and continued to rock on his heels as he laughed long and loud.

Justin faced Chrissie. "I'd no idea you ladies would even know such a book existed, let alone acquire a copy. Lady Stressing wrote and published her blasted book before I could stop her. And I assure you, she grossly exaggerated the stories about me."

"Do you mean you didn't do the things she wrote about?"

Justin was not prone to embarrassment about his wilder exploits of the past. What was done was done as far as he was concerned and he could not change his reputation now. However, he was disconcerted by the thought that Chrissie had read the book about Lady Stressing's affairs with not only him, but several other gentlemen. And not always at different times. Chrystal liked her men young, assorted, and together. As many as she could get in one room at the same time. And she was at this very moment languishing in one of the terraced Bath Houses just behind his house.

Feeling it was more beneficial to his health to ignore that particular question, Justin motioned for the group to walk with him. "When here, I assume the character of the prince for the entertainment of the guests. They like the pageantry to be realistic to a sultan's palace in the middle of the desert and as they pay a great deal of money for the exotic location, I am happy to oblige their desires. That is why you are also in disguises— and those very disguises are what will help you move freely around the various areas and observe without causing a disturbance. It would be unwise for the guests to discover that I have broken all my hard and fast rules for you. They would immediately become suspicious."

He led them inside and took them to his private wing in his own house. "You all have rooms here away from the other guests, so tonight, when the drink has been flowing and the level of debauchery deepens, I insist you all retire to your rooms. It is one thing for you to observe some of the more light-hearted pursuits, but I will not allow you to be present if anything too sordid takes place." He gave the three women a severe stare, daring them to contradict him. "Do you all agree?"

They nodded their heads in a meek fashion that didn't fool Justin for a minute.

"Bloody hell!" He looked at Edward who was also dressed in Arabic clothes. "I expect you to keep them under some sort of control. Act like you're here to serve food and drinks, nothing more. Keep your heads down and don't attract any attention to yourselves. There are plenty of secret viewing areas where you may sit unobserved."

Bart treated Anna to one of his most roguish grins and she, innocent that she was, returned it with another sweet smile. "I shall be delighted to accompany our delightful Anna, and to explain the events as they unfold."

Justin growled low in his throat and glared at Bart. Beside him Thomas stiffened, his fists tightening at his sides.

"Bart," Justin said, stepping between Bart and Thomas before Thomas decided to direct a punch at his friend's nose. "I thought you preferred Magdalene's company."

"Oh, I do. I adore Magdalene. But it occurred to me Anna may like to join us."

Thomas's shoulders heaved with barely contained fury and the color in his cheeks turned to a worrying motley red. Justin groaned. "Bloody hell, Bart, why are you doing this to me?"

Thankfully, Anna seemed ignorant of how high the tension between the two men had risen. She placed her hand on Thomas's arm as she tilted her head in consideration. She addressed Bart, her tone sweet and innocent, naïve in fact. Justin could see disaster looming as his two friends eyed each other over Anna's head.

"Perhaps," Anna said, oblivious to the opposing ways her words would be construed, and most likely twisted, by the two men. "I might find that interesting. We will see."

With a strong sense of foreboding, Justin showed the group to their rooms and after they had refreshed themselves, accompanied them to the gardens. He explained the area was attended by different servants who catered to the needs of the guests during the entertainment. After that, individual guests or groups could request particular entertainment for viewing, but for the first afternoon, public displays of intimacy were forbidden in the gardens. After the dancing girls, people would wander up to the terraced levels of the Bath House and relax in the hot spring waters that flowed down the mountainside.

"If any of the men or women accosts you, keep your veils over your faces and your trays close to your bodies. Don't speak to them. Pass them by with your head dipped. The guests know better than to annoy anyone who is not one of my paid courtesans or a willing guest."

Thomas frowned at him and Justin knew his more conservative friend was envisioning all the problems that he himself could also foresee. Only Bart seemed happy with the prospect of throwing three naïve women amongst the lions. But then, Bart had always had an appreciation of the absurd. And what could be more absurd than a man who had decried sex, avoided women's beds, and was trying to live down his reputation yet now was forced into this bizarre state of affairs? A circumstance where he would offer three ladies, not demi-mondes or whores, a chance to see things forbidden from being discussed aloud in the world they inhabited.

"Edward, I fear you may be the biggest problem of all. You do not look like the burly men I bring to entertain the women—"

"Now see here," Edward objected.

"I mean no offense, but I only employ very large men to go with the groups of women. Much bigger in every aspect than any of us." He waved a hand to include himself and Bart and even Thomas. "I feel it would be better if you pretended to be a participant but kept your face covered."

Gillian's face dropped and for the first time she looked distressed. "But I did not intend ... I mean, what if one of the courtesans offers to do things with my husband?"

Justin reassured her as best he could but he knew they were taking a risk. If Edward's identity were uncovered, other gentlemen present would be more than happy to spread the gossip that his marriage was already failing. That would leave both Edward and Gillian as targets for the rakes and widows of the ton. The ones who delighted in preying on spouses who were left alone. Gillian did not realize the trouble she might unwittingly unleash for them both.

"I will ensure that no one, woman or man, will touch Edward in an inappropriate way, Gillian."

"My dear, I am perfectly able to protect myself from a group of tittering women," Edward announced.

Justin exchanged a glance with Bart and Thomas. The three of them knew how demanding these people could become when fueled by lust. Gillian and Edward resembled babes-in-arms amongst these degenerates. He prayed for guidance from above and hoped Bart and Thomas would help keep the other out of trouble. The sights they were about to behold would be shocking enough on their own, but to be enticed into participating in the more raucous activities would send them into a tailspin.

"Now," he said, trying one last time to instill some wisdom to the ladies, "when we reach the gardens, you three women take up positions around the perimeter and try to remain out of sight if possible."

He groaned at the three over-eager faces before him, then moaned louder when he looked at how much of their three bodies was exposed, despite his efforts. With their breasts straining at the leather of their skimpy vests, they looked lush and edible and worst of all, totally available. Like the most exotic and erotic harem girl any man could envisage. Sucking in a deep breath in a vain attempt to calm his now twittering nerves, Justin stepped into the large cleared area of the Pleasure Gardens. He readied himself to address the attendees and commence the first of what he knew was going to be three days of hell.

With a deep bow, he approached the cheering crowd and smiled magnificently at them, morphing into the ultimate actor he became on these occasions.

"Ladies and gentlemen, welcome to the Pleasure House."

10

Viscount Hawkesbury drew a deep breath, raised his arms heavenward, then declared, "I am Prince Zoltan." He made his announcement with as much drama as Queen Victoria when pronouncing her latest parliamentary bill against prostitution or child labor.

"My name means leader. I am the eldest son of the Sultan of Karamu. Please enjoy all the pleasures of my harem. Bathe in the heated waters of the Bath House and be anointed with oils carried on my ships from the far ports of the eastern seas. Recline upon pillows woven of the finest silk from the worms of China. Slave women will then be available to massage your bodies until you fall into sleep.

"By my command, your dreams shall be pleasant ones and your waking hours here will be filled with incredible joys. There is much to be sampled in and each day we will have displays for your viewing pleasure as I know many of you enjoy watching others dallying in the delights of the flesh.

"There will, of course, be ample opportunity for everyone to participate in the activities. As the sultan's regent, I remind you of our few simple rules. No one may venture into forbidden areas away from the Pleasure House. No one will use force in any manner to involve either another guest or one of my servants in proposed activities. I've brought the most talented concubines to every tent for you to enjoy." He lifted his arms skyward again. "So please, enjoy my hospitality. Eat, drink, and be merry."

He bowed and backed away as a long line of dancing girls wove their way into the first tent where the guests lounged. The air hummed with anticipation and a heady mix of perfumes filled his nostrils as tendrils of smoke rose from the large brass incense burners in each corner. The sandalwood was mixed with minute doses of a drug that had a sedative effect upon the muscles yet none of the addictive properties of opium. He'd no intention of turning people into drug-crazed opium smokers who haunted the dens in London craving their next dose. But the drug relaxed guests and ensured no one over-imbibed on wine and became drunk and abused the courtesans.

The tent was an enormous expanse of flimsy cotton in a variety of bright colors that draped across poles and covered the entire center of the garden. Around the outside, smaller tents connected with the main one, but curtains could be lowered to ensure privacy in smaller alcoves. Some people preferred more privacy on the first evening, but generally by the third day, all inhibitions were left behind and the garden resembled one giant orgy.

Justin's dearest wish was that long before the third day, the three women's minds and bodies would be so exhausted from the onslaught of sensations they'd have departed. He closed his eyes. The sort of debauchery some of the ton were used to was enough to turn even his hardened stomach, although anyone who came to his estate knew he didn't tolerate any extreme perversions. Those who followed the more disgusting practices visited low-class brothels in Cheapside or other London slums. He'd tolerate none of it near him.

Men who'd debase children or destroy young lives were the lowest of the low, and by choice, he'd see them hanged. That caveat included his own father, if he still lived. Not that his father's form of sensual pleasure counted as extreme in seedy London or in more liberal parts of the continent. And especially not in eastern countries from which Justin's alter ego Prince Zoltan originated.

Justin had visited those countries and observed firsthand the practices of men who shared beds with men, performed with animals, or did what English church-going people considered unholy and unnatural practices. Over his years of travel, he'd witnessed sights that caused a man's eyes to pop from their sockets and had gladly left them behind. He refused to drag the stink of those depravities back to taint his gardens.

He'd been willing, three years ago, to bend the rules of society in order to make a fast fortune so he could search for his family. Despite stretching himself to those limits, he wasn't willing to compromise his entire moral belief structure. Nor would he dirty the morals of his friends to that extent, knowing they'd both need to take wives one day in the future.

Leaning back against one of the strong poles supporting the tent, he closed his eyes and wished for the hundredth time he'd never had such a wild idea as to start this. A soft hand touched his back and made him start in surprise. Chrissie stood in the shadows beside him, a slim figure dressed in the same colored cotton as everyone else. Yet even in the falling dark, every nuance of his being recognized her and knew her scent.

The smell of lavender filled his nostrils, a welcome relief to the heavy and exotic smells filling the air around them. Cloying perfumes were not something that he enjoyed, especially on his lovers, but he'd immured himself to these scents as he'd immured himself to the sights of naked bodies writhing on his manicured lawns.

"My lord, I'm deeply sorry to cause you so much distress," she said in a soft whisper. "I'm afraid my friends and I didn't think through the consequences when we made this plan. We thought only of our own goals. We failed to consider how difficult this might prove for you. To do this once again when you'd stopped holding galas here."

Justin straightened. "Thank you. It means a lot to me that you understand at least why I was so reluctant. The whole idea of the Pleasure House was so I could locate my mother and sisters quickly. Yet here I am, three years later, still clutching at straws. Still trying any road to find where they went."

Chrissie nodded. "I know. In four days' time, I hope I'll have good news for you. Even while we stand here, I've three men investigating different areas where I was told they might be. So far, each time I've sent my men out to check, they've returned empty-handed, although they've narrowed the area down considerably. I know this frustrates you and you probably hate me for doing this to you, holding up your own search, dangling carrots in front of your nose."

"Huh. You're correct there, sweetheart."

"I do understand. And I'm trying my best to help. The people who are out looking know me better than they know you. They're working day and night to assist me." He sighed, nodded, then peered around the corner of the pole to see where Gillian and Anna had secreted themselves. "Where are the others?"

"They found a quiet corner to watch, from up there." She pointed to a raised area slightly behind the tent where they could look down upon the dancers without anyone being able to see them. "Thomas and Edward are with them."

"And Bart? I expect he's in the tent where he can get the closest view of the belly dancers. He has a fascination with Eastern girls and their costumes and jewelry."

"I don't know. I didn't see him. I was more worried about you." She touched his arm. "You look exhausted."

Her concern touched him, touched a place deep inside him that craved a woman's love and care. Most would never say he didn't possess a heart, yet that spot in his chest ached. With one hand, he rubbed the area, but it didn't ease. Chrissie's hand covered his, held his motionless, halted the nervous circles he'd rubbed so viciously his chest hairs pulled tight and hurt. He removed her hand from his chest, kept it firmly in his, and tugged her behind him around the tent and toward the sloped area rising from the garden.

"Where," she gasped, "where are we going?"

"Don't you want to watch?"

He took her quick nod as consent and continued to pull her to the safety of the trees. There was a small stone bench hidden there that he knew from past evenings spent watching proceedings would give a perfect view. The dancers moved backward and forward across the tent in time to the pulsing rhythm of the music being played by the pipes while the bells from their tambourines jangled and sang.

Justin pulled Chrissie down beside him and snuggled her close to his side, placing his finger over her lips when she tried to object. "Shush," he cautioned. "Be very quiet. I'm trying to avoid being pulled into participating in the show."

"Why are you avoiding it?" she whispered back.

"Because I hate making a spectacle of myself, and the women always accost me when I dress like this." He gestured at his costume and grimaced. "The whole Zoltan thing went crazy after Chrystal wrote her book."

"I can imagine."

Chrissie's smirking face irritated him more than anything else about this whole evening— and a lot of it had irritated him.

"You may find it amusing," he snapped, "but I don't. I cannot go to the park without having my ride interrupted by some widow pretending to fall off her horse in my path. Young chits stare at me in the street or giggle when I walk past them. If I inadvertently touch any part of them or their clothing, they swoon."

Chrissie chuckled but when he glared at her, she attempted to smother her amusement behind her clasped hands.

He groaned and dropped his head to his knees. "Why bother explaining? You're yet another reader of the tall tales of Zoltan. You're probably under the spell of the Sultan's Palace magic that has spread by word of mouth from woman to woman throughout the land."

"My lord, how poetic."

"I was being ironic, not poetic."

"Perhaps you'd like me to—" He leaned closer to find out what Chrissie was offering to do, but at that moment, his worst nightmare came true as Chrystal burst through the bushes.

"Justin, my pet, why are you hiding up here?"

He jumped to his feet and placed his body in front of Chrissie. "Why aren't you with the dancers?"

Chrystal pushed him aside and peered around him at Chrissie, who dipped her head and pulled her veil higher over her face. Only her eyes were exposed but those eyes were wide with fright.

Chrystal pointed an accusing finger at Chrissie and spoke to Justin in an accusing voice. "Why is one of the dancers here with you when everyone else must obey your ridiculous rules? No watchers, only participants. No one is allowed outside of the performance areas. Justin, I don't understand. If you wished for company ... " She stepped closer and ran her hands over his body. "You only had to ask."

Chrystal then spun away to speak to the three people behind her, people Justin had failed to notice. Damn. If he allowed her to dwell on the inconsistencies in his rules, Chrystal and her annoying curiosity would start spreading the story and asking questions.

He needed to distract her and her followers, and do it quickly. He grasped Chrystal's elbow and bent to her and produced his most seductive smile as he guided her toward the tent.

"Amira was nervous about dancing for the first time in front of so many strangers but I've assured her she'll do well." He turned back to Chrissie but gave no signs of any acquaintance other than master and servant. "Come, Amira, stop twittering and join the other dancers."

Chrystal attempted to look back over her shoulder at Chrissie but Justin kept his grip firmly on her arm and forced her to walk away.

"Amira looks like a succulent morsel, Justin. Is she new?"

"Ah, yes. New to performing here. She'll be used to amuse select guests only."

Chrystal tittered and pulled sideways to glimpse Chrissie's features. Chrissie dipped her head. "But, Justin, my sweet, you know as I'm your extra special friend, you've never denied me anything before. Especially not here in the gardens."

She giggled in an irritating manner and laid her head on Justin's shoulder, peering up at him through her thickly blackened eyelashes.

Looking down, he thought of Chrissie's unadorned countenance and her lack of face paint, and realized with an inward sigh that it was just one more thing to add to a long list of things he preferred about Lady Wellsby.

"No matter what has happened here on previous occasions, I make the rules and I expect everyone, including you, Chrystal, to abide by them."

Chrystal was oblivious to the edge to temper in his voice and giggled again, raising his level of irritation for all things frivolous of the ton to an even higher level.

No wonder his distaste for London life increased daily. And little wonder he wanted to locate his family and bring them with him to the country. He longed to retreat here, to his estate, so they could all recover. Hopefully he'd have a chance to wash away the multitude of sins clinging to his skin like mud. Hopefully he could start to cleanse their minds of the wrongs committed to them and cleanse his soul of the sins he'd committed. He looked around him and shuddered. Those wishes may still come true as soon as he could rid himself and his estate of the pests invading it for the next three days.

"But I do so adore our gatherings," Chrystal said, her nasal whine grating on his nerves more than ever before. "And our naughty group romps in your luscious gardens. Your tents are so positively perfect for playing our little games of peek a boo. I get such a thrill from discovering a new harem slave hiding behind a mound of pillows. Arthur and I are so thrilled to be here again. We miss the House, and you, so, so much."

Justin flinched as she ran her nails up and down his arm in her over familiar and possessive way. Three days. That was all he had to last. Right now, it seemed like a life sentence.

"And where is your husband, Chrystal?"

"Ooh, Arthur's waiting over there," she waved vaguely in the direction of the larger tents, "for me to bring you back. You know how much he admires seeing you perform. For dear Arthur, the highlight of his visit is your marauding Arabian prince act when you throw off your robes and mount a captured slave girl and then like a stallion in heat you—"

"Enough!" Justin realized too late the story Chrystal revealed. He'd no intention of re-enacting any of those old Arabian fables tonight, or on any future nights. His days as the arrogant desert ruler Prince Zoltan were finished. And he certainly didn't need Chrissie being regaled of the erotic fantasies he'd played out before audiences here before.

Unfortunately, Chrystal wasn't going to give up her fantasies without a fight. She grasped his arm and pulled him toward the tents and straight into the path of her leering husband. Arthur, true to past form, didn't hesitate. He reached down and grabbed Justin's balls in an eye-watering grip.

"Jesus, Arthur," Justin shouted as he pulled away, bending over to protect his private parts from the idiot. "What the fuck are you doing?" He heard the gasps from around him and realized many pairs of eyes were trained upon him. Arthur laughed, an over hearty laugh that sent shudders down Justin's spine.

"Merely checking if you still have the balls to perform as Zoltan. Been hearing plenty of tales of your lack of prowess with women lately, Winchester. Been worrying me." Arthur raised his brows in his most lecherous look. "Still, couldn't resist the chance to see if my prize stallion could still plough a mare or two."

He grabbed his wife around the neck and tugged her closer to him, and when she was within easy reach, covered her breasts with his two beefy fists. "And you know how my darling Chrystal treasures your shaft prodding her, eh, Prince Zoltan? A sight to behold it is." He pulled a roll of notes from a pocket he must've sewn into his costume especially for the purpose, the old bastard, and pushed some money toward Justin. "You know me, Hawkesbury. Willing to pay, and to pay well, for the privilege of watching you fuck my wife every way I decree for the next week."

The older man laughed, his fat stomach wobbled, and the raucous sound caused Justin's stomach to knot and heave. Not only was Justin aware that Chrissie could hear every word the old letch spoke, but a few minutes more of listening to Arthur's sordid description of their previous threesomes, or foursomes, and he would cast up his accounts all over Chrissie's feet.

Arthur turned to the waiting crowd and raised his arms as he announced in a booming voice, "Prince Zoltan is about to perform his opening ceremony. As he is our sultan, and ruler of the palace where we seek our pleasure, he chooses the first concubine. Or if he runs true to form, Zoltan may take many concubines before the night is over. He is an inspiration to us all to go forth and procreate."

The middle-aged lord nearly fell over while laughing at his own stupid jest. Justin grimaced as he debated with himself at which stage he should intervene. At present, it was far easier to let the lecherous Arthur babble on and make a complete fool of himself before Justin was forced to fix the problem. If only he knew the best way to protect Chrissie.

11

P rince Zoltan raised his arms to the sky and prayed for inspiration.

"My fellow pleasure seekers," Arthur said. "You realize that was merely a jest. Our great leader Prince Zoltan doesn't allow anyone to procreate. Precautions will be taken as usual, so you may remove that scowl from your face, my worshipful sultan, our gracious ruler."

Justin forced a smile to his face before he stepped forward and spoke, addressing his audience with arms spread wide in true theatrics.

"Indeed, now that his lordship has mentioned the problem, let me explain. On the tables are preparations to be drunk before participating in any activities. They contain my own secret recipes carried back from the Orient to prevent conception and disease. Drink these ancient medicines often and freely, as they are both aphrodisiac and malady prevention."

Justin backed away, hoping to escape and take Chrissie with him but Arthur and his perverted wife refused to allow him to leave. They blocked his departure and with their friends, made a mockery of all his intentions to avoid performing his usual rituals.

Bart, seated on pillows close to the row of dancers who still wiggled their brown bellies enticingly for the crowd, jumped to his feet. "Perhaps Zoltan would allow his general to perform the rituals for him this evening."

"Or me," Thomas added, bravely facing the crowd as well.

Justin gave them both grateful glances. His friend's attempts to save him from breaking his promise to himself to never perform those acts again were gratifying. His family may be far away, but at least he could count on these true friends to get him through the tough times. He dipped his head in acknowledgement of their sacrifice, especially Thomas's. Knowing the idea of performing a sexual ritual in public would terrify shy Thomas, the gesture became all the more poignant. He clapped Thomas on the back and thanked him in a soft voice.

"No, my friends. I must untangle myself from this dilemma." He turned and spoke to two of his servants before he stepped into the center of the billowing tent and bowed to the crowd. Men and women lounged in relaxed positions around the tent's outskirts, stuffing themselves with excellent food and befuddling their head with vintage wines from his cellar. Unfortunately, they were also exciting themselves into a lather waiting for more of the spectacle for which he was famous. If he failed to provide it, there'd be a riot and the three women's presence—plus his reason for reopening the palace—would be revealed.

"My people, the tradition has always been for the sultan to thrust the first knife in the sheath of the first virgin at the commencement of the festivities. Far be it from me to break with the customs laid down by my ancestors centuries ago."

He lifted a golden goblet from the table, raised it above his head, displayed it for the crowd, and drank deeply. As he went through the ritualistic part of his display, a deliberate ploy to gain time, he searched for a way to change the situation. But whatever happened, his servants needed more time to make adjustments to the night's adventures.

"I shall drink from the potions of love and endurance given to me by my ancestors. My stamina is already legendary amongst my people, and tonight I shall demonstrate why I'm known to have fathered the largest family in the history of my people. The great Zoltan shall outdo himself tonight. I'll take not only one virgin, but also every woman I desire here tonight. One after the other. Until I tire."

He laughed hilariously for the crowd, as if the thought of a prince tiring was absurd.

"Then, as my honored guests, I will grant you a great gift. You shall share the exquisite bodies of my slaves alongside me. You shall slake your lust with the most beautiful women and men the Pleasure House has ever seen."

At his elbow, he could hear Bart and Thomas voice their objections to each other and to him.

"What the hell are you doing?" Bart hissed in his ear. "Are you mad? I thought you'd finished with all that."

"I have. Trust me. Follow my lead and it will all work out. Between the three of us, we're going to work the others into such a frenzy there won't be a woman, or man, left standing for me to fuck."

"But you still have to fuck the first one," Bart said, his face contorted with lines of worry.

Beside him, poor Thomas looked terrified. "Justin," he hissed in a frantic effort to attract his attention, "You're going to have to do it in front of the whole crowd, like you used to, but this time with our three more innocent friends watching every move you make."

"Ah, but they'll not be watching. They'll be bent over and being ploughed like all the other women."

Chrissie still stood close enough to Justin that she overheard his crudity. He heard her shocked hiss of breath. "Justin," she said in a croaky voice that sounded nothing like her normal confident tone. "You ... you cannot expect us to display ourselves like ... like them." She waved at the crowd who now stood, stomping their feet and clapping hands in a clamorous din. "Please," he murmured close to her ear, "trust me to keep you safe. We're going to give the illusion you're participating, but in reality you three ladies shall be with us, and no one else. Bart, bring Gillian and Edward, and Thomas, escort Anna. Make certain they're wearing full costume."

The men nodded, understanding his hidden message even if Chrissie didn't. He drew her aside. "Are you wearing the undergarments I sent for all of you?"

When she nodded, he placed her in the center of the tent and ran around collecting his props. When the men arrived with Gillian and Anna, Justin went into his supposed trance for his performance as Zoltan.

To the women he commanded, "Come, come, every one of you. Come to Zoltan, the greatest sultan ever known. My rod is the longest and the strongest and every woman will bend before my prowess." He waved his arms to signal for all the women to crowd around him in the middle of the tent. "My beautiful harem, fall to your knees before your ruler."

He smiled his most radiant smile and rotated in a circle, arms upraised as the women scrambled for positions close to him. "I call upon the most powerful gods in the kingdom to give me the stamina of a hundred stallions so I may touch the womb of every mare in my stable." He looked down at them. "And you, my beauties, do you promise allegiance to your prince? Do you pledge to obey me this evening in my palace of pleasure?"

The female guests, already excited by the spectacle unfolding around them, lost their remaining inhibitions from the drug in the incense and the effects of the wine. A loud cry went up from the women.

"Yes!" The word filled the air, while the male guests provided background noise by stomping their feet and cheering, seemingly as aroused as their women.

Justin prayed the three ladies for whom this spectacle had been arranged would understand, and forgive, what he was about to do. "I command my harem women to unwind the veils from their upper bodies, so I may see your beautiful bosoms, so my staff will rise up as strongly as maize growing to meet the sun. For now though, you will keep your faces veiled, as the sight of your combined beauty will be far too shocking for these men to view just yet."

Starting the disrobing process, Justin drew his heavy outer robe over his head. The most uninhibited women, ones who'd romped naked around these gardens many times before, threw off their veils with gleeful shouts. Several were almost naked in seconds. Some clung to a small remnant of dignity by retaining a sheer veil around part of their bodies.

Justin caught the eye of Thomas and Bart, who nodded and helped Anna and Gillian discard one outer garment so they stood in their specially designed leather undergarments. While the strips of leather may shock these conservative women, the corset-like top supported their breasts adequately while the pants fitted like tight pantaloons. He nodded at the three women as he drew off the remainder of his own top garments.

He stood proudly before the cheering crowd clad in his sheer loose pants, thrust his hand through the hidden front opening, and drew his penis from the folds of material of his pants. The gasps from Chrissie and her friends made him flinch, but he ignored them and concentrated on pulling off his performance. It would be the performance of his life if he could fool his paying guests into thinking the three straight-laced ladies present were part of the audience. It would be a miracle if he could convince them the ladies were participating and yet keep them out of the activities.

"As the most lowly slaves in my harem, it's your task to ease your master's tired body when I return to the camp after a hard day's ride in the desert. My men, and my visitors, need to be tended as well. This is your opportunity to please me, to please my guests." He waved his hands to indicate the excited men standing around the tent watching the performance and waiting their chance to join in.

The most decadent of the women, with Chrystal leading them, rushed at him. With a resigned sigh, he pretended this was nothing more than a momentary relapse into the debauched world he was determined to leave behind. He lifted his gaze above the crowd so he didn't need to look anyone in the eye, didn't need to show his shame. He loosened the string of his trousers and let them drop to the carpet.

He may no longer be emotionally driven to demonstrate his virility in every second bed in the city, but his physical equipment seemed to once again be in working order. Though, he recognized it had only sprung back to such vigorous life for one driving reason. Since he'd met Chrissie and started having nightly lurid and erotic dreams about her, what could be termed his manly vigor had been resurrected with a vengeance.

And since he was forced into this display, he was eternally grateful that his dick stood proudly rather than hanging limply in his trousers as it had done for several months.

Not even to Bart and Thomas had he admitted that he'd become deeply concerned, that he'd believed impotency to be his deserved punishment. Though some part of him had still longed for the day when he'd have a wife he'd be able to service enough to produce an heir—and possibly even the spare child. Some part had still longed for the conventional society life he'd been so long denied. Ridiculous, really, that after all the disgusting things he'd observed in this same society he still wanted to join it in some small way.

He shook his head and mentally fortified himself to face the forthcoming events with his head held high. After all, he was already notorious, so what he could he possibly do to worsen the situation? He glanced once again toward Chrissie. Oh, yes. He groaned and dropped his head. There was plenty he could do to disgrace himself. He could become less of a man in her eyes.

At least before when Chrissie had come searching for him she'd believed him to be a scum on the face of the earth—but a virile one. After three days here with these greedy, grasping women to endure, he may just become the scum of the earth with not a sign of his previous vigor left to him. His virility seemed directly dependent on Chrissie, and his whole aim was to protect her from any close physical participation in these games. Not to bring her closer and closer to him so that his own arousal grew and grew and so to the onlookers he became the invincible sultan he portrayed.

He flinched, winced, as anonymous hands grabbed and groped at him. Fingers stroked every part of him, especially his penis, which now bobbed straight and high, a contrast against his tanned workman's skin. Determined to ignore the assault upon his body, he stood to rigid attention. In fact, every part of him stood to attention. He clenched his jaw and tamped down his impatience, waited for them to finish. He'd endured it before and he could endure it this time.

Glancing over, he saw Chrissie had looked away. However, Gillian and Anna stared, wide-eyed and open-mouthed, at his penis as if his protuberance was a giant ham on the bone cured especially for a picnic for the hungry hordes. They looked up at him, and he winked to relieve the tension of the moment. Gillian laughed behind her veil and he sensed the cheeky enjoyment she drew from this mad moment of his exposure. He'd call it humiliation but after three years, the word no longer suited. Apathetic resignation seemed more apt.

Anna appeared transfixed with what he presumed was her first eyeful of a man's naked form. She stood still, eyes wide and fixed on the direction of his groin. He caught Bart's amused grin, and he shrugged. There was little he could do but grit his teeth and endure the agony until they could be finished with it all.

Chrissie still refused to look at his body, nor would she meet his gaze. He watched her pick a path around the edge of the crowd of women and keep her gaze fixed on the ground.

Damn her. He couldn't decide which was worse—to have her avoid looking, or to know that she looked at him and suffer the agony of his body being aroused beyond bearing. Finally, she took the place furthest away from him and stood with her head bowed like a supplicant in a convent praying for forgiveness for her future sins. Although, to him, she looked anything but a penitent woman of the cloth as the many patches of bare skin he could see were pale white, lush, and alluring. A body made to experience every sort of sin he could deliver to it.

At the remembrance of his latest erotic dreams, the ones about the many different places on his estate he longed to take Chrissie's supple body, his shaft swelled and lengthened.

While he'd been helping his workers prepare the areas, his mind had constantly envisioned Chrissie posed in every area he prepared. He saw her body, oiled and perfumed, reclined upon the rocks and warmed by the hot steam of the underground springs. Imagined her lying naked in the field of wildflowers where the maids picked bouquets to scent the rooms.

Thought about bending her over the carpenter's bench, spreading her limbs as though he had her chained in the vice, and plunging into hot, tight pussy from behind.

Each hiss of the blacksmith's dipping water reminded him of the noises she made when he kissed her. Those little inhaled breaths at first, and then the escalation to hisses and whimpers and begging words. His arousal grew and the women cheered and called lewd encouragements.

Knowing he had to continue, had to hurry and finish this pantomime before he lost control entirely, he raised his arms to address his subjects in a commanding manner. "Kneel, my slaves. Kneel and give me your allegiance."

He waited until each woman dropped to their knees before him, noting the very last to do so was Chrissie. For her own sake, he hoped she'd follow his directions or he'd not be able to guarantee her safety. "Each of you will have one chance to touch my staff, with your hand, your tongue, your mouth, however you choose. The one who arouses me the most, and who excites the lust of every man watching ... " He waved his hand at the men crowding closer, their lust palpable in the heated air. "The one who stirs me beyond bearing from a single touch, a lick of their soft tongue, a suck of their wet mouth, will be the one privileged to receive my staff first. I will plow my rod into her tight passage and give her my royal seed. This slave will then be blessed for evermore.

"If, however, you do not entice me enough to draw out my seed, you must attempt the same with my generals, each one in turn, over and over, until you satisfy one of us. Only when one of us spurts our come into your body will you be granted your pardon."

Drawing a deep breath for courage, Justin moved down the line and braced himself for the onslaught of sensations. When he'd invented this game to start the first night's play three years ago, he'd never dreamed that it would come back to haunt him like this. Luckily, his staff had been able to locate enough of his old medicines from the Orient and he'd anointed his genitals with the ancient Chinese recipe. His balls were mostly dead to the touch and his rod, while painful, was mostly numb and immune to the torment inflicted by these ravenous carnivores.

Hungry hands gripped him hard and he winced. Greedy mouths sucked him sloppily until a steady stream of wet saliva dripped from his balls to the Persian carpet. For several minutes, he ducked and weaved his way around the line of female attackers.

"Christ!" He flinched, and cried out when someone's sharp teeth ripped skin from his penis as he tried to drag it out of a grasping mouth. Rolling his eyes, he looked toward Bart who gave him a solemn and commiserating wave of his fingers.

Justin looked to where Bart pointed. Hell! Now he stood before Chrystal, who'd deliberately placed herself near the end of the harem line in the belief she'd be the one he stopped at. In past times, he'd done just that. He'd spent several nights in lusty romps that involved her, her extremely rich husband, and whoever else he'd invited and paid for. Arthur 's cheers were often the loudest as Justin swived Chrystal before a group of their friends.

Poor miserable Arthur, who became aroused as a viewer rather than a doer, gained the most return for his money when he stood dead center of a romp. And that romp became all the better if his own wife was the center exhibit. Arthur was a man who exalted in owning the best of everything, and being able to brag about his possessions to others. His town house claimed to be the largest in Berkley Square, his balls and soirees the most lavish entertainments of the season, and his wife possessed of the most succulent fanny to fetter that Arthur could buy.

Justin managed to avoid Chrystal's excited gestures and calls, much to her obvious disgust, and he moved to stand before Anna. He closed his eyes and clenched his fists at his sides, praying to any god who'd listen for guidance. For the first time, the supposedly emotionless Hawkesbury felt shame and embarrassment. Not merely for himself, but for her.

Past experience had taught him to cope, but Anna was different. She wasn't a hard-hearted schemer like him but a pure-minded innocent unused to seeing a man's flesh exposed. Probably not even a glimpse of bare chest in private. To endure the mortification of a stiff penis jiggling inches before her eyes would be as far from her normal evening's activities as sailing the seven seas.

And tonight, Justin's consciousness continually pricked, knowing the intrusive eyes of a lusty crowd watched him, observed his every movement and registered his every emotion. Wrenching open his eyes, he looked down and prepared to whisper something to Anna, anything to put her at ease. He stopped, taken aback. The look on her face wasn't anything like what he expected. Instead of revulsion, he saw what looked to be awe. His own face must have looked thunderstruck, not hers.

He swallowed deeply, once, twice, before he was able to face Thomas, expecting censure. And yes, on Thomas's face there was definitely that, plus disgust and anger. Plenty of anger, directed not at the innocent woman bowing at his feet, but at him. Thomas's well-placed fury was directed at the idiot who'd thought this little performance would extricate them from a sticky situation.

But damnation. All he'd managed was to alienate one of his best friends, and he certainly didn't have enough of those that he could afford to lose one. In direct contrast, Bart's face glowed with admiration for Anna. As if he couldn't believe an innocent angel had turned in to such a sexual woman, one intent upon learning about the male body in that public way.

Justin glanced down again, bending his knees a little to whisper to the golden-headed angel. "Pretend to touch me so I can move on before anyone notices."

Her hand flashed out from her side and with the softest of touches ran one finger across the purple tip of his penis. "Oh," she murmured with a surprised gasp as his body reacted.

His shaft bobbed and bucked like a bee-bitten horse. He jerked back from her fingertip, but Anna didn't hesitate. She followed him, reaching out again and again to caress him again with her fingers. Her sweet and subtle touches aroused him so much more than the practiced grasps and grabbing of the others, that a dribble of liquid oozed from his slit.

"Jesus," he gasped, and backed away.

"Oh, no!" Thomas moaned from somewhere close by.

Justin understood his friend's anguish, and felt a sharp stab of shame and self-loathing. Good- hearted Thomas revered saintly Anna, and he, the most unsaintly of men, had cheapened her by letting her touch his exposed member in front of this lewd and screaming crowd. He looked at Thomas, who stood open-mouthed with shock and horror, and lifted his hand in apology and appeal.

"I'm sorry," he mouthed to his friend. "I tried to stop her." Thomas's face twisted into a grimace of pain, but after a moment's hesitation, he nodded.

Justin glanced down to Anna where she still kneeled in the line of women, expecting to see disapproval, embarrassment. Good Lord, he didn't know what else. He stared. Anna's face glowed. Red for embar-rassment, definitely. Her cheeks were flushed with color but on her complexion and with her angelic looks, it looked beatific. In fact, her whole demeanor was one of a serene Madonna. How could that be?

He stepped back to her and bent to whisper in her ear, "Anna, are you well?"

She looked up at him with her angelic smile and nodded. "Very well, thank you, my prince."

He swallowed hard, not sure what she thanked him for, not sure what to do or say. He gave Thomas a helpless shrug and looked to Bart for assistance. If he had to guess, he'd say that Anna, sweet and innocent Anna, had thoroughly enjoyed herself. Too bloody much for his sanity.

Bart started to laugh, a small rumble becoming louder and louder until he was laughing in a full- throated roar. Trust Bart to find it so amusing. Thomas alternated between glaring at him and smiling reassurances at Anna. Chrissie ... oh God, he didn't think he could bear to look at her. Bracing himself, he stepped away from Anna and once again managed to skirt around Chrystal but that put him directly before Gillian. He sucked in a quick breath, bent to her ear, pretended to nuzzle and tease her for benefit of their attentive audience.

Gillian's eyes glittered with amusement and naughtiness. Before he could speak, she whispered, "It will be all right, my lord. Trust me."

He pulled back a little. Trust her? He glanced sideways at Edward. Oh, double damn. Edward was a picture of seething fury. Now what the hell was he going to do? And what happened to his plan for these women to play act in the harem line, not to take an actual physical role?

"Christ!" A wet tongue darted out and touched him several times, not as tentatively as Anna, but in sloppy licks. Gillian was more determined than Anna to get him strung up by his friends.

"Enough," he murmured, bending close to her ear and hopefully putting his dripping shaft out of her tongue's reach. "You've proved your point, Gillian. You're now officially a worldly wise woman."

With a majestic wave of his hands, Justin addressed the girls in the line that he'd already passed.

"Arise, my beauties. You've performed well. Now go forth and spread your pleasures with others." He particularly addressed the last words to Chrystal, hoping she'd take the hint and find other playmates to spend her next hours with. The line of girls dispersed as the giggling mass rose and rushed away to the eager crowd of men to find partners. Gillian blew Justin a kiss, sashayed over to Edward, took his hand and dragged him toward a dark hedged area. Justin grinned and gave Gillian a small wave. Edward's luck had just changed for the better and if this excursion had done nothing else, it had at least accomplished that. He'd brought a husband and wife who obviously adored each other back together. He smiled again. This Good Samaritan thing was okay after all.

He looked to where Anna had risen with Thomas's aid and was excitedly describing the details of her first sexual adventure to Thomas and Bart. Anna appeared jubilant, Bart aroused, and Thomas alternated between lust and anger. Justin wondered idly which man Anna would chose for her practice session tonight, for he was certain there'd be one. He'd seen that same look of eager anticipation on too many women's faces before not to know what it indicated. It was the recognition of female power all women grew into with maturity and experience. The knowledge that by giving pleasure, they also received pleasure.

He sighed. Two women remained in his line. Chrystal, who had come back around for more, and Chrissie. Chrystal drooled with eagerness and now that he'd moved closer, reached out and grabbed him by the bollocks.

"Hell." Her other hand wrapped around his cock and pulled him toward her in a physical command he was unable to resist without doing permanent damage to his equipment. Though he mightn't have had much use for his genitals lately, he didn't want them damaged.

He raised a finger in warning to Chrystal. "One touch, remember. Nothing more."

He knew what this scheming woman was capable of when in the grip of frenzied lust. Three years ago, in the beginning, he'd convinced himself it was exciting, amusing, and not just a money-making venture. Now it appeared low-class, sordid, and shameful.

Chrystal's reddened lips opened wide, as if she was about to gulp down a glass of the best French champagne. She leaned forward and engulfed his shaft, but without touching him. With a cunning move, his sneaky adversary had neatly circumvented his one touch rule.

He stiffened his lower body, anticipating what would follow. She'd had her mouth on him enough times in the past for him to know Chrystal turned oral sex into a hedonistic act. How the hell was he going to survive this without letting it appear she'd won the ultimate prize? Namely him. He'd be forced to plunge into her body in front of everyone. Not that he cared who saw Chrystal being pleasured, but he minded that Chrissie watched him and assumed he wanted this, when all he wanted was to protect her and her friends. His grand plan had exploded in his face. She'd probably never forgive him for this stupid miscalculation.

He braced with his legs apart and readied himself for the moment when Chrystal lowered her mouth to the base of his shaft because he knew from experience her mouth opened to encompass not just his rather large length, but part of his balls as well. He groaned. He was doomed!

At the very moment Chrystal's teeth bit into his engorged flesh and Arthur led a loud cheer group, Chrissie caught his eye. She didn't reproach him with scowls or sneers or taunt him with her eyes. She, too, blew him a kiss, as Gillian had done. Her mouth opened to tell him something, a soundless command. He sucked in a breath as he understood her message.

"Save it for me," she said with her face, her eyes, her whole body. "Save yourself for my mouth."

Her encouragement made it easy to resist Chrystal's determined ministrations and a moment later, jerk back from her mouth. Still, he heaved a sigh of relief as he stepped across to stand in front of a kneeling Chrissie.

Lifting his arms, he made another announcement. "So far, there hasn't been a woman who excited me enough to perform my masterly sexual acts, and there remains only one woman. A novice. I'm sure she'll not manage it either, so I now give permission for all subjects in my kingdom to join with others. Take up your partners and relish the pleasure they'll bring to you."

"No, stop," a lone voice cried out from behind him.

He spun back to see Chrissie rise and address the fervent group. She lifted her arms in an identical theatrical gesture to his own. Her eyes gleamed brightly in the light of the torch flames, flaming locks flowed over bare shoulders to dance around barely contained breasts, and he was mesmerized. The hide-skin trappings he'd devised for the three women was enough for the smaller figures of the other two, but for Chrissie, there didn't seem to be enough leather to stretch around.

His mouth dried with an instant rush of desire and his arousal reached upward and toward her seeking the perfect match to his body. He wanted to grab her and drag her away to his lair, out of sight of any of the lecherous men now drooling over the sight of such a sensual goddess. Before he could will his frozen limbs to move, to scoop her up and carry her away out of sight, she stepped around him.

"I demand a chance, my great ruler, to service your needs. I may be only a novice, yet I feel certain that I am the one harem slave who can bring you to your knees. Who can make you writhe in ecstasy."

"No, no. It's not necessary. You are my slave and I command you to go back to your other tasks. It is time to bring forth the roasted pig." He signaled to his waiting servants and they rushed off to hasten forward the elaborate repast he'd ordered.

Bart walked forward and clasping Chrissie's hands he raised both her arms with his and held them aloft. "My friends, should not such eager willingness to serve our royal master by a girl come newly to the harem be rewarded?"

There were loud cheers from men and women alike. Chrystal stood alone and pouting but even her husband ignored her to rush forward and shout out lewd advice to Chrissie.

"Use your teeth on the man. A little pain heightens the pleasure." "Good God, Bart," Justin said, grabbing his friend by the arm. "What the bloody hell are you playing at? I wanted her out of here."

Bart indicated to where Chrystal was deep in conversation with five or six of the women from the earlier harem line. On their faces, Justin recognized insult and fury.

"Trust me," Bart said. "I organized something in anticipation of just such an unwelcome outcome. Chrystal and her compatriots will be demand blood, or your hide, if you don't see this pantomime through to the end."

"Damn!" Justin muttered. "Very well, let us proceed. But I must find a way to protect Chrissie's privacy."

Bart nodded and once again addressed the not caterwauling mob.

"Zoltan and this supplicant will perform a ceremony for us, my friends, such as you have never before witnessed. It will whet your appetites for the food that is being served momentarily. And prepare you for all the games and romps and pleasures that Zoltan has been gracious enough to provide this evening."

Bart led them to the side where swathes of silk had been arranged to resemble a desert tent. He pushed them inside and then addressed the few in the group who were objecting to the location of the ceremony. The silk was sheer but the many layers blocked a direct view for any of the onlookers.

Justin realized immediately what Bart had planned and sent silent thanks to all Arabian gods for giving him Bart as such a good friend. In their cocoon of fabric, the audience would see nothing but moving shapes and would be unable to discern the action unfolding in any great detail.

"We can pretend to make love in here and no one will be the wiser," he whispered to Chrissie, leading her to the mound of plum pillows in the center of the space.

"No. We will not pretend. We will have sex, Justin. Wild passionate sex, of the sort for which you are so renowned. I want to sample, just once, the enjoyment and satisfaction of having a proficient lover to ignite my senses and stir my arousal."

Justin groaned and dropped his head to his chest. "Christ. You've no idea what you're asking me. Don't you see, I want you so badly if I come near your naked body for even a moment, I'll lose control. I may not be able to stop."

She frowned at him. "Do you mean you may not be able to pull away and spend your seed outside my body?"

"Ha! That may be the least of your worries, my love. What I meant was I'll want to use your body in every position. I'll want to plunge into you from every angle and I'll not want to stop until I hear your screams of pleasure echo through the air. I'll want to make every man standing outside and listening experience such white-hot jealousy they'll orgasm from listening to us. Just from knowing how easily the succulent curves of your body can excite and arouse the hunger in a man. Even in a man who'd sworn off sex."

Her eyes widened and he hoped that the prowling predatory cat he portrayed had frightened her enough she'd turn and run. A country mouse scurrying back to its hole.

She laughed. Threw back her head and gave a deep-throated howl. "Oh, yes, my lord and master," she called in a loud voice, playing to the listeners outside. "My body is yours to command. Do with it what you will."

Hell! Once again, he'd miscalculated her reaction. The woman was a demon who outwitted him at every turn. Who excited him unbearably and turned him into a ravenous beast.

"Very well," he whispered. "I'll call your bluff and you'll suffer the consequences of all your weeks of teasing my control. Because know this, my lady, I will take you as I said. From every direction. Until you scream louder than Chrystal and all her friends together."

Chrissie looked pensive for a moment and then she shocked him again by saying, "Ah! Despite your reluctance to reveal any names about your past conquests, my lord, I now know for certain who paid you such an enormous sum of money to service her and all her friends."

He groaned aloud and wondered at his own stupidity. Inadvertently, he'd given her the identity of his past lovers, something he'd always been careful to keep secret. The ton made up stories willy-nilly about his prowess but the actual number of women he bedded was only known by a select few. His butler Perkins, and Bart and Thomas.

Now, instead of Chrissie looking afraid of the consequences, Justin felt a shiver of apprehension as he recognized that gleam of determination to rise to a challenge. Suddenly he was afraid his past had come back to haunt him in an unexpected way. She had told him more than once that she'd heard many, many stories about his bedroom antics and his prowess between the sheets. Or, for that matter, in linen closets and on library floors.

If what he suspected she was thinking was true, he was in for a thrilling encounter. And quite probably the ride of his life, one to outshine anything from his long and debauched years. In his mind, he could already picture a wild and thrilling sexual ride on Lady Wellsby's, Chrissie's, beautifully naked back. For sure, the woman would kill him this time.

12

Chrissie studied Justin's expression with interest. He appeared undecided as to whether he was about to shot at dawn or about to die from extreme pleasure. A hard choice. She prayed he'd choose her, and the option of expiring with pleasure during intimacy.

"So," she said, trailing a finger over his bared chest. "If I'm to be a more memorable harem slave than any of those other women out there ... " She waved a hand toward the shadows moving beyond the tent.

Chrystal's voice came to them clearly as she bemoaned the fact the great Zoltan had chosen Amira, a novice harem slave, to be serviced by the great and powerful ruler this evening. "It should be me!" Chrystal screamed, presumably at her long-suffering husband. "I'm the one who's wet and eager and waiting to be filled by his princely prick. Just as he used to do."

Chrissie watched Justin close his eyes and swallow deeply, his embarrassment obvious. She, however, was amused. "I see even the great Zoltan can be brought undone by a woman's emotions. Her fury and her jealousy." She ran her fingers lower and let them circle the tip of his bobbing penis in a lazy fashion until she felt his shivers ripple, one after the other, up his lean body. He opened his mouth to reply but she placed her finger over his lips.

"Hush, my lord. Those other women mean nothing to us in here. This is our private land of pleasure, is it not?"

Justin nodded, robbed of speech for now. Good! Exactly how she wanted him. Slavering over her body. Speechless with desire. "My master doesn't need to speak except to give me his commands, to convey his wishes and desires. Nod if you comprehend my language."

Wide eyed, and with his breath coming in hot pants, he nodded. "I am your master, Zoltan. Chrystal—"

"No, no, my lord," she cried out, nodding her head to indicate to Justin the listening crowd. "Please, Zoltan, do not speak another 's name in here. I cannot bear to hear it."

He nodded again. In a loud voice, he called out so the waiting guests could hear his commands, playing his part again. Chrissie was also acutely aware the lecherous men waiting outside would grasp any opportunity to enter the tent. They'd also welcome any indication that Zoltan was unable to perform as he used to and they'd step into his role. The thought of any of them touching her made her shudder.

If they weren't convincing enough in this performance, it could spell disaster for her reputation, and for that of her two friends. No one must discover their true identities and so for that reason, her act must ring true. They must believe outside that she was being taking by a domineering Arab ruler who had little regard for the sensibilities of women. Apart from that, she longed to feel Justin's hands on her, not those leering men's rough and coarse caresses. She yearned to feel the stretch of the viscount's famously long cock as he rammed it home inside her in wild abandon.

Above all, her secret wish was that he would forget the names of all the other women he'd ever taken in a tent, a bed, a park, and only remember hers. Lady Wellsby, Chrissie, or Amira. She cared little by which name he recalled her face and body.

Chrissie only knew she'd feel even more devastated after they parted, as they would invariably do, if their shared intimacy were another notch on his bedpost. Another faceless woman who had a warm body for him to use.

"Amira, my other harem slaves hover in anticipation outside this tent."

From outside came Chrystal's loud voice demanding she be admitted instead of the untried Amira. Her husband's voice added to the rising noise as he also showed his preference to see his wife's body being plundered like a captive by a conqueror.

If this were what Justin had dealt with for three years while he amassed enough money to search for his family, Chrissie felt sorry for him. It was easy to understand why he had become quickly jaded with society. These people who dined with the queen one day would be at their rank antics the next. For them, money and position meant the freedom to indulge their perversions and extremes without a second thought. No wonder Queen Victoria despaired of the dissipated morals of her court. Moreover, it was little wonder the lower classes were in revolt. To see money and time wasted in these games and romps through nothing more than the boredom of the elite troubled Chrissie and her long-held values of every man's right to a fulfilling life. She was startled out of her reverie by the viscount's—rather, by Zoltan's—impassioned words.

"My latest concubine, a nubile young girl stolen from her tribe on the edges of the desert," he called loudly, "has stated for everyone to hear that she is also wet and ready for my shaft. However, my loyal followers, before I take her she will need to prove that she is also ready."

Inside their haven, Justin spoke to the world. Nevertheless, his eyes remained locked with her, giving her strength. Asking her in silence if she still wanted this. She held no doubts that if she objected in any way, baulked even at this late stage, he'd find a way to extricate herself, and her three friends, from the danger.

Chrissie had never met three more noble men that Justin and Thomas and Bart. Oh, she knew well enough the things they'd done.

The extreme means they'd employed to raise capital for first Justin's brothel, then his Pleasure House, and last his vast railway investments. Thomas and Bart both held regal titles so they'd done it through their friendship with Justin.

In her eyes, men only showed that sort of ongoing loyalty to others if they were noble themselves. Moreover, if the men they helped were deserving of their loyalty and devotion. Therefore all the signs pointed to the idea that they were three honorable men who had been trying to make the best of a terrible situation—to extricate Justin's family from whatever danger they were in. In addition, to make retribution for the wrongs inflicted by Justin's father on his family. Women who'd been unable to defend themselves from a bully. Another disgusting man like her late husband had been, Chrissie thought with a shudder. If Justin's mother and sisters had endured a lifetime of

that sort of bullying, she felt very sorry for them. Men took delight in degrading women by using harsh words and large fists. It sickened her.

She prayed that she would not be too late in reaching his family. She prayed that her investigators were even now entering the village where his mother and sisters had been thought to have last taken refuge. The place they had hidden themselves after running from the late viscount's heavy-handed methods of discipline, she was sure.

Chrissie yearned to do something good for Justin, something kind and decent to restore his faith in the humanity of mankind. To be able to bring him together again with his lost family would be a miracle. She longed to be able to offer him a miracle after his life of disappointments. He had persecuted himself long enough for not being able to stay at his ancestral home for longer than he did.

From what she had heard of the story, if he'd stayed, the honorable young man in him would not have allowed his father 's cruelty. And according to British law, his father held total rights over his wife and two daughters. Please, God, let me find them for him.

Goodness, she must concentrate. He spoke again. " ... and as you all know, my prick is the longest and thickest and most randy in the

entire kingdom. Slaves have fainted under the onslaught. Before I
waste my valuable time I need to be assured that you, Amira, are
strong enough to receive the blessing I bestow upon your hitherto
unworthy body ... "

She raised her eyebrows in silent question, not sure where this
over-the-top monologue was headed. " ... and to that end, I command
you to test your own readiness for me. I fear I'm too lethargic to do so
myself as I'd normally enjoy doing. A man loves nothing more than
to feel a woman's rush of liquid arousal trickle hotly through his
fingers. I like to lick my fingers free of the thick moisture, finding it
sweeter than the very best of oasis dates."

Chrissie did indeed feel that rush of hot liquid of which he spoke
begin between her legs. At first, she felt embarrassment at her whore-
like response. Then she realized something.

Justin did this deliberately. He'd thought she might not become
aroused with the crowd outside hanging on their every word and
every movement. He prepared her physically without touching her,
so she'd carry this off with aplomb. She nodded, letting his see the
gratitude in her eyes.

His shoulders slumped as he heaved out a deep sigh, which
reconfirmed her assumptions. Even in this situation, the man was
honorable to the core. His first instincts had been to do whatever
necessary to protect her from more embarrassment, despite the fact it
had been she who goaded him into it.

"Now," he demanded, "touch yourself. Tell me how ready you
are."

Now was the moment she'd anticipated. Would she have the
courage to carry it through though? Yes, she would, for Justin's sake
and for her own. Plus, it was what she wanted most. To create an
exciting and sensual memory of her time with Justin to carry away
with her. Something good to hold in her heart and bring out in her
darkest and most lonely moments later.

He reached down and his finger slipped past the leather strap-
ping around her groin and through her curls, but she shook her head
and stepped back. She placed her own fingers on the spot where his

had dallied. His gaze fixed there. Dark inscrutable eyes suddenly became easy to read. One touch had caused his penis to stiffen even higher, and as she watched, it jumped and twitched like an eager child awaiting a treat.

She smirked. He glanced down, and then back at her with a rueful smile. He shrugged. What can I do? She laughed aloud as she dug her fingers deeper into her mound, and gave a very loud and exaggerated groan. From beside the whippy folds of tent fabric several men moaned with her.

She lifted her eyes to meet Justin's. He too had realized that the guests had moved closer, desperate to catch every noise of action they made. He gave a resigned shrug and she understood. The sooner they carried on and finished with their act of intimacy, the sooner the guests would pair off amongst themselves and leave the main players alone.

"Oh, my lord. I didn't know. Didn't understand before. No one told me being with you ... and hearing your masterful words ... " She gave several little pants. " ... would make me melt inside. I can feel gushes of hot liquid running over the leather you strapped between my groin. It stiffens the leather and tugs tighter through my ... "

She raised her hands in helpless appeal as she realized that despite her courageous performance, she lacked the actual words of sexual display.

He grinned and licked his lips. "Your pussy, Amira?"

"Oooh, is that the word you use, my lord?"

Justin rolled his eyes over her over-the-top theatre antics. "I fear, Chrissie, you'll never be good enough to tread the boards of Covent Garden," he whispered in her ear.

She giggled and then a stab of mischief occurred to her. This was her performance, hers to dictate. Therefore, it was also her one and only chance to make his squirm. More theatre dramatics were needed. Not less!

"Zoltan would call it other more intimate things with his favorite concubine, is that nor correct, oh good and mighty, high ruler?"

His eyes widened and his mouth dropped open as he realized her intent. No, he furiously signaled by his shaking head. Don't you dare take this any further, his darting eyes warned. She ignored his unvoiced threats and spoke even louder. "My pussy... my crevice ... my—"

His mouth descended over her in a hard and punishing kiss, one that he meant to silence her but one that instantly aroused them both. They broke away, panting and awed, staring at each other. At the same moment, they both reached between her legs and when their wet fingers touched in there, in that soft bush, they both halted and swallowed. It was as if their actions were being seen in a mirror, two halves of the same motion. As if their minds knew what the other thought, the level of excitement each one felt. When they registered it in each other's eyes, that level increased rapidly.

Justin pushed one longer finger up further inside her and she squirmed and moaned. "Ah, yes, Amira. You did not lie to your leader. Never have I felt a tighter, hotter, more enticing female quim. I rotate my fingers now, Amira ... " As he spoke, Justin matched his actions to his words and Chrissie was robbed of speech and of breath. With his free hand, he reached down and thrust her own fingers higher, sliding them beside his, upwards and inwards, until she screamed.

"Her first scream!" Arthur called out from outside and once again they realized how close to the tent fabric he'd pressed his eager ear. Possibly also his intrusive eyes.

"Make her scream louder, Zoltan," Arthur's friend called out. "Fuck her hard with those agile fingers of yours. We've seen them in action before, so we know how quick you can be with them."

"And I know how they feel inside me," Chrystal's voice came clearly and smugly.

Justin groaned and dropped his head but Chrissie nuzzled his cheek until he raised his gaze again.

"Ooooh, master. Oooh, how wonderful that feels. Oooh, what is happening to me? I feel something rising up in me, something hot and powerful."

Forgetting their acting, Justin cried out, "Let it come for me, Amira."

He plunged his fingers into her, higher and higher, over and over, setting up a faster rhythm that caused everything to fade except the feel of him. The scent of aroused male as he leaned closer and breathed heavily with her, his breath hot and rapid against her neck.

She panted and arched into his fingers as the first spasm shot through her. She screamed again, this time longer and louder. One of his arms remained wrapped around her as held her through the tremors and she sagged against him and let out a long sigh of pleasure.

Justin stiffened against her, and pushed her away. She felt a waft of cooler air as the ends of the tent flap were lifted a foot away from the opening, leaving a viewing hole. The next seconds were a blur as he turned her and pushed her to her knees, her rump in the air pointed to the door. His lithe muscled body stretched to cover her, his hips pushed tightly against her bottom and his arms outstretched beside hers. He tilted her head down into the pillows to hide her face.

"Onlookers," he whispered in her ear.

She sucked in a sharp breath, realizing what he'd done. He'd covered and hidden her body and face so no one could see her. All that would be visible would be Justin's long muscled thighs molded over hers and his brown back spread across hers.

"Forgive me," he added, and pushed his penis into her in one long, hard, quick thrust.

The momentum carried her forward and her forehead hit the pillows with a thump.

"Ouch," she cried, reaching up to touch the bump. Before she could think about that small hurt, Justin pumped into her from behind. The position had forced him deep, deeper than her husband had ever managed, and ripples of pure pleasure shot through her from her groin up. Her womb clenched under each hard push, her vaginal muscles tightened and tried to cling to his shaft, to halt any retreat. From behind her he groaned, but then must have recalled the audience.

"Amira, oh my God. Your passage is tight, just as a virgin's should be. And as I pump myself into you, you clench and squeeze around

me and bring me to ecstasy far too fast. I can see, my young concubine, I'll want to use your body many times this night. How many
times can your tight passage accept me? How many times can I spill
my hot seed into your woman's receptacle before you tire? Will you
allow your master to plunder your body through the night until the
sun rises?"

Chrissie moaned. Her loud noises were echoed from many voices
outside and she heard the grunts and groans of people already
engaged in sex. They hadn't waited for permission, but had taken
whoever had been closest. Chrissie prayed Edward and Thomas had
managed to slip her friends away from the crowd in time.

Justin's groans came faster, louder, until he shouted and thrust
hard, once, twice, three times. The rush of hot male sperm filled her
womb and by instinct she tightened her muscles, clamped them
together. She held onto his warm life-giving seed for as long as possible, all the while praying for a miracle. If she became impregnated
with his child, she'd be overjoyed. Justin would no doubt be horrified, but for her, becoming enceinte would be a miracle. A welcome
one.

The sounds of completion were evident everywhere outside, as
men and women alike screamed, yelled, and made noises of collapse.
The tent flap had dropped back into place when the guests had
coupled and moved away to find their own small space to fuck in.
Chrissie wasn't naive. The noises were obviously men calling to men,
and women to women, cheering each other on. Outside, she knew
people were engaged in every sort of uninhibited sex, one of the
orgies Anna had thought they'd observe.

Justin moved off her and slid them both sideways to lie face to
face on the pillows. A finger over her mouth stopped her speaking,
though she didn't think she was capable of coordinating her thoughts
and words just yet.

"Don't move. Wait until they finish and forget about us. Hopefully, they'll move away and find other partners."

She nodded, although their audience's departure wasn't the
reason she lay contentedly in his arms and wanted to delay their

departure. In that moment, she accepted the truth. She'd fallen in love with a rogue and a scoundrel. A man who couldn't possibly be interested in her, not for other than a brief affair, anyway.

Sane and sensible Lady Christina Wellsby had stupidly fallen in love with the totally unsuitable Virile Viscount.

13

"Oh, hell no." Justin grabbed Chrissie's hand and pulled her to her feet. With his free hand, he scooped up what he could of their discarded clothing and guided Chrissie out through the tent's back flap. Ignoring her obvious reluctance, he tugged her six or seven steps up the hill behind where they had just performed.

When Justin slumped down onto the grass, Chrissie lowered herself beside him although she clearly didn't understand what had prodded him into their hurried escape from the tent. She'd not heard Gillian's voice. Not realized that Gillian and Edward had imagined the tent was empty and were about to make use of it in the same way Justin and Chrissie had when they performed for the crowd.

Justin lifted his head from the grass and watched Gillian, the normally easy-going countess, drag her husband inside the tent. Where Justin and Chrissie sat was dark and above eye level for anyone walking around, yet every word uttered inside the tent could be clearly heard.

"I demand to be allowed the same liberties as Chrissie," Gillian was saying to her husband. "You will make love to me, Edward, just as

Justin did in here with Chrissie! Like a man possessed. Like a man who wants me above all else."

"Gillian." The poor Earl sounded shocked. The flimsy coverings of the tent lifted and blew in the rising breeze. "But, my love, the entire world will be able to see us."

"I don't care, Edward. I want you to prove you want my body above all the others ... " The exasperation in Gillian's voice was evident. "Every one of those women who stare at you and lick their lips as if you're their next meal. I want to be treated like the others. I want passion, Edward, and lust. I want to be thrown on the ground and ravished by you."

Justin could well imagine Edward's surprise, and then his excitement, at the image his wife portrayed. Beside him, Chrissie gave a small gasp before covering her mouth with both hands. They both knew Edward would now be seeing Gillian as she was here and now. Not dressed in a prim and proper gown and layers of petticoats but in the tempting and indecent eastern barely there garments.

Justin and Chrissie exchanged knowing glances as Gillian moaned and said, "Yes, Edward, that's the look I want to see back in your eyes. The one that tells me that you love me and want me the way I do you."

For nearly an hour, the now happily reunited husband and wife made full use of their time alone in the tent while Justin lay with Chrissie's soft and supple body pressed against his own still naked form.

"Oh my goodness, Edward," they heard Gillian say. "Your education at the Sultan's Palace has stood you in good stead. That was amazing."

Edward's voice boomed out from the tent. "I was rather astounding, wasn't I? Even surprised myself."

"Ah, yes," Justin murmured in Chrissie's ear as they cuddled closer and tried to suppress the sounds of their laughter. "Seems our reluctant groom is once again besotted with his bride."

"But you," Edward said loudly, "my one and only love, were magnificent. And I adore you, every pink inch of you."

She giggled. "Well, my darling, do you think we might improve on our magnificence next time?"

"Oh, yes, my sweet. I rather think we can create an even bigger tilt in the equilibrium of the known world this time."

"And Gillian will be ecstatic," Chrissie quietly replied to Justin. "With her newly acquired knowledge, Edward will never again leave her bed. It's obvious that Gillian knew who Edward was from the start, despite their disguises, so your plan worked, Justin. Very well indeed. And for that, I'm truly grateful."

"It's not gratitude I need from you, Chrissie."

Chrissie rose, dressed, and walked away from Justin, leaving him reclining on the small hillock by himself. He looked skywards and announced, "At least I managed to solve Gillian's problem."

Now he only had to figure out what to do about Chrissie. She'd left him alone. Lonely and confused. Where the hell did they go from here?

14

Chrissie stumbled across the grass, desperate to escape from Justin's presence and get her emotions under control before she spoke with any of the group again. Gillian and Anna were bound to read on her face what she thought of Justin, what she felt for him. Her two friends would most likely pity her for being enamored, for the second time, with a man who wasn't the type to reciprocate her feelings. She heard Thomas arguing with Anna and came to an abrupt halt, concealing herself behind a tree while she debated with herself the wisdom of eavesdropping on her friend's conversation.

"No, absolutely not," Thomas said. "I refuse to let you participate in such things. Not in a tent, nor rolling on the grass for the entire world to observe and report upon. Your reputation would be ripped to shreds."

Bart happened to walk past in the middle of their heated debate and Thomas grabbed his arm. "For God's sake, Bart, tell Miss Anna. Explain to her why she cannot possibly join an orgy."

"Stop, my friend! I'm not the right person to convince Anna of something like that. I believe every woman has the right to make her own decisions regarding when, and where, and with whom, she indulges herself in pleasure for the first time. But, Anna, my dear girl, I will say, have a care with your reputation. This place could ruin you in minutes if anyone discovered your identity."

"Humph! My reputation no longer matters though, does it, gentlemen? Not if what you've told me about my captain is true. If he truly is a cad, I cannot marry him. Yet, what other man will want me?" Thomas opened his mouth to speak but no words came out. Bart groaned and looked heavenward the same way Chrissie had watched Justin do on several occasions. Looking to the sky for inspiration.

"Thomas, you great slow- witted oaf," Bart said to his friend, "that's what is commonly called a leading question. A woman's way of bringing a man to heel. To get him to voice his approval of her."

Chrissie peeked around the tree trunk and watched comprehension slowly seep into Thomas's brain. Bart waited, a hopeful look on his face. Anna stared at Thomas, her eyes wide with excitement and appeal. Thomas remained silent and Chrissie felt an urge to giggle at the ridiculous situation.

"Heaven preserve me," Bart muttered, "I imagine it's now up to me to save the situation. And to save Miss Anna any further embarrassment." He turned to Anna and took her hand. "Miss Anna, it would be my great privilege to educate you in any matters you wish to learn, be they mildly sensual or wildly erotic. I'm known to be rather an expert in both. And, as a gentleman, I'll not press the point. You may call a halt to our little adventure whenever you feel uncomfortable, as I for one, still believe most girls are happier going to their marriage night as a virgin."

"Balderdash, Bart," Thomas exclaimed. "The only reason you leave virgins alone is because you can't bear the thought of being leg-shackled to one of those young innocent chits who'd bore you to tears in a night."

Far from being insulted, Bart grinned like a cheeky schoolboy. "There is that, of course. But if Miss Anna feels she wishes to learn more, or if she feels this is the appropriate place, I shall endeavor to overcome my normal reservations about virgins. I'd be delighted to conduct her experiments." Bart flung his arms wide and smiled at Anna. "Take me, my dear, my body is yours to do with as you wish."

"No, no!" Thomas blustered in horror. "Absolutely not. We may be friends, Bart, but I'd never trust you with the sensual initiation of someone as sweet and innocent as Miss Anna. If she so desperately needs to experiment with a man tonight, it should be with someone like me." Anna's eyes went wide and her mouth pursed. "Someone who cares for her," Thomas added, warming to his subject. "Yes, I feel I'm the perfect one for Miss Anna. After all, I've spent as much time at Justin's Sultan Palace and our beloved Viscount's Pleasure House as you have. I may have a trick or two of my own to show Anna."

Thomas turned to face Anna with a grave expression, one that Bart was certain belied the rising excitement his friend felt. Even if Thomas wasn't ready to admit it, he was in love. Head over heels in love with the pretty girl staring at him with adoring calf's eyes.

"Miss Anna, I believe I'm the best choice of partner for you here tonight. I vow to protect you from all the vices displayed everywhere. I'll allow you to ask any questions you may have regarding the relationships between a man and a woman."

Chrissie heard Bart's slap on his friend's back and sighed with relief. Things were going to come right for Anna after all.

As Bart walked away, Chrissie heard Anna say, "Oh, Thomas, how big and strong and manly you are tonight in that costume. Why, I do believe the muscles on your arms are larger than any other man's here tonight. Even large Matthew."

Chrissie smiled. Anna had come out of her shell. And sweet Thomas was in good hands.

15

The next morning, a line-up of carriages pulled around to the front entrance of the estate, ready to convey Chrissie and her friends to their homes and Justin, Bart, and Thomas back to London. Justin had sent the other paying guests on their way the evening before, deprived them of even their last night at the Pleasure House.

He'd dispatched them without notice after becoming overly sickened by the level of debauchery some of his cruder guests had suggested. Their new ideas for even wilder romps, to include his new members of staff, had proved the final insult. The drunken revelers had finally followed his advice, and his not-so-subtle hints, and driven away in a raucous group to spend a night at the nearest inn where the hostelry benefited from wealthy peers eager to pay for the company of bar maids and stable hands in their beds.

Free of those responsibilities, he'd encouraged Chrissie and her friends, along with Thomas and Edward and not to mention Bart and his new fancy, Magdalena, to stay another night and enjoy their seclusion. The eight of them had spent a quieter night, breakfasted and then walked through his grounds to the lake, rejoicing in their few last moments of serenity before setting out on their respective journeys.

Justin took Chrissie's hand and drew her aside. "Come with me."

Without giving her a chance to argue, he led her down the path and away from the other six, who were so engrossed in each other they failed to realize two of their party had slipped away. They walked, hand in hand, around the edge of the old maze and climbed the steps of the white-washed summerhouse. Standing on the edge of a small pond, Justin's favorite retreat was less than half the size of the lake the others visited, but beautiful nonetheless.

Justin kept a firm clasp on Chrissie's hand and when they reached the top and stood in privacy near the ornate fret-work railing, he swung her about and dipped his head to hers. His mouth closed over hers with a hunger that seemed ridiculous considering she'd spent the night in his bed.

He'd claimed her, over and over. Attempted to show her, with his hands and mouth rather than any of the false-sounding words of flattery she abhorred, how much he enjoyed her body. How aroused he became each time she screamed out her pleasure as he brought her to one peak after another until she'd collapsed, limp and satisfied, in his arms. How his own climaxes had been stronger and far more important to him than any of the hundreds he'd had in recent years.

He hoped she knew. Prayed she'd understood his silent messages. Because with Chrissie none of his usual glib speech was relevant. With her, between them, there needed to be only truths.

"Oh, bloody hell, I miss you already."

He pulled her tightly against his body and thrust one leg between her thighs. Already aroused, he moved against her in a mimicking motion of what he wanted to do to her. What he'd done to her several times in the past twelve hours. Though it still wasn't enough.

He wanted her again. Now! Despite knowing he needed to use the information on his family's whereabouts that Chrissie had provided and set out to bring them back to their former home. He shouldn't be thinking of anything but restoring them to their rightful place in London.

She drew back to smile at him, reached up, and touched his face. "How could you miss me? I've been with you."

"Oh, yes, silly me. How could I forget?" Justin declared with heavy sarcasm. "We breakfasted together. Just you and I. With Edward and Gillian acting as if they married just yesterday. Thomas grinning from ear to ear and ready to kiss Anna's feet each time she moved or spoke. Bart leering like a fool down Magdalena's neckline with every movement she made. Not to mention the three footmen who served us breakfast, plus the butler and various maids."

When she laughed, he frowned. "You, my dear, have a very strange sense of humor. I didn't find it in the least amusing."

"Oh, but it was funny. If you could have seen your face when Bart decided he wanted Magdalena to join us in the breakfast room. And then she felt too embarrassed to come and sit with us there, unless all the others ..."

"Yes, yes. Unless the other thirty people I employed for last night's performance were also invited to join us. Good Lord. The bloody room was busier than the Stock Exchange when a new share package is released."

She giggled, a girlish sound that sent renewed desire straight to his loins. Although everything she did, or said, seemed to have a similar effect and excited him to fever pitch. The terrifying part was not knowing if she shared his intensity of feelings. He'd dragged her out here because he dreaded spending the days until he next saw her tormented by insecurities and doubts. He needed some indication of her thoughts, her feelings.

"You loved every minute of it," she said, waving an admonishing finger, "so don't pretend you didn't. You love your friends dearly, and you'd do anything for them."

"True. Without Bart and Thomas, I wouldn't have survived the agony of following up lead after lead while trying to locate my family. So many dead ends. So many loose threads that unraveled whenever I came close to solving the mystery."

Her face crinkled and she bit down on her lip, expressions of sympathy that earned her another quick kiss. And then another flick of his tongue across the reddened patch on her lip to soothe it.

"I really did miss you," he murmured as he nibbled the lobe of her tempting ear, "for those three agonizing hours this morning when I was forced to play lord of the realm for the staff."

She swished her skirts against his legs, shimmied closer, and pressed against his groin, stirring him instantly to semi arousal. "Chrissie," he murmured in a raspy tone, "if you continue doing that you'll be tossed to your back on the grass, and in two shakes I'll lift your skirts and—" He broke off and took a step backwards without letting go of her forearms.

"Are you wearing petticoats this time?" She nodded, a small smile of amusement dimpling her cheeks. Once again, he abandoned his questions and kissed each little dent in her face, nuzzled each tiny hollow. "Drawers?"

In a slow, teasing motion, she shook her head from side to side. He moaned, grasped two handfuls of skirts, and lifted them to her waist. He extended his hand downwards to trail a finger through her soft curls, and kissed her again, deeper. His tongue thrust into her mouth, over and over, until she trembled and shuddered. He eased her onto the wide ledge around the viewing window, lifted her a little so she could sit securely there and lean back against a post.

"I don't want you to fall," he murmured, before he dipped beneath her petticoats. Using his thumbs, he separated her folds and sighed. He popped his head back up high enough to look her in the eyes. "You're so beautiful there. So pink and wet, and glistening in the sunlight. Do you know what I'm about to do to you?"

Her eyes went wide and she swallowed and shook her head.

"I'm going to taste you. Lick up your love juices, savor them, and swallow them down so that for the next few days when I can't see you, I'll remember what you look and taste like. How sweet and salty and delicious you are down here."

He swiped his tongue over her from bottom to top, held still her thighs when she squirmed under his invasion. This may be new to

Chrissie but the wriggles of her plump white bottom, plus the extra moisture that ran from her crevice and dribbled down her thigh told him how much she liked it. As he applied himself to her sweet little nub, now swollen and risen to meet his tongue's invasion, her breathing became small rapid pants. She pushed up with her hips, a silent demand for him to continue.

He felt more than happy to oblige and knew he'd be happy to oblige her every whim sexually for the next fifty or sixty odd years. Leaving his fingers to do the work where his mouth had been, he shifted up toward her mouth once more. He let her taste her own essence on his lips, their two flavors mingling. The same way he wanted them to mix and blend for a long time to come. "Come for me, my sweet," he murmured close to her ear. "Let me see it once more before you leave."

When the peak of pleasure hit her, she grabbed at him and held his shoulders while she rode it out. He nuzzled, kissed, and held her, and it felt so good, so right.

After a few minutes, he raised his head and looked her in the eye. "Chrissie, I realize this probably isn't the time or place to ask this, but I need to know. You still haven't told me everything about why you came to me, why you did this."

She dropped her gaze and hid her face. When she finally spoke, her words shocked him. Never in his wildest dreams had he expected this.

"You didn't remember me and I didn't expect you to, though I knew you as I was a friend of your sisters. That's why, when I heard what had happened to them, that your mother had taken the girls away before your father passed on to protect them, I was concerned. Worried." She shrugged. "I don't know why, but some instinct told me I needed to find them. I'd been asking questions around the village for some time before I knew about you."

He raised an eyebrow. "Hmm. And how did you come to hear about me? I've been wondering that."

She gave him a small smile. "That was a stroke of luck. Your prowess was spoken about, even in our small corner of the country, by women who came to visit from the city. You have many admirers."

"Hell! I had no idea."

She gave another shrug. "Women confined to country entertainments for weeks at a time tend to discuss anything and everything. It helps pass the time and avoid total ennui."

"I remembered we were neighbors, but little else."

"Distant neighbors, yes. While you were away at school, I often stayed with your sisters but only occasionally when you were home after term finished."

His eyes went wide. "My God. You're Tiny Tina, the one who used to follow me around like a puppy."

A red flush spread up her neck and onto her face. "I've tried to forget that time in my life. I was a typical silly girl who had a large crush on an older boy."

"But then you were there when I was older too. When I was at university."

"I hoped you'd have forgotten about that too. I used to watch you, you know, when you went to visit the innkeeper 's daughter in the village. You waited until her father was busy serving and the two of you would sneak around the corner of the barn. You kissed her. There was also the widow down road you paid regular visits to."

He closed his eyes with an embarrassed groan. "I'm not sure I need to hear anymore. I feel a fool. I'd no idea you knew. Did my sisters also know all this?"

"Of course. How else could I sneak away from your mother? We planned it together, all our little adventures. The side window on Widow Jensen's house still hasn't been repaired and men still climb in her window at night."

"Good God! She was a mature woman even then." He grinned and gave her a quick pecking kiss. "But very, very experienced. A wonderful teacher for a green young man trying to prove his sexual worth before his friends. How the hell does she still manage to entice men to her bed now?"

"Ah, well, rumor has it that Widow Jensen used to be a highly paid London courtesan before she married her husband. So the young men of the district still rely upon her expertise to teach them before they venture up to town for their first bachelor season."

"I'm afraid, Chrissie, I cannot remember trying to steal a kiss from you. Did I?"

"Oh, goodness, yes. You tried with every girl for miles around. But after that one memorable kiss, you ignored me."

"Not entirely. I did watch you sneak down to the pond one day to swim nude with my sisters. Gave me all sorts of ideas about what girls' bodies looked like, and all the delectable things I might do with them. Unfortunately, my father discovered my spy hole in the hedge. Made sure I understood dallying with any of my sisters' friends would be the quickest way to end up married, long before I'd enjoyed bachelorhood. I left home straight after that."

"Yes, you did. No one was allowed to discuss the real reason you left but everyone knew of your father 's cruelty, so it took little to put the pieces of the puzzle together. To be truthful, for many years I indulged myself with the fantasy that you became my lover, instead of Widow Jensen's."

"And now we have become lovers."

She gave him a strange look, a long considering one that worried him. "Yes, you've fulfilled my every fantasy. We can part friends and I can return to my ordinary life. And you can start a new life with your family."

"What do you mean we can stay friends? We're a lot more than that, Chrissie, and you can't deny it. Last night was amazing. There's no reason we can't keep on seeing each other."

"Justin, there are dozens of reasons. For one, I live mainly in the country, a very quiet life. Secondly, your mother and sisters will be back living with you very soon." She stared at the water. "Then you'll need to marry a suitably titled girl who isn't scarred by her history." She waved her hand, a show of nonchalance he didn't believe. Between these dire pronouncements she swallowed hard, each time, and telling him the words didn't come easily. "And then, naturally, you'll be required to produce the expected heir and spare."

"Then you could marry me. Give me those children."

Her face creased with lines of distress. "No, Justin, no. It would be unfair to you. I didn't conceive during my marriage. Chance are I'll never bear a child. It's best we go our separate ways. After we're assured that your family is safe and well, returned to your home, there'll be no need for us to contact each other."

He opened his mouth to deny everything she said, yet couldn't summon any convincing arguments quickly enough. His chest ached with unvoiced emotions. With any other woman, he'd have kissed her cheek, thanked her for the night they'd spent together, and walked away. Or in earlier days when he desperately needed money, he'd have continued a casual liaison whenever it suited them both. The thought of never seeing Chrissie again, or only as a meeting of glances as they twirled down the length of a ballroom didn't sit well. He shuddered at visions of having to pretend to his future Countess of Hawkesbury that he and Chrissie were passing acquaintances, nothing more. Unfairly, she seemed determined to bid him farewell here and now and then to walk away without looking back. Did she not feel it as he did? Did she not feel the heart's wrench he suffered when she mentioned parting?

He stood and stared at her until she touched his arm and broke into his thoughts.

"Justin, let us part as friends and let the future eventuate as it will."

Left with no choice, he nodded, helped right her clothing and lift her down.

"Justin," she said softly, reaching down to run a caressing hand over the noticeable bulge in his trousers. "Do you want me to relieve you?" She squeezed gently and he sucked in a sharp breath.

Oh, hell yes, he wanted her hand on him. Though not like this, and not after she'd announced they wouldn't see each other in the future. In a snap of perverseness, he decided if he wasn't good enough for her bed, then he didn't want a quick tug and release in his summerhouse. A pity climax wouldn't be enough, and would be bound to leave him feeling even more frustrated and thwarted.

He removed her hand and shook his head, although he was unable to summon a pleasant demeanor as they walked back to join the others. Consequently, the air was so thick with an unprecedented tension between them it was a miracle he could even draw a breath.

Time to get away from here before he did something also unprecedented, and fundamentally stupid, and fall to his knees before a woman and beg her to stay.

16

---

our weeks later, Viscount Hawkesbury again walked to the summerhouse on his estate. This time he was accompanied by three different women—his mother and his two sisters. True to her word, Chrissie had traced the whereabouts of his family fairly rapidly, despite his mother hiding behind her maiden name in the village where they were living in seclusion.

A runaway wife was illegal under British law and frowned upon by small-minded people, so she'd presented herself as a widow to save scorn being heaped upon the head of not only her, but also her two daughters. As his mother had explained, they'd settled in a place they liked and where they were accepted, and decided to stay.

When they heard rumors of his father 's drunken fall and perhaps even his death, they'd tried to make discreet enquiries. They'd feared making open enquiries in case it proved yet another trick by their father to find them and drag them home. Not because he wanted his wife and daughters around for any loving reasons, more to ensure their solicitor believed the countess to still be alive. The inheritance coming to her from a doting great- uncle held stipulations that it was not to be given to her fortune- seeking husband under any circumstances.

If she died, the money would be held in trust until her son and daughters could be located. Lady Hawkesbury had thought it better to wait until they could be sure either her greedy husband was dead or they could assure themselves that Justin had returned. Or more importantly, that he had not changed to become tarred with the same brush as his father.

Justin now knew his elder sister had taken a post teaching at the local school and was eager to assist at the village school near his estate. His younger sister had also been ill with the same fever that had affected his mother so badly, and was now enjoying a more restful life walking and riding the fields.

Previously, the three women had vowed to stay hidden in their low-key lives on the assumption Justin may have perished when on his eastern travels as no word had come from him for so many years. For his own part, Justin had stayed away because he thought his father still lived, and his mother hadn't written to him because she'd no desire to see him return home. No wish for the resumption of tiring family conflicts. He lamented the time they'd all wasted at cross- purposes but he now had a chance to put things right. Consequently, his last month had been tempered with high and low points.

Having his family returned lifted an enormous burden from his shoulders, both mentally and financially, and allowed some joy to fill the dark recesses of his heart. However, the consequences of Chrissie severing contact with him prayed on his mind every day as he rode the fields and made new plans for the estate. Plans that should be including his future wife. The torment of giving up her body, and the passion they'd briefly shared, saw him tossing and turning each night in his lonely bed.

Their last meeting had been brief, and crowded with people. Before he'd known it, Chrissie had declared it time for her to depart and leave him to enjoy the comfort of his newfound family. She'd left him bemused, confused, and devastated. Now, he sat with his mother in his drawing room and tried to divert his thoughts from spinning back to Chrissie too many times every hour. An impossible task.

"Mother, I've been foolish, and I've made so many mistakes.

Chrissie— Lady Wellsby—was right to run from me, wasn't she? I mean, what could a man like me offer a lady like her? I've done nothing for years but disappoint others."

His mother raised her eyes from her sewing and shook her head. She looked utterly fetching in one of her newly purchased gowns from London and totally different from the scared shadow of a woman she used to be. The band around his heart eased a little more each time she smiled, each time she added a little more food to her plate at meal times and a little more flesh to her thin frame. And those times he now caught her admiring herself and her new clothing in a mirror without fear of being discovered and ridiculed, his own spine stiffened. He stood a little taller, felt a little prouder. At least this woman who had given birth to him could now hold her head high without fear of having an eye blackened or a sleeve ripped from a dress.

"Utter rubbish, my dear boy," she said with a fond smile. "You've never disappointed me, or you sisters. You searched for us all this time. If not for your love and persistence, we would still be living in a poor cottage and Lucille would still be coughing. We owe you so much."

"You're my family. And I had a large debt to repay to all of you for leaving you to face father 's wrath without me."

"Justin, do not beat your breast upon our account. We understood why you needed to leave. It was either that or die on the gallows for murdering your own father, which would have been much harder to bear. And I've not forgotten the number of times you stepped between your father's fist and my face. Nor the beatings you took for one of the girls."

"I couldn't let that bastard continue to lay his hands on you. I regret I couldn't stay longer and protect you until he was dead."

"It matters little, my son, as after you left he was a changed man. You had stood up to him and threatened his manhood. As a bully, he was unable to continue to use force on us as he lived with the knowledge of your threat to come back and kill him if he touched us again. You spared us anymore misery for those last months."

He dipped his head in acknowledgement of his mother 's praise and the look of love she bestowed upon him. "I'm glad at least in that small way I was successful."

"And we're also grateful to Lady Wellsby. We're indebted for everything she did to bring the three of us back home."

He closed his eyes. He, too, owed Chrissie and he'd never had the chance to thank her properly. "Yes, Lady Wellsby is a very generous woman. Loyal to her friends, and kind to others less fortunate."

His mother raised a brow at him. "If we're agreed she's a remarkable young woman, why, my dearest boy, are you still here? Why haven't you gone to ask for her hand in marriage?"

"It's a complicated situation, Mama. She didn't believe me serious in my intentions, and I … I couldn't rid myself of the stink of my old reputation."

Chrissie believed he merely lusted after her body, as he'd either done or pretended to do with many, many others. Certainly physical attraction was part of it, because their lovemaking had stirred a passion in him he'd never experienced before her. Yet, the largest part of his yearning to be with her was to gain her respect, her love.

His mother reached over and touched his arm. "Justin, if you love her, prove it to her. Make her realize she means a lot more to you than your normal passing affair."

He chuckled. "Mama, I'm not certain this is the correct conversation for a mother to have with her adult son, one reputed to be a scoundrel. Nevertheless, I thank you for your council. If only I could convince myself I deserved her, I'd chase after her in the blink of an eye."

"And what of Chrissie? Did you ask her what she wanted before you let her leave? I saw the way you looked at each other, Justin, and it warmed my heart to see the love that flowed between you. Are you going to sit and mourn for what might have been? That's not the stubborn and single-minded boy I remember. Don't let her escape, Justin. Not if you truly love her. Take a chance she feels the same way, or at least give her a chance to deny it."

He gave her a small hesitant smile. "You're right. I've always fought for everything. Why am I not fighting for her, for the woman I love?" He jumped to his feet and grinned, more light-hearted than he'd felt in weeks. "If you'll excuse me for a short time, I have a pressing matter in the city that requires my immediate attention."

His mother smiled. "Go, my darling, go. Court her, woo her. Do anything you can to get her to marry you. Use the seductive charm the notorious Virile Viscount became famous for."

"Good God, Mother! Where did you hear about that name?"

She laughed. "Sweetheart, mothers always discover everything about their offspring. We have clandestine methods."

Justin laughed. "Now you're terrifying me."

As he strode from the house, he felt enervated for the first time in days by having a productive plan in his mind. What did he have to lose? Nothing—except perhaps his dignity. Pride he'd long since abandoned. Having to make his money by catering to the sexual whims of the rich had made him acutely aware that beneath their expensive clothes was the same flesh and blood as every ordinary man. Arrogance and conceit mattered little if it meant he'd spend his life alone, without her, without Chrissie. The woman who filled his mind and soul and made his body yearn.

At the stables, he ordered his horse to be readied, arranged for his bags to be packed as quickly as possible and sent by carriage to his London house. Then he drafted a letter, the most important missive of his life. When it was finally done and his first two attempts nothing more that crumpled sheets of vellum in the fireplace, he bid farewell to his family. With a much lighter heart, he rode away from the estate, eager to start on his plans to secure his future.

He refused to consider the possibility she'd ignore his invitation. After all, she'd already visited the Sultan's Place one night in disguise, so he saw no reason for her to balk at his chosen venue, or his command. Come at midnight and wear the red dress. Nothing else!

After he arrived at his town house, he'd need to move quickly to put his plans in place as he'd have little time to prepare for their forthcoming night and he wanted it to be perfect. He spent the ride deep in thought about the best way to seduce a woman who'd, not long before, declared herself incapable of being lured into passion and intimacy.

He'd taken great delight in disproving her beliefs, and tonight he'd also dispel any ideas she clung to about being past marrying age, or even past bearing children. Not that the latter particularly worried him, because after dealing with prostitutes for so many years, more than anyone, he knew the number of unwanted babies given away each year. They could fill his house with a dozen adopted babies and he'd be outside himself with happiness. As long as Chrissie was there to be their mother. To be his wife.

In his mind, he planned her seduction, something to shock her out of country complacency and yet maintain her ingrained conservatism. He'd control himself, not leap upon her body like a starving lion, but take his time in wining and dining her. Soften her up and fill her belly with course after course of exquisitely prepared French delicacies. Mellow her mind with champagne and wine. When she was replete and relaxed and her physical needs attended to, he'd lead her to his row of prepared activity rooms to feast her sensual senses. He'd need the help of his friends, and possibly every available staff member he could muster at short notice.

Ah! And, of course, Matthew the Large should take center stage. Because no matter how much Chrissie had denied it, her eyes had almost popped out of her head when she'd viewed Matthew servicing two women. He smiled in remembrance. His prim and proper lady experienced a complete change of character whenever she was treated to a visual feast, despite men supposedly being the more visually oriented of the two sexes and women more attuned to emotions. Nevertheless, the Virile Viscount knew how to delve into the recesses of a female's mind and read her thoughts, so he'd discovered Chrissie's secret fantasy.

Lady Wellsby dreamed of being swept up in a whirlpool of sex, to have it happen all around her at a vigorous pace, to be surrounded by sin and debauchery, to be close enough to it to reach out and touch it. And she wanted it all without being physically caught up in it. Watching, considering, absorbing, followed by touching and tasting.

Oh, yes! He thrust his fist upwards to the sky. His hard-earned reputation as the foremost authority on sexual sins in the whole of London would prove useful. If anyone could arrange the perfect night for a perfect princess, it was he, notorious Hawkesbury.

Sheer bravado carried him through the rest of his busy day while he sent servants scurrying all over London delivering messages and calling in favors. At fifteen minutes past the witching hour of midnight, he paced the foyer of the Sultan's Palace and checked his pocket watch for the twentieth time. He'd tugged it from his fob pocket so many times, Bart advised him to leave it dangling from its Prince Albert style gold chain. Otherwise, his high and mighty valet would be reduced to the lowly task of mending clothing.

When a radiant Gillian had arrived with Edward an hour ago and announced they may be anticipating a happy event not too far in the future, he'd attempted to send them home. But even Edward, resplendent in his rich red waistcoat, an exact match for his wife's gown, had stood firm.

"No, Hawkesbury, my countess and I owe you a great deal. You saved our marriage and have possibly hastened the arrival of another addition to our family. Gillian's mother has been dispatched and order returned to our home. You wanted everyone here dressed in red, and here we are. Although I must say, red simply is not my best color."

"But for Chrissie," Gillian said in a rush, "we'd gladly dress in old rags."

The party seemed almost jovial, especially when Anna joined them. Accompanied by a beaming Thomas, the pair was also attired in shades of red, and, added to Bart's brilliant red hunting coat, they created a fiery vision.

The group ignored Justin's half-hearted protests that he didn't expect them to participate in the festivities but vowed they'd come to support him in his quest to win over Chrissie; they refused to leave until they witnessed her acceptance of his betrothal ring. Justin sagged with gratitude. The waiting was unbearable, but with this show of solidarity from her friends, he allowed himself to feel a glimmer of hope.

He clung to a positive attitude. She would accept him. She must. That optimism carried him through another anxious ten minutes until Bart, standing as lookout at the house's front window called out, "A carriage has arrived." He peered out to the street again. "She's here. And she's wearing red."

Justin sucked in a breath and said, "Let the show begin."

Amidst a chorus of "Good luck," he strode to the door to greet his last guest. He tugged down his own red waistcoat and adjusted the ostentatious ruby pin fixing his cravat in place. The formality above his waist looked out of place with his wide harem trousers but the ruby pin was a gesture of defiance to his father who'd defiled the Hawkesbury titles. And also a bolster to his self- esteem in his attempt to convince Chrissie he could play the part of titled gentleman and mix with the higher echelons of society when the occasion arose.

If they married ... no! Be positive. When they married, she'd expect her husband to take some part in the social arena that bored him, but that he'd been driven to mixing in out of desperation for quick funds. Although if he had Chrissie at his side, and in his arms, he'd take a new perspective on evenings spent talking and dancing.

He yearned to have her back in his arms in any, and every, way possible.

17

J ustin sucked in a raw breath at the sight of the lady who entered through the doors of the Sultan's Palace. He'd deliberately retained ownership of this house of pleasure for one last night, though he'd restricted entrance to all but his special guests. And to the beautiful and desirable lady crossing the greeting parlor.

When he'd planned this, he'd not expected his first glimpse of her to suck the air out of his lungs in quite such a dramatic fashion. He'd imagined being excited and aroused in her presence, though he'd not imagined seeing her would send his well-known control skittering out the door. With effortless grace and a regal air, the red-gowned lady swept past him. She ignored his frozen immobility, and open- mouthed awe, and strode toward the receiving room to greet her friends.

Wafting perfume filled his nostrils and he inhaled, drew her essence into his lungs like a drinker sucking up his first ale of the day. His senses filled and swam with the sight and smell of her. Damnation, he acted like a mindless idiot around her. Scurrying after her, he caught her arm to pull her to a halt. But his steps faltered, slowed, and ceased all motion. He gulped, stared down at her neckline. Christ, once again the lady had out-witted him.

"What ... what ... did you do to that gown?"

She glanced down at herself, gave a nonchalant shrug, spread her arms out wide. The gesture sent the slashed to the waist gown even lower on her bosom, where the fabric caught and held on her nipples alone. A deep slice of bare skin shone, tempted and taunted, between the two sides of fiery red silk.

"This old thing?"

She wiggled and tilted forward to smooth down an imaginary crease on the skirt but he noticed the gleam in her eyes before she bent. Ah, a deliberate move then. This time, she'd kill him for sure. From his higher angle, his view was directly of her nipples, twin ruby peaks barely held inside the rich red silk of her bodice. The two rounded buds wavered for ten long seconds, as if deciding whether to retreat and hide or tip out into his waiting palms.

Closing his eyes, he threw back his head and moaned. "Why me? Why am I destined to be tormented this way?"

"I do hope, my darling," she said, touching his face to bring his gaze back to hers, "you're not going to waste precious time doing that groaning thing again." She softened her words with a smile, stretched up to her toes to touch his lips, butterflies wings flitting softly. "You know, those pleas and moans you insist on directing at angels frolicking across your ceiling."

For the first time in weeks, he relaxed his tensed muscles and let a true grin split his face. He understood the significance of her slashing a piece out of the already daring neckline of the red gown. Or at least, he hoped he interpreted her meaning correctly.

Lady Christina Wellsby wanted him and was sending him a clear signal, one even an obtuse idiot such as himself couldn't fail to comprehend. He chuckled. Perhaps she also sent another message, one to tell him he'd stupidly missed too many cues before. Misunderstood the depth of her feelings for him when she'd given herself to him, body and soul, in the harem tent at the Pleasure House.

Bloody hell! He cursed slow wit and the time he'd wasted. As notorious Hawkesbury, he'd prided himself on grasping every nuance of women's convoluted thinking and had believed his best asset to be an instinctive knowledge of how best to respond, or act, to gain whatever suited him best. And yet now, when it mattered most, he'd wasted precious weeks prevaricating. He'd sat in the fields with his sisters as, like playful children, they'd sung an old song and plucked petals from daisies. She loves me, she loves me not.

A huge grin split his face. "Cupids," he murmured, glancing once again at the sheer fabric inserted across her bosom in the place of impenetrable lace and ruffles.

One layer of red organza wasn't nearly enough to hide such bountiful assets from a rogue's eager eyes. In fact, his eyes were so eager to devour every inch of this magnificent woman they could have penetrated several layers of this flimsy fabric.

He swallowed again, hard, before risking a quick sniff near her neck. "Ah! A lavender day. My favorite."

"I beg your pardon?"

He laughed and shook his head. "Mere mutterings of a besotted idiot, my dear. Ignore them." Taking her red-gloved hand, he raised it to his lips for a kiss. "However, my beautiful lady, before I can allow you to enter my harem tonight, I fear I must correct your misassumption. On the ceiling in all my rooms, I have cupids painted. They symbolize purity and innocence and joviality and ... "

A finger trailed down his cheek, making him shiver, as she leaned closer to whisper, "And love? I've always sensed love when I stand under your cupids. Do you remember the first night when I came to your library and you appealed to your sage cupids?"

"Oh, sweetheart, I remember everything about us. Every moment and every touch. And, Chrissie, I want more, lots more." Their gazes met and held and something passed between them, something intense, wonderful, and special. Everything faded except the reality of the two of them begin together again." I notice your red gown is still too small."

She glanced down again and drew his eyes down with hers. Unable to help himself, he ran his fingers over the puckered nipples pouting through the sheer red fabric. Backwards and forwards, until her breath came in short pants and his arousal swelled painfully. She pushed her groin against his and in the space of a breath, his control slipped faster down the slippery slope toward insanity.

"Tell me why, my love. Why you've come to me as you were before, with your breasts spilling over your bodice and begging me to take them into my mouth. I need to hear you say it."

"When I first read your letter, I immediately thought no, no, no. I'm far too old to risk marriage again. Too settled in my spinster existence to enter an unpredictable, yet permanent, relationship. My biggest worry was that I might rob you of the chance to have a child. Or children, lots of them, as every man with your titles is expected to do."

"Chrissie, if we cannot have a child of our own, there are many, many children we can take into our lives and create a family with. The most important thing to consider is us, and what will make us happiest."

"That's why I came here, Justin. I tried really, really hard to convince myself marriage wouldn't be good for either of us. Most especially for you. But I discovered that deep down I'm not a good person—"

"Chrissie, you're amazing," he said, taking her hands in his. "The most wonderful person I've ever encountered."

She shook her head. "No, I'm not. I'm selfish. I want you. Far too much to do the right thing and give you up. You've no idea, Justin, of the thoughts that now rush through my head. All hours of the day and night. Of all the things I want to do to your body. To do with you."

He snorted. "Believe me, my love, I've a fair idea. I'm continually distracted from my accounts by picturing how you'd look bent over every piece of furniture in my office. I go to bed and wish you were there, tied to my bedposts. Never able to escape. Never wanting to escape. Begging me to plunge inside your dripping pussy and fill you to the hilt. I can't even hide it anymore. Bart and Thomas think it's amusing that my balls ache all day and that I'm reduced to using my hand each night to relieve myself."

She smiled. "Really? And I imagined I was the only one suffering. Though I should warn you, I'm likely to be voracious, to resemble a gluttonous pig in my need for you. The thought of any other women having you in their lives, or in their beds, is too much for me to contemplate."

She ran her hands, now divested of gloves, around his bare waist and under his embossed red vest. Her nails dug into his back, an exquisite pain, as she clasped him in a demonstration of her need.

"So, I thought if I could become the sort of woman you wanted, the wild, barely there red- chiffon type, you may be prepared to over-look my many faults and flaws. Ignore what a greedy, grasping person I've turned into since encountering you again."

Justin threw back his head and laughed, relief making his body go limp, before he recovered enough to slide his arms around her waist and tug her as close as possible to his eager body. Widening his stance, he pulled her into his crotch and let her feel his arousal, his own need and want.

"No. I don't think I can overlook your greed. Not if it means you want to be with me as badly as I need you in my life. Oh, my love," he dropped his head to kiss her, "I want nothing more than to have you, faults and all, as long you'll accept me with all of my past indiscretions." Keeping hold of one hand, he dropped to his knees before her. "I love you, Chrissie. So much. Will you please, please, marry me?"

As he raised his gaze to hers, two fat tears plopped from her eyes onto his cheeks. His heart ceased beating. Did this mean he'd upset her again? Would she refuse him even now when he'd laid bare his soul for her?

With a loud sob, she fell to her knees in front of him and wrapped her arms around his neck. Her shoulders heaved as she cried, loudly and wetly. His chest tightened and his heart skipped another beat as he forced himself to wait. He'd misinterpreted her motives, her actions, before and he was determined to not make the same mistakes. Beneath his titled head, he felt her give a small nod, and then she nodded again, and again until they were both nodding and shaking and holding onto each other for support.

"Are you saying ...," he said, his voice sounding wispy and uncertain. "Is that a yes?"

"Yes, yes. A thousand times yes."

He clasped her face between two hands and kissed her deeply, his lips moving with hunger over her open and eager mouth, his tongue searching for and finding hers in an age-old mating game. Their breaths rose and fell in unison, short pants between bouts of kisses he didn't want to end. Their upper limbs were entwined and their lower bodies pressed together, his hard penis pushed so tightly into her groin she'd be left in no doubt of the desperate state of his arousal. He slid one hand behind her derriere and tried to push her against him even harder still, anything to relieve a little of the incessant pulse and ache in his shaft.

Visions of the beds above them swam into his mind, if only he could summon the where-with-all to stand with her and carry her there. He wanted to lay her back on the red carpet and spread the flimsy bodice apart so his eyes could truly feast on the offerings of her breasts. So his mouth could feed on her cherry nipples, so his hands could wander over bare skin, soft and pliant.

He wanted— oh, God, he wanted everything at once.

Loud clapping sounded from behind them. Startled, they pulled apart a few inches and turned to the noise. Damnation. Only then did he remember the group who hovered in the outer room, only then did he realize they'd moved closer into the drawing room to watch them. He'd been so caught up within their small arena of love he'd completely forgotten the rest of the world existed.

He gave a self-derogatory laugh as he helped Chrissie to her feet. "When you walked toward me in that indecent gown, I forgot everything else. Completely forgot about the romance part of this evening I'd planned."

He waved his hand to indicate their audience and the room decorations. Red flowers overflowed huge vases, and rose petals strewn down the center created a trail to take Chrissie from room to room. "We didn't get past the receiving room. Even my poorest paying customers advance to the larger drawing room."

Her head was still partly buried against his chest, yet he heard muffled chuckles that grew from giggles into loud laughter. Around them, her friends joined in with a chorus of happy laughter as Gillian and Anna rushed forward to hug them.

When he was finally able to get a word in over the chatter of the excited ladies, he said, "I've arranged dinner, and performances, and even Matthew. Anything and everything I could think of to mellow your mood, Chrissie. I wanted you relaxed for the end of the evening when I proposed to you, so you'd be content, blissful, and ready to accept me as your husband." He looked around and groaned. "Yet here we are, standing in the entrance of the last brothel I will ever own and I have a fiancée whom I adore." He sucked in a long slow breath and spoke directly to his new bride-to-be. "And it's the happiest moment of my life."

She smiled at him. "Mine too, my lord. Mine too."

Unable to help himself, he kissed her again and another loud cheer broke out from their audience. "Do you want to see the performances?" he asked, half afraid of her answer.

He wanted Chrissie to experience every sexual adventure she'd missed in her life, and yet, at the same time knew jealousy would make him long to rip the arms from the sockets of any other man who touched her body. He swallowed hard, forced himself to continue. After all, this was the grand finale, the big climax to her evening of pleasure.

"I've had the entire staff costumed in red tonight in deference of you, and to the red room, the one final room in my house of pleasure you've not visited."

Chrissie grinned cheekily but before she answered, Anna called out. "You're correct, Justin, much to our regret you whisked us away before we'd completed our tour of the rooms."

Thomas exclaimed, "I say, Anna, I thought in light of our recent—

"

"Friendship?" Bart asked with an ironic lift to his brow.

Thomas glared at him. "I was speaking of my close relationship with Anna, in light of which I'd rather Justin didn't show her the red room."

"Oh, how intriguing," Gillian said. "May I, as a married woman, see it?"

"No," Edward said with a snap. "I shall gladly demonstrate, at home, anything you might see there." He held up an imperious hand. "Not that I've ever viewed the infamous red room, mind you. I wouldn't do that to you, Gillian. We are married."

"Yes, Edward, and we will remain that way if I have anything to say about it," Gillian announced smugly.

Justin rolled his eyes and stepped forward to interrupt. "If you don't mind, this night is for Chrissie— my fiancée." He rolled the word over his tongue and savored the feel of it. It felt wonderful. He grasped Chrissie's hand tighter, reluctant to ever let go again even for a moment. "I still worry someone as wonderful as Chrissie will realize her mistake, and renege on our betrothal if I give her a moment to contemplate it. Therefore, I'm in a hurry to move the evening's entertainments along."

He turned back to Chrissie. "Now, my darling, I have Matthew ready to show off his talents with several of my female performers. I even coerced him into a harem uniform, although he refused to dress like a eunuch."

She laughed. "I can well understand a man of his size and reputation being reluctant to be viewed as dismembered."

He grinned. "And the other rooms are set up with the girls at the ready. Name your pleasure." He sucked in a breath and braced himself for the jealousy sure to follow. "And, of course, you must feel free to join any of the entertainments this evening, even Matthew's. After we marry, I'll be too possessive of all your lush curves and tempting crevices to let any man near you, but for tonight, I intend making your every fantasy come true."

She sighed, tilted her head to the side in consideration, and then shook her head.

"No, my deepest love, my only lover. My fantasy for tonight is not to view any of your entertainments, no matter how arousing I'm sure they'll be." She waved a hand to her friends. "They shall want to see them, however." She turned back to face him. "I don't need to see other men's naked bodies, nor do I wish to use them, or be used by them."

He drew in a sharp breath in anticipation. "What then?"

"You!" She reached up to kiss his mouth but he held perfectly still, holding his breath, waiting, needing to hear it all. "I want you, Justin. You alone."

He groaned, a thankful groan, and swept her up into his arms.

"Oh, but there is one more thing I require to make my night perfect."

He raised his eyebrows. "Anything, my love, anything."

She giggled, leaned closer to his ear. "I want you, naked, tied with those red silk cords to the biggest bed, the one in nearest approximation to our shared divan in the tent at the Viscount's Pleasure House." She waved a languid hand to indicate the brothel they stood in. "I want you to perform the role of my sex slave in the infamous Red Room." She licked her lips. "I want to test for myself the much fêted stamina of the Virile Viscount. All night long."

He didn't hesitate, but scooped her up and strode for the door. As he walked, he called over his shoulder to their amused friends. "Please feel free to entertain yourselves in any fashion you wish. My future wife and I are going to be occupied in the Red Room where I intend on introducing my inquisitive bride-to-be to as many exotic forms of pleasure as I can possibly imagine."

He smiled down at the bundle of woman lying trustingly in his arms, and dipped his head to brush his lips over her pursed ones. She smiled, a siren's smile of feminine knowledge and anticipation. He laughed.

What a pleasure it would be teaching beautiful Chrissie all the tricks of his former trade.

EXCERPT LOVING LADY KATHARINE

I lived in Vanuatu, previously the New Hebrides, in the South Pacific for nine years and loved the island life and its fascinating history. Kelly's Justice is set in contemporary Vanuatu and Loving Lady Katharine in historic Vanuatu. I hope you enjoy reading both versions of Vanuatu.

1860 New Hebrides, Pacific Ocean.

At first, all Lord Alexander St. John had gleaned was that Lady Katharine Montgomery was the young widow of a British Lord and yet she now ran, efficiently and unobtrusively, her father's extensive businesses in the largest town in the New Hebrides, a large group of islands in the South Pacific. Her father, a cruel Scots man estranged from his family, beat her whenever he was drunk or whenever something reminded him of their forced and hasty departure from London.

But less than twenty four hours ago, Robert McLeish, Katie's father, had been laid to rest in the small burial ground beside the open-sided erection that passed for a church. Father Bryan struggled to speak complementary words of the man as the coffin was lowered into the ground, yet Katie stood dry eyed, her only feelings being those of profound relief. She was finally free.

Robert McLeish, with his usual arrogant disregard for the native's warnings, had pushed his horse through dense undergrowth on his distant plantation and a wild boar had startled his horse into throwing him, where after he had sustained repeated attacks from the monstrous animal.

People had moved around her at the house, offering tea and sympathy, mainly speaking pathetic lies of what a good man her father had been. No one believed them, least of all his only daughter. The European population on the island was small so Katharine's situation with her father had been well understood although never spoken of as in some way they all depended on their trade business to supply goods to the town. MacLeish's temper was legendary and none had dared to interfere.

'Katharine, please let us know if we can help in any way.'

'Lady Katharine, will you now be returning to England?'

She stared at the speaker intently before replying. 'I have nothing to return to.'

'It is impossible for you to remain alone in the house now. Certainly not fitting for a lady.'

Now she almost laughed, her thoughts mixed with a touch of hysteria. If they only knew. This hell hole was fitting for a woman like her.

Katie stifled rising feelings of frustration and anger with their questions to mingle with her guests, finding it easier to fix her face into her normal unemotional mask and agree with their lies about her father rather than acknowledge the unspoken truth.

Finally the house emptied, except for Alexander. She'd been polite, formal and firm at her first attempt to get him to leave, to leave her alone with her thoughts, but he insisted on staying, worried about her state of mind. After plying her with three whiskies from her father's best bottle, a bottle she'd never been allowed lay a finger on before, he drew her unresistingly to the large bamboo settee on the front verandah.

'Sit, Katie! Rest a while. You're exhausted.'

She stared at him with unseeing eyes. He sat close to her, his thigh almost touching hers through the skirts of her black mourning dress. This dress, like everything else he'd seen her wear, was practically threadbare and hopelessly out of fashion but here on her beloved island, Katie wouldn't have given such frivolous things a thought.

'I know you didn't like your father...'

Expressing the first real emotion he'd seen all day she yelled, 'Like? I despised him. My father was a tyrant just like...'

His stroked her arm. 'Like your husband?'

She shot off the settee, gaping at him. Unused to alcohol, she rocked on her feet but when he reached out to steady her, she jumped backwards. 'No, don't touch me. What do you know about my...my husband? No one knows. Only my father and he's dead. He's dead and I'm happy! Do you hear me, happy!' The last came out as as a shout and she looked skyward, as if expecting to be struck down. Though if she wanted her father to hear, she should have shouted at the floor because a man as evil as her father would be looking up, not down.

Watching closely to make sure she didn't hurt herself, he gave her the space she obviously needed to be able to tell her story. And even then, he didn't think she would have unburdened her hidden story of shame and grief if she hadn't been slightly inebriated. Her arms wrapped her waist in a defensive manner and he tried to picture her life. Being under the control of two men who'd alternatively ignored and then abused her must have been a living nightmare.

Keeping his words soft, he'd encouraged her to share with him. 'Katie, I know your father beat you but I never understood 'why.'

Katie clutched the bamboo railing wrapping the verandah. This house had been her father's pride and joy. 'My father loved to stand here and look down on the town and the docks. High enough to spit on the world down below. High enough for him to feel superior to everyone.' Flinging her arms wide, she nearly toppled over the balcony but waved away his aid.

This was where Katie had first met Alex, less than two months earlier, and from that moment her mind had constantly drifted to him, hoping his ship would return soon. Her father's pompous voice had been disgustingly boastful as he announced one morning, 'I am bringing a guest for dinner tonight. Alexander St.John. Soon to be the Duke of St John as I have heard that his father's health is failing quickly. Alexander will inherit the title, the properties and ships that go with it.'

His sneering glance raked Katie's thin figure. 'It's a pity you are so ordinary or I may have entertained the thought of giving you to him as an incentive to trade, but unfortunately he has been betrothed from birth to some chit in England.' Katie had inwardly flinched at the insult from her father, but she schooled herself to not give him the satisfaction of seeing her mortification.

'Be sure to instruct the cook to prepare an excellent dinner. Mr. St. John will one day be a man of great importance. Work in the back room at the warehouse today but return to the house in good time to ensure everything is in place for dinner. We will be at the house at six o'clock. I expect everything to be perfect because if you embarrass me in any way, you know the consequences.'

Katie knew exactly how many lashings her father would deal out for each imaginary sin she committed. Her father enjoyed inflicting pain and even the mildest protest would see him double the lashings. She depended on the healing lotions Tong Lee prepared to prevent further scarring on her back.

The menu had been perfect, her father drooling with greed at the memory of the lucrative business deal he had just concluded with his guest. Conversation had been intelligent and enjoyable and for the first time in many years, Katharine was able to relax in the company of a well bred man. For the first time in her twenty six years, she felt a flutter in her stomach, her body heating as she met his direct, appraising glance. Something flashed between them. Something she had no knowledge of previously and didn't know how to deal with now.

Then the unthinkable had happened. Alex had spoken directly to her. Simply addressed a question towards her across the dinner table, unleashing a chain of events.

'Lady Katharine, your father tells me you attend to his accounts in the warehouse. I am impressed with your talents. Do you enjoy working there?'

Even as she raised her eyes to answer, a fleeting smile on her lips, her father burst in with his malicious evil. 'Of course she doesn't enjoy it. Who would enjoy living in this God forsaken hell hole, but it is because of her...Lady Katharine...that we are both forced to endure here. She had it made in London, a Lady married to a Lord of the realm with a powerful and influential family. All she had to do was lie in the marriage bed and open her legs to produce an heir. But would she do it? No! She was too good for that, too above herself, thinking she was better than any of his family just because she is educated, reads books.'

Katharine gasped, her face burning and her mortification complete as she staggered out of her chair, knocking it over in her haste but bravely facing her father. 'You forget!' Her voice was reaching hysteria, yet she stood her ground firmly. 'It was your greed that forced me into that situation. You gave me to that man knowing what he was. What he expected.'

Her father's swift answer was an open handed slap across her face that knocked her sideways. Without looking their shocked guest in the eye, Katharine covered her reddened face, regained her footing and turned to escape the room. Alexander sprang to his feet, trying to capture her arm before she fled. 'Lady Katharine...' But she lifted her skirts and flew out the door and into the garden.

Alexander was outraged on Katharine's behalf. In his experience women were to be protected. 'Mr. McLeish! I hardly think this is suitable dinner table conversation. She is your daughter.'

'Daughter! Daughter!' He was choking on the words, drunk on wine and whiskey as he flung back his own chair, slamming his fist on the table and spewing his rage. 'She is no daughter of mine. She disgraced me. I now have to live my life here.' He threw his arm wide to indicate the small cluster of houses grouped below the hill where his house stood. 'This nowhere!' A malicious gleam sprang into his bloodshot eyes. 'But soon I will be rich. Rich enough to return to

London. Then my stupid daughter, the Honorable Lady Katharine, can stay here. She can repay me by continuing to run my business interests here.'

Alexander had been even more shocked. 'You can't be serious! The port is full of rough seaman and unscrupulous men. You can't mean to leave your daughter here by herself, with no one to protect her?'

'Protect her? Protect her from what? You've seen her. No man would want her. I could never imagine why Lord Percival married her in the first place until I understood the true situation later. She should have been grateful... despite what he was.'

Alexander's question was deceptively quietly spoken. 'What he was?'

Under the weather with drink, Robert let his tongue run away with him for a few minutes.

'Well who would have guessed what persuasion he was? How could I have known?' His look was sly, almost evil, and Alexander knew without doubt that this man had known exactly the situation he had sent his daughter into. 'Anyway, it should have made no difference to Katharine. She was his wife regardless and should have done her duty. If she had, the truth would have stayed hidden. That...that... other man's wife would never have found out. Never have found them together and taken a gun to them.'

Belatedly recalling who he was talking to, another peer of the realm, Robert pulled himself together. 'Never mind that now. How about another shot of my fine whiskey?'

Nearly choking on rising bile, Alex forced himself to exit politely. 'I thank you sir, but as I sail on the first tide tomorrow, I will bid you goodnight.'

He desperately wanted to race to the gardens and search for Katharine. To assure himself she was all right, but he couldn't afford to be anything but detached with her father. He'd heard the stories of his repeated cruelty. Yet if he remained in the same room as that vile man for another minute, there was no saying that his rage could be contained and the only thing that held him back was worry.

He strode down the flare lit path away from the house until out of sight and then turned into the gardens to search. When a sound-less shadow stepped out of the bushes in front of him, he jumped. Tong Lee put a finger to his lips in a gesture of silence and beckoned Alex to follow. Wordlessly, they descended to the small cove where Tong Lee simply stopped and pointed. Huddled on the beach, Alex could make out a small figure sitting in misery and staring fixedly out to the ocean. Not wanting to scare her, he cleared his throat softly to announce his approach... but still she started in fright and fear.

'It is only I, Alexander. Please do not fear me. I didn't wish to alarm you but I needed to be assured of your well being before I left.'

'If my father knows you have spoken to me, he'll...he'll...'

Shuddering at the stories of the man's harsh treatment of his daughter and miserable at the thought that he had been the hapless cause of yet another beating for her, sickness overwhelmed him. While he had fought often with his own father over the years, one of the main reasons he'd gladly left England behind, his father would never inflict physical pain on either he or his three sisters.

He cleared his throat and struggled to settle his agitation before speaking. 'He'll what? Beat you? I am so sorry. I didn't mean to cause you any more distress. Is there any way I can help?'

The look in her eyes as she now fully stared at him was a picture of helplessness and hopelessness. 'There is nothing anyone can do for me. Please leave now before he finds you here or it will be worse for me tomorrow.'

Without moving, he raised his face heavenwards as he searched urgently for an answer, any answer. 'I sail with the morning tide, but I return in a month. May I have your permission to search you out privately then, away from your father? I wish I could help. I wish I knew how.

Please know that I will think of little else during the next month, but you. Lady Katharine, I deeply regret the suffering I have caused you.'

Receiving no reply, he gave a little bow, turning to walk away.

Finally the moonlight lit her face with the ghost of a smile as she whispered. 'Katie. Call me Katie. My friends do.'

He halted. Turned to her. Gently, he reached out to touch one finger to her swollen cheek. 'Thank you Katie. My friends call me Alex. Keep well until I will see you next. Watch for me at the next full moon. Perhaps we could ride together.'

She didn't reply, yet as he walked mutely along the sand to the harbor he heard the faintest of whispers, 'Farewell Alex.' The finality in it wrenched at him. She never expected to see him again. In her whole life, she had never been able to depend on any man and she fully expected the same from him. Guilt washed over him at the thought that he may have unwittingly caused such torment in any other woman in his past life. Never again would he be casual with the feelings of women he knew. All women were treasures and deserved to be treated as such.

Tong Lee fell in silently beside him to match his stride. He was becoming accustomed to the Chinaman's shadowy presences and spoke quietly to him. 'Will she be safe? Will he beat her?'

'Yes, he will beat her tomorrow when he wakes and his head is sore. But after I will take care of her as I always do.'

Alex reached into his pocket and pulled out ten gold coins. 'Use these to buy what you need to look after her.'

Tong Lee merely averted his eyes from the money and bowed. 'I will care for her as I always have. As if she is my own daughter.'

Alex insistently pressed the money into his hand and closed his fingers around the coins. 'Please! Keep her safe until I return.'

The ship's sailing kept him too busy to reflect on what had happened but eventually they were under sail and he collapsed onto his bunk. He felt like a miserable coward, leaving a woman with that monster of a father. But what could he do? He had a betrothed awaiting him in England. A girl he hadn't seen for five years yet his family had committed him. To her and to the shipping business. If he stepped in to save Lady Katharine and lost the business, he may well cause the down fall of his entire family. Could he risk it. Two sisters in London depended on his money to give them a season to find a suitable match. Could he jeopardize it all. Risk the scandal by rescuing Katie from her father. But once he had rescued her, what then? What could he possibly do for her.

And so it was that around the next full moon, Katie's eyes drifted continually to the horizon, scouring every boat that arrived, hoping to glimpse Alex's arrival. Her back had healed once again from her father's lashing but this time a new hope blossomed inside her. Not that she allowed her expectations to climb very high. The past had taught her caution.

ABOUT THE AUTHOR

Tag Line - Making history fun, one year at a time.
I now live in a sunny part of Australia after spending many years in developing countries in the South Pacific. I love traveling, anywhere and everywhere, meeting crazy characters, and visiting the Australian outback.

My sexy heroes and feisty heroines challenge tradition, and though they might live a privileged life, they also understand the seamier parts of life.

I can be found in many Facebook groups talking about books and history and am always busy on Twitter, Instagram, and my personal favorite, Pinterest.

To learn more about Suzi Love and my new releases, join my newsletter at my suzilove.com. I am on Instagram and Goodreads and have lots of Pinterest Boards as suziloveoz. And please join my Facebook Group, Suzi Love's Lovelies, to keep up with my news on books and history.

Please visit my WEBSITE
Email me: suzi@suzilove.com

BOOKS BY SUZI LOVE

Fiction By Suzi Love

Embracing Scandal Book 1 Scandalous Siblings Series

Scenting Scandal Book 2 Scandalous Siblings Series

December Scandal Book 3 Scandalous Siblings Series

The Viscount's Pleasure House Book 1 Irresistible Aristocrats

Four Times A Virgin Book 2 Irresistible Aristocrats

Pleasure House Ball Book 3 Irresistible Aristocrats

Petunia and the Pearl Diver Book 4 Irresistible Aristocrats

Loving Lady Katharine Book 5 Irresistible Aristocrats

Love After Waterloo

Kelly's Justice

Outback Arrival

Old Sydney Town

Non-Fiction By Suzi Love

History Of Christmases Past Book 1 History Events

Easter In Images Book 2 History Events

History of Valentine's Day

Regency Overview Book 1 Regency Life Series

Young Gentleman's Day Book 2 Regency Life Series

Older Gentleman's Day Book 3 Regency Life Series

Young Lady's Day Book 4 Regency Life Series

Older Lady's Day Book 5 Regency Life Series

Self Publishing: Absolute Beginners Guide.

HISTORY NOTES SERIES

Here are some of the many titles in this Non-Fiction History Series.

Coming Soon:-
History Notes Underwear
History Notes Grand Tour
History Notes Mail Deliveries
History Notes Peerage
History Notes Food
History Notes Carriages
History Notes Money
History Notes Sewing
History Notes Hats
History Notes Mourning
History Notes Furniture
History Notes Shoes
History Notes Trades
History Notes Clubs
History Notes Fans
History Notes Sports

Historic London

Overview
Bridges
Hospitals
Churches
Famous

REVIEWS

Reviews are like gold to authors. I would appreciate it if you could leave a review, good or bad, for this book at any book retailer.

And don't forget, to get insider news about my book releases, any discounted books or contests that I am a part of, you should sign up for my newsletter. I promise you will only ever hear from me when I have exciting news, about me or my other author friends. www.suzilove.com

You can send me an email : suzi@suzilove.com.

Or send a letter : Suzi Love, 258/ 52 University Way, Sippy Downs, Queensland, 4556, Australia.

www.ingramcontent.com/pod-product-compliance
Lightning Source LLC
Chambersburg PA
CBHW071301250626
47159CB00004B/1258